THE METAMORPHOSIS IN THE PENAL COLONY and OTHER STORIES

Franz Kafka

TRANSLATED BY JOACHIM NEUGROSCHEL

SCRIBNER PAPERBACK FICTION
PUBLISHED BY SIMON & SCHUSTER

New York London Toronto Sydney Tokyo Singapore

SCRIBNER PAPERBACK FICTION
Simon & Schuster Inc.
Rockefeller Center
1230 Avenue of the Americas
New York, NY 10020

First Scribner Paperback Fiction Edition 1995

SCRIBNER PAPERBACK FICTION and design are trademarks of
Simon & Schuster Inc.

Designed by Anne Scatto
Manufactured in the United States of America

5   7   9   10   8   6

Library of Congress Cataloging-in-Publication Data
Kafka, Franz, 1883–1924.
The metamorphosis and other stories / Franz Kafka;
translated by Joachim Neugroschel.
p.   cm.
Translated from the German.
1. Kafka, Franz, 1883–1924—Translations, English.
PT2621.A26A258   1993
833'.912–dc20   92-43912
CIP

ISBN 0-02-021807-9

Selections from this translation first appeared in the Forward.

Contents

Contents

INTRODUCTION

On-Site Migration

"Our grandparents spoke Yiddish, our parents spoke German, and those of us who are left speak Czech."

That statement by a Prague Jew sums up the linguistic and cultural history of not only the Prague Jews but, by extension, the vast majority of European Jews since the end of the eighteenth century. During this period, the various Jewish communities in Europe and its colonies have passed from Jewish languages to a few simultaneous and/or sequential non-Jewish languages and perhaps ultimately back (or forward) to Hebrew in Israel. Outside Israel, this process has shifted the Jews from an ethnic category with a core religion and multiple Jewish subcultures (Ashkenazi, Sephardic, etc.) to a religious category whose various communities are scattered through many countries, where they are largely assimilating into the local non-Jewish cultures.

Franz Kafka was born in Prague at the end of the nineteenth century, and for most of his lifetime Bohe-

mia and Moravia belonged to Austria-Hungary—until
1919, five years before Kafka's death in 1924. During
that era, the Jews in Prague, like many Jews within
the Dual Monarchy and most Jews in the German
empire, were discarding Yiddish in favor of German,
the language of the dominant culture, while holding on
to their own religious practices and identities. Parallel
developments were taking place wherever Jews were,
in fact, allowed to assimilate into the language and
culture—especially throughout Western Europe, but
far less so in the tsarist empire.

This process of what I would like to call "reaccul-
turation" began when Napoleon offered French citi-
zenship, nationality, and complete civil rights to the
Jews in France: they would thereby become French
Jews if they agreed to give up their own Jewish culture
and languages, their peoplehood, and maintain only
their religious identity. They agreed—under great
pressure—thus abandoning some centuries-old Jewish languages and cultures in France: Jehudit (Judeo-
Provençal), Western Laaz (Judeo-French), and Alsa-
tian Yiddish. (Western Laaz, incidentally, had helped
to provide the substratum of Yiddish during its birth
phase in Alsace-Lorraine.)

In the nineteenth and twentieth centuries, new gen-
erations of Central and West-European Jews spoke a
Jewish tongue with their parents but a non-Jewish one
with each other—and of course with Christians. When
Karl Marx or Heinrich Heine wrote to their parents,
their letters (still extant) were in Western Yiddish
(misnomered *Judendeutsch* in German). Much later,
Bernard Berenson wrote an article about his childhood

experiences with Yiddish and its literature—which, however, like many assimilated Jews, he dismissed as irrelevant. Elias Canetti, in his memoirs, *The Tongue Set Free*, describes his Sephardic family in their native Sofia and the Ladino they spoke—which, however, he eventually replaced with German. And Primo Levi, in his autobiographical collection *The Periodic Table*, touches on the Judeo-Italian language used by his family and the local Jewish community.

Those are better-known exemplars of the countless Jews whose families passed from Jewish to non-Jewish in language and society, thus becoming, perhaps unwittingly, a transitional minority. Such on-site migration paralleled the mass migrations of Jews, especially from Eastern to Western Europe and then to the New World. Franz Kafka was a member of the on-site migration—while Karl Rossmann in "The Stoker" (*Amerika*) acts out the geographic migration.

Language in modern Europe became a defining national and then political characteristic—especially with the emergence of the nation-states in the nineteenth century. A "natural," i.e., biological, rationale was supplied by Darwin, for whom language—and English in particular—was a sign of higher evolution. When describing some aborigines whom he brought back to London (in *The Origin of Species*), he explains that the ones who managed to pick up some English were obviously the more highly evolved in the group. Such thinking pervades all modern politicizing of language, especially imperialism—not to mention on-site imperialism: by giving up their own language and assimilating to the surrounding languages, Jews became more acceptable to their host nations and to themselves, both socially and civically—and economically.

Internally, however, religious Jews looked forward to the coming of the Messiah and/or a return to Palestine and thus saw their given Jewish language as part of a transitional condition. Then again, many Jews regard(ed) their Jewish language as culturally inferior to either Hebrew or a non-Jewish tongue, especially the national/administrative language of a country. For Jews throughout Central and Eastern Europe, German was the language of enlightenment, civilization, modernity.

For Kafka, language is likewise viewed—sardonically—as the hallmark of being "human." When Gregor Samsa is turned into an insect, his speech can barely be understood and the family members act as if he cannot understand them; only the (uneducated) housekeeper addresses him directly, though teasing him. The ape in "A Report to an Academy" takes his first step toward becoming a human being by saying, "Hey!"; this makes him virtually the embodiment of the assimilating Jew. Kafka satirized the European attitude toward language yet employed language as his foremost instrument.

Born in the multilingual Austro-Hungarian city of Prague, the site of the first German university, Franz Kafka was raised and schooled in German in his assimilating Jewish family, although unlike most Prague Germans—Gentiles or Jews—he was somewhat fluent in Czech. Kafka made wondrous use of Prague German, which itself became a transitional tongue in the Czechoslovakian capital. The Nazi regime, ban-ning Kafka and murdering most of the Jewish speakers of Prague German, ultimately precipitated the expulsion of the Germans from Prague, thereby abolishing a very old and very rich area of German culture. As a result, Kafka's oeuvre has now become a monument to Prague German, which, like so many dialects and regional variants of German, was liquidated along with the Fascist era.

The language of these Prague Germans differed crucially from what was spoken in the "German lands": Prague German was never fed by a local German dialect, which, perceptibly or not, infiltrates the speaking and writing of every German, even the most fastidious writer—down to the very forms, genders, syntax, stresses, and inflections. Surrounded by Czech but by no German dialect, Prague German has been described, half derisively, as a "holiday German," because, for better or worse, it lacks the slang, colloquialisms, and dialectal influences that color High German in most areas. Still, Prague German was lovingly influenced by the forms and phrases, the quirks and cadences of Austrian, especially Viennese, German—that is, a regional standard usage but not a substandard dialect. More colloquial in their speech than they realized, the Prague Germans nevertheless saw their tongue as a "pure" linguistic and stylistic model that they used in their literature— which therefore sounds *more* colloquial than its authors sensed, just as their spoken language sounded *more* literary than that of most German speakers. "We write the way we speak," they said. Indeed they did— and they almost spoke the way they wrote.

Kafka's prose likewise reveals a careful and lucid

Prague German with an Austrian tinge. In his earliest stories, he tested certain expressionist and even surrealist innovations, shredding syntax, short-circuiting imagery, condensing emotions and tableaux into brief, sometimes even tiny shards and prose poems, to evoke a moody and sometimes wistful lyricism that patched these various fragments into a world of jocular mystery. Ultimately, however, especially in his master tales, "The Judgment" and "The Metamorphosis," he settled into a generally traditional language that paid scant homage to contemporary stylistic upheavals in German and French.

Thus, less than twenty years before Kafka began writing, the interior monologue or stream of consciousness had been invented in French literature by a Belgian novelist, Edouard Dujardin (*Les Lauriers sont coupés*, 1887) and in German literature by a Viennese Jew, Arthur Schnitzler (in his short story "Lieutenant Gustl," 1890). Ultimately reaching British literature and thriving in the fiction of James Joyce and Virginia Woolf, this innovation affected Kafka as little as most other modern linguistic experiments. Compared with the far more realistic contents of Joyce, Woolf, and Schnitzler, the world of Kafka's writings is so bizarre, so alienated, so grotesque that a both humorous and anguished incongruity arises from the juxtaposition of subject and style, absurdity and realism. Kafka's shock effects (and shock *is* a major component of modernism) were powerful enough in those times— and by sticking to an everyday, sometimes impartial prose that takes the nightmares for granted, he intensifies their overwhelming impact. Thus, in telling us that Gregor Samsa (whom we are supposed to know) wakes up to find himself turned into a giant bug, the author, commencing *in medias res* (like Arthur Rimbaud in *The Drunken Boat*, though not in the first person) reports in a cool, casual, objective tone that displays no surprise at this unnatural antimiracle.

However, the objectivity and matter-of-factness of the narrative voice are breached by a stylistic device that had a long tradition in European, especially Yiddish, literature. While commonly used in English, this device has no name here: we refer to it both by the French term, *style indirect libre*, and by the German term *erlebte Rede*. Fusing the author's objective omniscience (third person, past tense, etc.) with the character's innermost mental view, this device offers "empathy" in its older (pre–Madison Avenue) sense: a process of total mental and spiritual identification. "Tomorrow was Sunday." The past tense, *was*, stakes off the narrator's viewpoint, the noun *tomorrow* evokes the character's viewpoint. Otherwise the use of a past tense with "tomorrow" would be a logical discrepancy. By now, *style indirect libre* has become so overused in European languages as to be a flagrant symptom of pulp and kitsch. However, by skillfully exploiting this method, Kafka manages to lead us from poker-faced protocol to subjective angst, forming a bond between tragicomical protagonists and desperately smirking readers—only to alienate the characters even more, since the bond is unilateral: the *persona* can never leave the imaginary world and can therefore never link up with the real author and the real reader. Empathy becomes alienation.

The sources of alienation in Kafka and in his characters (they are not necessarily identical with him)
have been thoroughly investigated by scholars. His
attempts at being universal are taken for granted; after
all, literature, since Aristotle, has been seen—often
purblindly—as a "universal" category. John Updike
even praises Kafka for avoiding "Jewish parochial-
ism" (*The New Yorker*, 1983). Although well-meaning
and certainly sympathetic with Kafka's predicament
as a Jew, Updike expresses the bias of the dominant
culture, which takes itself for granted: it subliminally
sees itself as universal and axiomatic while viewing
external and smaller cultures as parochial and relative. This prejudice likewise extends to the "other,"
to colonized and marginalized groups like women and
homosexuals, racial and religious minorities. Black
writers like Willard Motley or Frank Yerby were not
African-American authors: they mainly depicted
whites. Female authors have been criticized for writing about women—and then praised or castigated for
writing "like a man." Book reviewers, if no longer
boycotting gay novels, will nevertheless chide them
(as does *The New York Times*) for not including more
heterosexual characters. (When was the last time they
attacked heterosexual fiction for not including more
homosexuals, or accused Balzac or Proust of having
too many French characters?)

In most countries, Jews have written about Jews
when working in Jewish languages and about non-
Jews in a non-Jewish language. Canada is a good
example: until recently, its English-language Jewish
writers (like Leonard Cohen, though unlike Mordecai

Richler) have dealt with Gentile themes, its Yiddish
writers with Jewish themes. The one country that flouts
this rule is the United States: a specifically English-
language Jewish literature has evolved here (next to
a Yiddish and also a Hebrew literature). Nevertheless,
even in its heyday, the American Jewish novel, whatever its worth, was derided as "clannish" by certain
Jews and non-Jews. The post–World War II era has
produced something of a German-language "Jewish
literature" in Germany and Austria, but with only a
few thousand German-speaking Jews left, the audience is chiefly Gentile.

Franz Kafka went along with this skewing and
masking of cultural subjectivity. Had he written about
Jews, his audience would have been vastly reduced;
after all, in his day, less than one percent of native
German speakers in Germany and Austria-Hungary
were Jewish. Like most Jews writing in German (say,
Hermann Broch or Elias Canetti or Ernst Toller),
Kafka tended to depict explicitly non-Jewish, indeed
often Christian characters. Still, we can't be sure that
these aren't disguises—just as the names of his protagonists sound suspiciously like "Kafka": e.g.,
Samsa; and just as Raban, being almost homonymous
with German *Rabe* (raven) is a quasi-translation of
Kafka, the Czech word for "raven." The Jewishness
of Kafka's themes and figures is open to interpretation.
"Persona," from the Latin word for "mask," can, as
in C. G. Jung, refer to the role that a person is playing
in life.

Take the filmmaker Josef von Sternberg: when he
transformed Heinrich Mann's novel *Professor Unrat*

into the film *The Blue Angel*, the director had a hidden
agenda in delineating the authoritarian German high
school professor. As he explains in his memoirs, *Fun
in a Chinese Laundry*, the film character was partly
suggested by a Hebrew teacher under whom von Sternberg had suffered as a boy. Not so dissimilarly: when
Kafka wrote "The Judgment" in an all-night session,
he composed it, according to his diaries, on the eve
of Yom Kippur, the Jewish Day of Atonement, which
is also known in Hebrew as Yom ha-Din, the Day of
Judgment. It is such secret itineraries, conscious or
not, that make art less than universal, more than
parochial, leaving it open to multivalent readings that
may unearth an intrinsic and perhaps necessary
"closetiness." Still, like the Oscar Wilde heroine who
dons a beautiful mask, which then becomes her face,
the underlying strata are finally replaced by the surface disguise. Albert Einstein (who spent some time
in Prague) left us with a modern metaphor for that
phenomenon when he described our physical world as
the three-dimensional surface of a four-dimensional
universe.

On Translating

No matter how much space can be devoted to a
stylistic and linguistic analysis of any writer, at least
twice as much would be required for investigating a
translation: along with the discussion of the original
text and the English text, we would have to delve into
the actual migration from one language and culture

into another. Let me therefore limit myself to focusing on a couple of facets, which, I hope, will show the confusions and complexities of any translation.

"Natural(ly)" and the Nature of Nature

Natürlich—both adjective and adverb—is a normal, indeed fairly bland and bromidic word in German. It means: natural(ly), of course, by all means, sure, needless to say, etc. As an interjection, a concession, it goes almost unnoticed. Yet it conceals an intricate reference to cerebral and behavioral manipulation by Western culture and religion.

During the nineteenth century, as traditional absolutes were being replaced by new (usually scientific and technological) absolutes but also by numerous relatives, the concept of "nature" and "natural" changed in meaning and power. Often, the word "divine" was replaced by "natural."

"Nature," says Katharine Hepburn in *The African Queen*, "is something we were put on this earth to rise above." For Christianity and European civilization, "nature" has always been something to be overcome, conquered, tamed, domesticated—subdued and subjugated for human use. The West draws an artificial line between "nature" and "human" or "man-made" —as if a beaver's "natural" dam and an engineer's "technological" dam were not subject to the same physical laws, the same "natural" laws. After all, whether you jump off the Jungfrau or the Eiffel Tower, you are prey to the same law of gravity and you will fall at the same speed. Naturally, this ancient distinction between "natural" and "man-made" gives *Homo sapiens* a special place in Creation—and the privilege of bending Mother Nature, and her children, to his will.

In an inconsistent yet compatible fashion, the "natural" was also seen as quite the opposite—an ethical imperative: not only in "natural law" (which nevertheless changes from culture to culture and era to era), but in human conduct. While religion and government attacked some forms of behavior as being "natural," they lauded others—likewise as being "natural": for instance, men's domination over women, whites' domination over blacks, Europe's domination over the rest of the world, the nuclear family, family values, etc.

To confuse things further, "unnatural" has always been a putdown no matter how good or bad the "natural."

In the United States, books and movies about the Wild West summed up this process as the subjugation by men of land, nature, and savagery—a process that was then complemented by the arrival of women, who brought Christianity, culture, refinement, breeding— i.e., civilization.

The cataclysmic upshot of this citing of "natural" and "unnatural" as ethical standards was European Fascism, which, in touting nature and natural man (yet deploying the most destructive prenuclear technology in history), set up life-and-death categories. The Nazi government even tried to change Nature's name, *Natur*, into the more Germanic (and therefore more "natural") *Allmutter* or *Werdemutter*. Rather than letting Darwinism and evolution take their alleged "natural" course, Fascism ("unnaturally") lent Mother Nature a helping hand: anything and anyone that a Fascist state declared "unnatural" was segregated and ultimately killed.

In Kafka, the protagonist often has to pay a terrible price when, willingly or not, he goes against "nature": not only by turning into a bug (Gregor Samsa), but also by, say, abandoning both his child and his parents (Karl Rossmann in "The Stoker"), or betraying his father (Georg Bendemann in "The Judgment"). Ultimately, "nature" takes its (or her) toll, and the punishment is no less severe than the ones meted out by vengeful deities in Greek tragedy. Kafka may assault and expose the nuclear family and its destructive patriarchal basis, yet he longs to restore it, to give the punitive father his "natural" place. Rossmann, orphaning his unborn child and orphaning himself by leaving home, seeks both father and family in the New World. Samsa, by dying, reestablishes the natural order of domestic things. Bendemann, by carrying out his own death sentence, puts his father back in power.

Now as a rule, one might render *natürlich* not necessarily as "naturally" but as "of course," or "needless to say." However, given the tradition that Kafka was working in and against, I've translated this adverb as "naturally" throughout. I have no choice: this innocent-looking word encapsulates a crucial pattern in Western and Kafkaesque thinking.

TENSE AND ASPECT

In its verbal structure, English, like the Romance and Slavic languages, divides motion and being into perfective and imperfective aspects. "I go" vs. "I am going"; "I went" vs. "I was going"; etc.

In an English narrative, the action, the bare bones of the plot, are rendered with the perfective tenses, while the background is filled in with imperfective tenses. This development in European languages seems to have begun at the same time as the introduction of spatial and mathematical perspective into European art: verbal tense and artistic perspective divided reality into foreground and background. Thus, a piece of fiction usually begins with an imperfective verb by way of introduction ("I was sleeping"); then, shifting into a perfective verb, the narrative launches into the plot ("I woke").

German verbs make no such distinctions. (The noun *Imperfekt*, applied to the simple past, i.e., preterite, is an inaccurate borrowing from Latin and Romance terminology; it is best ignored and replaced with *Präteritum*, preterite.) In a German narrative, foreground (plot) and background are distinguished by the syntax: the often Ciceronian sentence tends to devote main clauses to the plot and relative clauses to the background (of course, given the multiple, often myriad, and sometimes even contradictory tasks of each grammatical element, this division of labor is never entirely strict). As a result, hypotaxis, or syntactic subordination, has a very different role in German, which clearly marks each subordinate clause not only with commas but also by shifting its verb to the very end, so that we can easily tell which clause is describing foreground and which background. (Once again, this assignment of linguistic tasks is not always rigorous.) Similarly, whenever German offers a quick string of very brief sentences or main clauses, English would tend to subordinate some of them as present participles, which German seldom uses to introduce clauses, limiting participial clauses to extremely lofty, highfalutin diction.

Confronted with the cat's cradles and Chinese boxes of German clauses, the American translator has to figure out when to use perfective, imperfective, or participial verbs in English: you have to decide if a German clause or sentence (German uses the same word, *Satz*, for both concepts) is foreground or background, superordinate or subordinate—or somewhere in between. Kafka learned Kleist's lesson about the anxiety created by intricate hypotaxis and the suspense of waiting for the verb to drop like the headsman's ax at the end of a long and harrowing sentence. Hard to duplicate in English.

In the first sentence of "The Metamorphosis" ("Die Verwandlung"), the reader slides through the casual tone, confronts the words *ungeheuren Ungeziefer* (monstrous vermin), and finally crashes into the concluding past participle *verwandelt* (transformed), which ties the whole sentence together, telling us what has happened to Samsa and explaining what the title means.

"Als Gregor Samsa eines Morgens aus unruhigen Träumen erwachte, fand er sich in seinem Bett zu einem ungeheuren Ungeziefer verwandelt." (Literally: As Gregor Samsa one morning from agitated dreams awoke, found he himself in his bed into a monstrous vermin transformed.) That final and ineluctable past participle, *verwandelt*, "transformed," is horrifyingly relentless. It makes the sentence—and the story.

Incidentally, *Ungeziefer* means "vermin," not "insect," which is either *Insekt* or *Kerbtier* in German; and while the adjective *ungeheuer* means "enormous," the noun *Ungeheuer* means "monster."

Like Kleist, Kafka piles on the prepositional phrases to increase the tension; but in English (as opposed to German or French), a sequence of even two prepositional phrases can sound clumsy—and adverbs tend to be discarded in favor of adjectives. All of which make for syntactical headaches in a literary translation.

> One morning, upon awakening from agitated dreams, Gregor Samsa found himself, in his bed, transformed into a monstrous vermin. He lay on his hard, armorlike back, and when lifting his head slightly, he could view his brown, vaulted belly partitioned by arching ridges, while on top of it, the blanket, about to slide off altogether, could barely hold. His many legs, wretchedly thin compared with his overall girth, danced helplessly before his eyes.

The hermeneutics of translation are individual. Each approach is subjective, selective, and no single interpretation, however valid, holds the unique and absolute truth. Equally decent translations may exist side by side. Another translator may reassign the perfectives, imperfectives, and present participles in altogether different patterns, to form a different arrangement of foreground and background, shading the narrative in a different way. While there are many possible mistranslations, there are only a few possible correct translations, each one constituting a variation of the original theme. The trick is to find a cohesive and coherent variation that replaces the original theme for the new reader, who, having no access to the foreign language, must take the translation as a primary text.

While it would be exciting to dig into all the strata involved in translating Kafka, I'd rather let the translation speak for itself.

Acknowledgment

I am deeply grateful to my editor, Erika Goldman, for her patience and for her thorough and sensitive editing of my translation.

Joachim Neugroschel
NEW YORK, NOVEMBER 16, 1992

THE EARLY
STORIES

CONVERSATION WITH
THE WORSHIPER

There was a time I went to a church day after day because a girl I had fallen in love with would pray there, kneeling for half an hour every evening, when I could watch her in peace and quiet.

Once; when the girl had not come, and I was glaring at the people in prayer, I noticed a young man who had thrown his scrawny figure full length on the floor. From time to time, he would grab his skull with the full force of his body and, moaning, smash it into the palms of his hands, which were resting on the stones.

The only other churchgoers were a few old women, who often turned their kerchiefed heads sideways to peer at the worshiper. This attention seemed to make him happy, for prior to each of his pious outbursts, he would glance about to see whether the onlookers were numerous. Finding his conduct unseemly, I resolved to accost him when he left the church and to question him about why he was praying in this manner. Yes indeed, I was annoyed because my girl had not come.

However, he did not stand up until an hour later, crossing himself very meticulously and trudging unsteadily toward the font. I stationed myself between the font and the door, knowing I would not let him pass without an explanation. I pursed my lips as I always do when I intend to speak firmly. I put my right leg forward and leaned on it, while casually poising my left leg on tiptoe; this too makes me resolute.

Now it was possible that the man eyed me when sprinkling the holy water on his face; or perhaps he had already noticed me earlier, with some anxiety, for now he unexpectedly dashed outside. The glass door slammed shut. And when I promptly went outside, I could no longer see him, for there were several narrow streets, and the area was thronged.

He did not show up again during the next few days, but my girl did come. She was wearing her black dress with the diaphanous lace on the shoulders (the crescent of the chemise neckline showing underneath) and with a nicely cut silk bertha hanging down from the edge of the lace. And since the girl had come, I forgot all about the young man; nor did I concern myself with him even later, when he started coming regularly again and praying in his usual style. However, he always hurried past me, averting his face. Perhaps it was because I could only picture him in motion, so that even when standing still, he appeared to be skulking along.

One evening, I dawdled in my room. But then I went to church after all. I did not find the girl and I was about to go home when I spotted that young man lying there again. The old incident crossed my mind, piquing my curiosity.

I tiptoed over to the doorway, handed a coin to the blind beggar sitting there, and squeezed in next to him behind the open wing of the door; I sat there for an hour, perhaps with a cunning expression. I felt fine and resolved to come here often. During the second hour, I found it absurd to be waiting there for the worshiper. Nevertheless, growing angry, I sat for a third hour, letting the spiders crawl over my clothes, while the last few people, breathing loudly, quit the darkness of the church.

Then he came too. He walked gingerly, his feet cautiously testing the ground before treading.

I stood up, took a large, straight step, and grabbed the young man. "Good evening," I said, clutching his collar and pushing him down the steps to the illuminated square.

When we reached the bottom, he said to me in a completely unhinged voice, "Good evening, my dear, dear sir, do not be angry with me, your humbly devoted servant."

"Well," I said, "I want to ask you some questions, sir. Last time, you escaped; today, you will scarcely succeed."

"You are a compassionate man, sir, and you will allow me to go home. I am to be pitied, that is the truth."

"No," I shouted into the din of a passing trolley, "I won't allow you. This is the sort of encounter I like. You are a lucky catch. I consider myself fortunate."

Then he said: "Oh God, your heart is alive, but your head is a block of wood. You say I'm a lucky catch—how lucky you must be! For my poor luck is one that teeters, it teeters on a thin edge, and if anyone touches my poor luck it will fall on the questioner. Good night, sir."

"Fine," I said, clutching his right hand, "if you won't answer me, then I'll start yelling here in the street. And all the shopgirls who are now coming out of their shops and all their sweethearts who are looking forward to seeing them will come dashing over here, for they'll think that a cab horse has collapsed or that something similar has happened. Then I'll make a public display of you."

He now tearfully kissed my hands, alternating between them. "I'll tell you what you wish to know, but please, let us go over to that side street." I nodded, and that was where we went.

However, the darkness of the street with its widely separated yellow streetlights was not dark enough for him; instead, he led me into the low hallway of an old house, under a tiny, dripping lamp that hung in front of the wooden stairs.

There he self-importantly pulled out his handkerchief, and spreading it on a step, he said, "Do sit down, my dear sir; this way, you can ask your questions more easily. I'll remain standing, so I can answer more easily. But please don't torment me."

So I sat down and, squinting up at him, I said: "You are an utter lunatic, that's what you are! How can you behave like that in church! It is so annoying and so unpleasant for the onlookers! How can people feel devout if they have to look at you."

He was pressing his body against the wall, only his head was moving freely in the air. "Don't be annoyed—why should you be annoyed at things that aren't relevant to you. I'm annoyed at myself when I behave imprudently; but if someone else behaves imprudently, then I'm delighted. So please don't be annoyed if I tell you that the goal of my life is to be looked at by other people."

"What are you saying!?" I cried, much too loudly for the low hallway, but then I was afraid my voice would weaken. "Really now, what have you said!? Why, I can sense—indeed, since I first laid eyes on you, I have sensed what sort of condition you are in. I'm a man of experience, and I'm not joking when I say that your condition is a seasickness on dry land. It is such that you have forgotten the real names of things, and in your great haste you now pour random names upon them. Hurry, hurry! But the moment you run off, you forget your names for them. You called the poplar in the fields the 'Tower of Babel,' for you did not know or did not want to know that it was a poplar, and now it is swaying again without a name, and you would have to call it 'When Noah Was Drunk.'"

I was a bit stunned when he said, "I'm glad I didn't understand what you said."

Annoyed, I quickly said, "The fact that you are glad shows that you did understand."

"Of course it does, my good sir, but you too spoke in a bizarre way."

I placed my hands on a higher step, leaned back, and in this almost unassailable position, which is a wrestler's last resort, I said, "You have a strange way of wriggling out of a predicament—by assuming that other people suffer from your condition."

These words lent him courage. He folded his hands

together in order to make his body compact, then said, a bit reluctantly: "No, I don't act this way with everyone, for instance you, because I can't. But I would be glad if I could, for then I wouldn't need the attention of the people in church. Do you know why I need it?"

This question left me perplexed. I certainly did not know, nor do I believe I wanted to know. After all, I was not the one who wanted to come here, I told myself at this point, this man forced me to listen to him. So all I had to do was shake my head to indicate that I did not know; but I simply could not get my head to move.

The man, standing across from me, smiled. Then he dropped to his knees and talked with a faraway look: "There has never been a time when I could truly convince myself that I was alive. You see, I only have such flimsy notions of the things around me that I always believe they used to be alive but are now fading away. I always, my dear sir, long to see things as they may be before they show themselves to me. In their earlier state, they are probably still beautiful and calm. They must be, for that is how I often hear people describing them."

Since I held my tongue, and only involuntary twitches in my face showed how uneasy I was, he asked, "You do not believe that people talk like that?"

I felt I ought to nod, but was unable to do so.

"Really? You do not believe it? Oh, but listen. One afternoon when I was a child, I opened my eyes after taking a brief nap, and even though I was still half asleep, I heard my mother on the balcony, asking someone below, in a normal tone of voice: 'What are you doing, my dear? It's so hot.' A woman answered from the garden: 'I'm having coffee outdoors.' They were speaking offhandedly and not all too plainly, as if it were a matter of course."

I thought I was being asked a question, so I reached into my back trouser pocket as if looking for something. But I was not looking for anything, I simply wanted to change my position in order to show my interest in the conversation. While so doing, I said that that was such a strange incident, and that I simply did not understand it. I added that I did not believe it was true and that it must have been made up for some specific purpose that I could not fathom. Then I shut my eyes for they were aching.

"Oh, but it's good that you agree with me, and it was unselfish of you to stop me and tell me so. Just why should I feel ashamed—or why should we feel ashamed—that I don't walk upright and trudge along, that I don't strike my cane on the pavement or graze the clothes of the people who pass by so noisily. Wouldn't I actually be justified in complaining defiantly that I have to slink along the houses as a shadow with square shoulders, sometimes vanishing in the panes of the shop windows?

"What awful days I'm going through! Why are all our buildings so poorly built that high structures sometimes collapse and no one can find a cogent reason? At such times, I clamber over the rubble heaps, asking anyone I run into: 'How could this happen! In our city—a new building—that's the fifth one today—just imagine!' And no one can give me an answer.

"Often people collapse on the street and remain lying there dead. Then all the shopkeepers open their doors, which are hung with wares, they step out nimbly, whisk the corpse into a house, then reemerge with smiling lips and eyes, and speak: 'Good day— the sky is pale—I sell lots of kerchiefs—yes, the war.' I slink into the house, and after several anxious attempts at raising my hand while crooking my finger, I finally tap on the janitor's small window.

" 'My good fellow,' I say amiably, 'a dead man has been brought here. Please take me to him.'

"And when he shakes his head as if undecided, I say firmly, 'My good fellow. I am from the secret police. Show me the corpse immediately.'

" 'A corpse?' he now asks and is almost offended. 'No, we have no corpse here. This is a respectable place.' So I say goodbye and leave.

"But then, when I have to cross a large square, I forget everything. I am confused by the difficulty of this undertaking, and I often think to myself: If people build such huge squares out of sheer exuberance, why don't they also add a stone balustrade leading across the square. Today the wind is blowing from the southwest. The air on the square is stirred up. The spire of the town hall is reeling in small circles. Why don't they end the commotion? All the windowpanes are banging loudly, and the lampposts are bending like bamboo. The robe of the Virgin Mary on the column is twisting, and the storm wind is tearing away at it. Doesn't anyone see it? The ladies and gentlemen who are supposed to walk on the stones are gliding. When the wind stops to catch its breath, they halt, exchange a few words, and bow as they take their leave; but if the wind starts blasting again, they are unable to resist it, and they all raise their feet in unison. They do have to clutch their hats tightly, but their eyes twinkle cheerfully as if merely a mild breeze were wafting. I am the only one who is afraid."

Abused as I felt, I said, "The story you told me earlier about your mother and the woman in the garden does not sound the least bit strange. Not only have I heard and experienced many such stories, I have even taken part in a few. Why, it's a perfectly normal business. Do you believe I could not have said the same thing if I had been on the balcony, or responded in the same way from the garden? Such an ordinary incident."

When I said that, he seemed very happy. He said that I was dressed nicely and that he liked my necktie very much. And what a fine complexion I had. And that confessions were the most informative when they were rescinded.

CONVERSATION WITH
THE DRUNK

As I sauntered out the front door, I was ambushed by the sky with its moon and stars and sweeping vault and by the Ring Square with its town hall, its church, and its Virgin Mary on her column.

I calmly stepped from the shade into the moonlight, unbuttoned my overcoat, and warmed up; then, raising my hands, I silenced the soughing of the night and began to ponder:

"What is it you all are doing pretending to be real? Are you trying to make me believe that I am unreal, standing strangely on the green pavement? Yet it's been so long since you were real, you Sky, and you Ring Square have never been real.

"It *is* true, you are all still superior to me, but only when I leave you in peace.

"Thank goodness, Moon, you are no longer Moon, but perhaps it's negligent of me to keep calling you, who are named Moon, 'Moon.' Why are you no longer so frolicsome when I call you 'Forgotten Paper Lantern in a Strange Color'? And why do you almost draw back when I call you 'Virgin Mary on the Column,' and I no longer discern your menacing stance, Virgin Mary

12

on the Column, when I call you 'Moon That Sheds Yellow Light'?

"It really seems to do you no good when someone thinks about you; your courage and your health start waning.

"God, how wholesome it must be when a thinker learns from a drunk!

"Why is everything hushed? I believe the wind is gone. And these cottages, which often roll across the square as if on tiny wheels, are completely pounded down—hush—hush—one can't see the thin black line that usually divides them from the ground."

And I broke into a run. I ran around the large square three times unhindered, and since I encountered no drunk, I ran toward Emperor Charles Street without reducing my speed or feeling any strain. My shadow often ran, smaller than I, along the wall as if in a ditch between wall and street.

When I passed the firehouse, I heard noise from the Small Ring, and when I reached it, I saw a drunk standing by the ironwork of the fountain, stretching his arms out level and stamping his feet, in clogs, on the ground.

First I halted until I was breathing more calmly, then I walked over to him, doffed my top hat, and introduced myself:

"Good evening, gentle nobleman, I am twenty-three years old, but I have no name as yet. You, however, most likely come with an astonishing, indeed, a singable name from that great city of Paris. You are redolent with the quite unnatural smell of the dissolute French court.

"With your colored eyes, you must have viewed those great ladies who stand on the high, bright terrace, turning ironically at their narrow waists, while the bedizened trains of their gowns, spreading out on the stairs, trail off on the sand in the garden. Isn't it true that long poles are set up everywhere, and that footmen in impudently cut gray tailcoats and in white knee breeches climb those poles, wrapping their legs around them, but with their torsos often leaning back and to the side, for they have to pull up ropes to hoist huge gray linen sheets from the ground and span them in the air because the great lady desires a hazy morning."

When he belched, I said, almost startled: "Is it really true, sir, that you come from our Paris, from that stormy Paris, ah, from that effusive hailstorm?" When he belched again, I said, flustered: "I know I am being shown a great honor."

And with nimble fingers, I buttoned my overcoat; then I spoke in a fervent but timid voice:

"I know you don't regard me as worthy of an answer, but my life would be filled with weeping if I didn't question you today.

"Let me ask you, Sir, who are so nicely spruced up: Is it true what they say? Are there people in Paris who consist entirely of ornate clothing, and are there houses in Paris that have nothing but portals, and is it true that on summer days the sky is a fleeting blue, embellished only by small, white, heart-shaped clouds that are pasted on? And is there a waxworks, mobbed by visitors, that contains nothing but trees hung with small plaques bearing the names of the most famous heroes, criminals, and lovers?

14

"And now this news! This blatant pack of lies!

"Don't those Paris streets suddenly branch out, they're unruly, aren't they? Things aren't always all right—and how could they be! Sometimes there's an accident, people gather, coming from the side streets with their urban stride, their feet barely touching the pavement; they are all curious, but also afraid of being disappointed; they pant, craning their little heads. But should they touch one another, they bow deeply and apologize: 'I'm so sorry—I didn't mean to—it's awfully crowded, do forgive me—it was very clumsy of me—I admit. My name is—my name is Jerome Faroche, I'm a grocer on Rue du Cabotin—please allow me to invite you for lunch tomorrow—my wife would be so delighted too.' That's how they talk, while the street is dazed and the smoke from the chimneys wafts down between the houses. That's how it is. And if possible, two carriages halt on a bustling boulevard in an elegant neighborhood. Footmen gravely open the doors. Eight noble Siberian borzois prance down and dash across the roadway, barking and leaping. And people say that those are young Parisian coxcombs in disguise."

His eyes had shut tight. When I fell silent, he thrust both hands into his mouth and yanked at his lower jaw. His clothes were filthy. He had probably been thrown out of a wineshop, and it hadn't quite dawned on him yet.

It may have been that brief, utterly calm pause between day and night, when, without your expecting it, your head dangles from your neck, and without your noticing it, everything halts because you are not watching it, and it then vanishes. While you remain

15

alone with a bent body, peering around but seeing nothing, feeling no resistance from the air, yet mentally clinging to the memory of houses standing at a certain distance from us with roofs and, fortunately, angular chimneys through which the darkness flows into the houses, through the garrets into the diverse rooms. And it is fortunate that tomorrow will be a day when, incredible as it is, we will be able to see everything.

Now the drunk's eyebrows rose so sharply that a shiny glow formed between his eyebrows and his eyes, and he explained in fits and snatches: "You see, it's like this—I'm sleepy, you see, that's why I'll be going to sleep.—You see, I have a brother-in-law on St. Wenceslaus Square—that's where I'm going, because that's where I live, because that's where I have my bed.—I'm going now.—Only, you see, I don't know his name or where he lives—I guess I've forgotten— but it doesn't matter, because I don't even know if I actually have a brother-in-law.—You see, now I'm going.—Do you believe I'll find him?"

To which I replied without qualms: "I'm certain you will. But you're coming from abroad, and your servants don't happen to be with you. Allow me to guide you."

He didn't respond. I therefore offered him my arm so he could link up with me.

GREAT NOISE

I sit in my room in the headquarters of the noise of the entire apartment. I hear all the doors slamming; because of their noise, I am spared only the footsteps of the people running between them; I can also hear the banging of the oven door in the kitchen. My father breaks down the doors of my room and trudges through them in his trailing robe; the ashes are being scraped out of the stove in the next room; Valli, shouting word after word through the vestibule, asks whether Father's hat has been cleaned; a hissing that aims to be friendly with me raises the shriek of a responding voice. The apartment door is unlatched, rasping like a catarrhal throat, then opens further with the singing of a female voice, and finally closes with a dull, male thud, which is the most inconsiderate sound of all. Father is gone; now the more delicate, more diffuse, more hopeless noise begins, led by the voices of the two canaries. It already crossed my mind earlier, and now, with the canaries, I again wonder if I shouldn't open the door a tiny crack, slither into the next room like a snake, and remaining like that on the floor, ask my sisters and their governess for some peace and quiet.

CONTEMPLATION

For M. B. [Max Brod]

CHILDREN ON
THE HIGHWAY

I heard the wagons rolling past the garden fence; sometimes I also glimpsed them through the faintly stirring gaps in the foliage. How loudly the wood in their spokes and shafts groaned in the hot summer! Farmhands were coming from the fields, laughing outrageously.

I sat on our small swing, just relaxing among the trees in my parents' garden.

Beyond the fence, the bustle never stopped. Children ran by in the space of a moment; grain wagons, with men and women on the sheaves or around them, darkened the flower beds; toward evening, I saw a leisurely strolling gentleman with a cane, and a couple of girls, coming toward him arm in arm, stepped aside into the grass as they greeted him.

Then birds soared up in a sparkling spray. I followed them with my eyes, saw them rising for an instant, until I believed that they were no longer rising but that I was falling, and clutching the ropes because I felt faint, I began to swing a little. Soon I was swinging harder as cooler air began to waft and trembling stars appeared overhead instead of the soaring birds.

I was served my supper by candlelight. Often both my arms lay on the wooden tabletop, and I was already weary as I bit into my bread and butter. The large-meshed curtains bellied in the warm wind, and at times some passerby held them apart with his hands if he wanted to see me more clearly and talk to me. Usually the candle soon went out, and the gathered midges flitted about for a while in the dark candle fumes. If anyone at the window asked me something, I would gaze at him as if peering at the mountains or simply into the air, and he likewise did not much care whether I answered.

But if anyone then vaulted over the windowsill and announced that the others were already in front of the house, I would stand up—sighing, of course.

"Goodness, why are you sighing? What has happened? Is it some special misfortune that can never be made good again? Will we never be able to recover? Is everything truly lost?"

Nothing was lost. We ran to the front of the house.

"Thank goodness, you're finally here!"

"Well, you're always late."

"What do you mean *I'm* always late?"

"You more than anyone else. Stay home if you don't want to join us."

"No mercy!"

"What? No mercy? What are you saying?"

We poked our heads into the evening. There was no daytime and no nighttime. At times our vest buttons were grinding together like teeth, at times we kept a steady gap between us as we ran, with fire in our mouths, like beasts in the tropics. Like cuirassiers in ancient wars, stamping and leaping high in the air, we drove one another down the short street and then, with this urging in our legs, into the highway. A few stray people ran into the ditch; no sooner had they melted into the dark embankment than they were already standing on the dirt road like outsiders and peering down.

"Come on down!"

"Come on up first!"

"So you can throw us down—not on your life, we're not that stupid."

"You mean you're that cowardly. Come on now, come up!"

"Really? You? You of all people are going to throw us down? Says who?"

We mounted the attack, were sent sprawling, and collapsed on the grass in the road ditch, falling of our own free will. Everything was evenly warmed, we felt no heat, no cold in the grass, we only grew tired.

When you turned on your right side, with your hand under your ear, you felt very much like dozing off. You did want to pull yourself up, raising your chin, but only to tumble into a deeper ditch. Then, holding your arm out crosswise and flapping your legs to the side, you wanted to throw yourself against the air and be certain to tumble into an even deeper ditch. And you never wanted to stop.

You hardly thought about how you might properly stretch out your body, especially your knees, as far as possible, to sleep in the final ditch, and on the verge of weeping, you lay on your back, as if ill. People winked whenever a boy, his elbows at his hips, leaped over us, with dark soles, from the embankment to the road.

The moon could already be seen fairly high, a mail wagon drove past in its light. A mild breeze arose all about, you could feel it even in the ditch, and the nearby woods began to rustle. You were no longer so anxious to be alone.

"Where are you?"

"Come here!"

"All of us together!"

"Why are you hiding, stop your nonsense!"

"Don't you realize that the mail wagon has already passed?"

"Oh no! Already passed?"

"Of course, it passed by while you were asleep."

"I was asleep? Imagine that!"

"Shush, one can tell just by looking at you."

"Oh, go on!"

"Come."

We ran closer together, some of us held hands, we could not keep our heads high enough because the road descended. Someone let out an Indian war whoop, a gallop shot into our legs as never before, whenever we leaped the wind would lift us by our hips. Nothing could have stopped us; we were running so hard that even when passing one another we managed to fold our arms and calmly look around.

We halted at the bridge spanning the mountain torrent; those who had run further doubled back. The water below smashed against rocks and roots as if it were not already late in the evening. There was no reason why no one jumped up to the balustrade of the bridge.

In the distance, a railroad train emerged from behind some shrubbery, all the compartments were lit, the glass windows were probably down. One of us began singing a popular hit, but we all wanted to sing. We sang much faster than the train moved, we swung our arms because our voices weren't strong enough, our voices formed a scrimmage in which we felt cozy. If you blend your voice with other voices, you are virtually caught on a fishhook.

And so, with our backs to the forest, we sang for the ears of the distant travelers. The adults were still awake in the village, the mothers were making up the beds for the night.

It was already time. I kissed the one standing next to me, casually shook hands with the three nearest ones, and began to run back; no one called out to me. At the first crossroads, where they could no longer see me, I turned off and ran back into the forest along dirt roads. I was heading toward the southern city which our villagers talk about:

"There are people there! Just imagine, they don't sleep!"

"And why not?"

"Because they don't get sleepy."

"And why not?"

"Because they're fools."

"Don't fools get sleepy?"

"How could fools get sleepy?"

EXPOSING A CITY SLICKER

Finally, around ten at night, together with a man whom I had once known only casually, and who had unexpectedly joined me this time, dragging me around the streets for two hours, I arrived at the elegant mansion where I had been invited to a soiree.

"Well!" I said, clapping my hands as a sign that it was absolutely necessary to say good night. I had already made a few less pointed attempts. By now, I was quite exhausted.

"Are you going right up?" he asked. From his mouth, I heard a sound like clicking teeth.

"Yes."

I did have an invitation, I had told him so immediately. Indeed, I had been invited to go upstairs to a place where I would love to be, and not down here, standing outside the front door and gazing past my interlocutor's ears. Or now going mute with him, as if we were determined to linger on this spot for a long time. The houses all around us promptly took part in this silence, as did the darkness above them all the way up to the stars. And the footfalls of invisible strollers, whose routes one did not care to guess, the wind, which kept hugging the opposite side of the street, a gramophone, which sang against the closed windows of some room or other—they sounded from this silence as if it had always been and would forever remain their property.

My companion resigned himself on his behalf and also—after a smile—on my behalf, stretched his right arm upward along the wall, and closing his eyes, leaned his face against it.

But I did not wait until this smile faded, for embarrassment suddenly whirled me around. This was the smile that had first made me realize he was a city slicker, pure and simple. And yet I had been in this town for months already, believing I knew these city slickers through and through: the way they come toward us at night, from side streets, holding out their hands like innkeepers, the way they squeeze around the advertisement pillars where we stand, the way they virtually play hide-and-seek, spying on us with at least one eye from behind the curve of the pillar, the way they suddenly hover before us when we grow anxious, at street corners, on the curb of the sidewalk. I did understand them so well; after all, they were my first local acquaintances in the small taverns, and I owed them my first inkling of an adamant character which I could so little imagine as missing from the earth that I was already starting to feel it inside myself. The way they stood facing you even when you had long since slipped away from them, when there was absolutely nothing left for you to be tricked out of! The way they refused to sit down, refused to drop down, but instead looked at you with glances that were still convincing, albeit only from far away! And their methods were always the same: they planted themselves in front of us, as broadly as they could, trying to hold us back from where we were heading; preparing a substitute home for us in their own bosoms; and when the throttled feelings finally surged in us, they welcomed them as an embrace into which they threw themselves, face first.

This time, I had seen through these old tricks only after we had spent so much time together. I rubbed my fingertips sore to wipe away the disgrace.

My companion, however, was still leaning there as before, still thinking of himself as a city slicker, and his satisfaction with his destiny was making his exposed cheek turn red.

"You've got me!" I said, patting him on the back. Then I quickly mounted the steps, and the so groundlessly devoted faces of the domestics up in the vestibule delighted me like a lovely surprise. I looked at each one in turn as they removed my coat and dusted my boots. Then, heaving a sigh of relief, I loped into the parlor.

THE SUDDEN STROLL

When you seem to have finally made up your mind to stay home for the evening, have slipped into your smoking jacket, are sitting at the illuminated table after dinner, and have gotten down to the work or the game which you habitually follow by going to bed, when the weather outside is disagreeable, causing you to stay home as a matter of course, when you have remained quietly at the table for so long that going out would be bound to provoke general astonishment, when, moreover, the staircase is already dark and the front door is locked, and when you now, despite everything, stand up in a sudden fit of uneasiness, change your jacket, instantly appear dressed for the street, declare that you have to go out, and indeed do so after a brief goodbye, depending on how fast you slam the apartment door, believing that you have annoyed someone more or less, when you find yourself in the street, with limbs that respond so flexibly to this unexpected freedom obtained for them, when you feel that all ability to decide is concentrated in this decision, when you realize with greater significance than usual that you have more strength than you need

to easily prompt and endure the speediest change,
and when you thus hurry down the long streets—then
for this evening you have fully withdrawn from your
family, which fades off into nonexistence, while you
yourself, a sharply defined black silhouette, slapping
the backs of your thighs, rise to your true stature.

And everything is intensified when you drop in
on a friend this late in the evening to see how he is
getting on.

DECISIONS

Lifting oneself from a miserable state of mind ought to be easy even by sheer willpower. I wrench myself out of the chair, walk around the table, loosen my head and my neck, drive fire into my eyes, flex the muscles around them. Work against any feelings, exuberantly greet A. if he turns up now, amiably tolerate B. in my room, inhale all of C.'s words in long drafts despite my strain and suffering.

But even if I can manage like that, any mistake—and mistakes are inevitable—will bring everything, light or heavy, to a halt, and I will have to twist back into my circle again.

Hence the best course is to put up with everything, behave like a heavy mass, and even if you feel blasted away, not be inveigled into taking any unnecessary step, gaze at the other with animal eyes, feel no remorse—in short, push down with your own hands any ghost of life surviving in you, increase, that is, the final gravelike rest and let nothing else exist.

A characteristic movement in such a state of mind is to run the little finger over the eyebrows.

THE OUTING IN THE MOUNTAINS

"I don't know," I cried in a toneless voice, "I just don't know. If nobody comes, well, then nobody comes. I've hurt nobody, nobody's hurt me, yet nobody wants to help me. A bunch of nobodies. But that's not the way it is. Except that nobody's helping me—otherwise a bunch of nobodies would be just fine. I would love to—and why not—go on an outing with a bunch of absolute nobodies. Into the mountains, naturally—where else? How these nobodies crowd and jostle, those many arms jutting out at an angle and linked together, those countless feet separated by tiny steps! All of them, needless to say, in tailcoats. We walk along, free and easy, the wind blows through the gaps left open by ourselves and our limbs. Our throats become free in the mountains! It is a miracle that we do not sing!"

THE BACHELOR'S
UNHAPPINESS

It seems so awful to remain a bachelor, an old man barely keeping up his dignity when asking to be received if he wishes to spend an evening with other people, being sick and gazing at the empty room for weeks on end from the bed corner, always saying good night at the front door, never squeezing up the stairs next to his wife, having a room with only side doors that lead into other apartments, carrying home his supper in one hand, having to admire other people's children and not being allowed to constantly repeat, "I have none," modeling his appearance and behavior on those of one or two bachelors he recalls from his youth.

That's how it will be, except that in reality one will also stand there oneself, today and later, with a body and a real head, hence, also a forehead, to beat one's hand on it.

THE BUSINESSMAN

It may be that a few people are sorry for me, but I do not sense it. My small shop fills me with worries, making my forehead and temples ache, but offering no prospects of contentment, for my shop is small.

For hours in advance, I have to make decisions, keep the errand boy's memory alert, warn against mistakes that I dread, and during one season figure out which fashions will be in vogue the next, not among people in my circle, but among inaccessible populaces in the countryside.

My money is in the hands of strangers, their circumstances are beyond my ken; I have no inkling of the misfortune that could strike them; how could I ward it off! Perhaps they have become spendthrifts and are hosting a party in a tavern garden and others are attending this party for a brief moment before fleeing to America.

Now when my shop closes on a workday evening, and I am suddenly faced with hours in which I can do no work for the incessant needs of my business, then my agitation, a distant harbinger every morning, tosses inside me like a returning tide, but it cannot endure being inside me and it sweeps me away without a goal.

And then I have no use whatsoever for this mood and all I can do is go home, for my face and hands are dirty and sweaty, my clothes are stained and dusty, with my shop cap on my head and my boots scratched up by the nails of crates. I then walk as if on waves, drumming with the fingers of both hands and stroking the hair of passing children.

But the distance is too short. Soon I am inside my building, opening the elevator door and stepping in.

I see that now I am suddenly alone. Others, who must climb stairs, grow slightly tired, have to wait with hurriedly breathing lungs for someone to come and open the apartment door, giving them good reason to be annoyed and impatient; they now enter the vestibule, where they hang up their hats, and they are not alone until they walk through the corridor past several French doors and get into their own rooms.

I, however, am instantly alone in the elevator, and propped on my knees, I gaze into the narrow mirror. When the elevator starts rising, I say:

"Keep quiet, step back, do you want to melt into the shade of the trees, behind the draperies on the windows, into the vault of the bower?"

I talk through my teeth, and the staircase landings glide down the frosted panes like cascading water.

"Fly away; your wings, which I have never seen, may carry you to the village valley or to Paris, if you feel an urge to go there.

"But enjoy the view through the window when the processions converge from all three streets, not shifting aside for each other, but passing through one other, and letting the square emerge free again as their final ranks march off. Wave your handkerchiefs, be indignant, be moved, praise the beautiful lady driving past.

"Walk across the wooden bridge spanning the brook, nod at the swimming children, and marvel at the 'hurrah' rising from the thousand sailors on the distant battleship.

"Just follow the inconspicuous man, and when you have shoved him into a doorway, rob him and then watch him, each of you with his hands in his pockets, as he sadly goes his way into the left-hand street.

"The scattered policemen galloping on their horses rein in their animals and push you back. Let them, the empty streets will make them unhappy, I know they will. They are already riding away two by two, if you please, slowly rounding the street corners, speeding across the squares."

Then I have to get out, send the elevator back down, ring the apartment bell, and the maid opens the door while I say: Good evening.

ABSENTLY GAZING OUT

What will we do in these spring days that are now hurrying toward us? This morning the sky was gray, but if you go to the window now, you are surprised and you lean your cheek against the window latch.

The sun is already setting, of course, but down below you see its light on the face of the childlike girl who is just strolling and looking about, and at the same time you see the man's shadow upon her as he hurries up behind her.

And then the man has passed her, and the child's face is utterly bright.

THE WAY HOME

Just look how persuasive the air is after the thunderstorm! My merits appear to me and overpower me, although, admittedly, I offer no resistance.

I march along and my tempo is the tempo of this side of the street, this street, this neighborhood. I am rightfully responsible for all the knocks on doors, on tabletops, for all toasts, for the lovers in their beds, in the skeletons of the new buildings, pressed against the house walls in dark alleys, or on the ottomans of bordellos.

I assess my past against my future, but find both of them excellent, I can give neither one the preference, and I can carp only at the inequity of providence, which has favored me in this way.

It is only upon entering my room that I get to thinking although without having found anything worth thinking about while climbing the stairs. It does not help me much if I open the window all the way, and the music is still playing in some garden.

THE PEOPLE RUNNING BY

When we stroll through a street at night, and a man, already visible from far away (for the street rises in front of us and there is a full moon), comes running toward us, we will not grab hold of him, even if he is weak and ragged, even if someone is running after him and yelling; we will simply let him run on.

For it is night, and we cannot help it if the street rises in front of us in the full moon, and besides: perhaps these two people are staging the chase for their own amusement, perhaps the two of them are pursuing a third, perhaps the first man is being pursued through no fault of his own, perhaps the second one wants to murder him, and we will be accomplices to the murder, perhaps the two of them know nothing of one another, and each is simply running home to bed on his own account, perhaps they are sleepwalkers, perhaps the first man is armed.

And anyway, don't we have the right to be tired, haven't we drunk a lot of wine? We are glad that we no longer see the second one either.

THE PASSENGER

I stand on the platform of the trolley car and am
completely insecure about my footing in this world,
in this city, in my family. Nor could I indicate even
casually what demands I might rightfully make in any
direction. In no way can I defend myself for standing
on this platform, clutching this strap, letting this trolley carry me along, defend people for scurrying out of
the way or walking quietly or window-shopping. Of
course, no one is asking me for a defense, but that's
beside the point.

The trolley approaches a stop, a girl comes over to
the steps, ready to get out. She is as obvious to me as
if I had run my fingers over her. She is wearing black,
the pleats of her skirt barely stir, her blouse is snug
and has a collar of white, fine-meshed lace, her left
hand is propped flat against the side of the trolley,
the umbrella in her right hand is poised on the second
step from the top. Her face is brown, her nose, slightly
pinched on the sides, has a broad, round tip. She has
a lot of brown hair and small, stray hairs on her right
temple. Her small ear lies close to her head, but by
standing near her I can see the entire ridge of her
right ear conch and the shadow at its root.

I wondered back then: How come she's not astonished at herself, how come she keeps her mouth shut and says nothing along those lines?

FROCKS

Often, when I see frocks with manifold pleats, ruffles, and ornaments, fitting so beautifully on beautiful bodies, I think they will not remain that way for long, instead they will develop wrinkles that cannot be ironed out, thick, unremovable dust will settle in the adornments, and no girl will want to appear so dismal and ridiculous as to slip into the same, precious frock early in the morning and take it off at night.

Still, I see girls who are certainly beautiful and display many attractive muscles and small bones and taut skin and masses of fine hair, and yet they sport that same natural masquerade day after day, always propping that same face on the same palms and letting their mirrors reflect it.

It is only on some nights, when they come home late from a party, that the frock looks frayed in the mirror, puffy, dusty, already seen by everyone and scarcely to be worn again.

THE REJECTION

Whenever I meet a beautiful girl and ask her, "Please come with me, do," and she walks on without a word, her drift is:

"You are no duke with a soaring name, no four-square American with an Indian's stature, with level eyes, with a skin massaged by the air of grasslands and the rivers flowing through them; you have never traveled to or on the great seas, which are goodness knows where. So please tell me, why should a beautiful girl like me go with you?"

"You are forgetting that no automobile carries you through the streets, rocking in long sweeps. I see no retinue of gentlemen, pressed into their clothes, blessing you in murmurs, walking behind you in a precise semicircle; your breasts are snugly laced in your corset, but your thighs and hips make up for that abstinence; you are wearing a pleated taffeta dress, the kind that certainly delighted all of us last autumn, and yet from time to time you smile—that mortal danger emanating from your body."

"Well, we are both right, and rather than having it dawn on us irrefutably, don't you think that each of us should really go home alone?!"

43

REFLECTIONS FOR
AMATEUR JOCKEYS

Nothing, once you think about it, could tempt you to be the winner of a race.

When the orchestra strikes up, the glory of being hailed as the best horseman in a country is too delightful to prevent remorse from setting in the next morning.

The envy of our opponents—cunning and rather influential men—is bound to cause us pain in the narrow enclosure through which we ride after that vast expanse of the racecourse, which soon stretched out empty before us, except for a few straggling riders from the previous round, who were tiny now as they charged toward the edge of the horizon.

Many of our friends are hurrying to collect their winnings and so they merely shout their hurrahs to us over their shoulders from the distant betting window; our best friends, however, did not even bet on our horse, for they feared that if they were to lose, they would be angry at us; but now that our horse has come in first and they have won nothing, they turn away as we pass and they prefer to gaze along the stands.

Our rivals, behind us, steady in their saddles, are

trying to overlook the misfortune that has struck them and the injustice that is somehow being done to them; they are putting on cheerful expressions, as if a new race had to begin, and a serious one after such child's play.

Many women find the winner ridiculous because he struts about and yet cannot cope with the endless handshaking, saluting, bowing, and distant waving, while the losers have shut their mouths and are casually patting the necks of their mostly whinnying horses.

Eventually, the sky clouds over, and it actually starts raining.

THE WINDOW FACING THE STREET

If a person leads a desolate life and yet would care for some sort of company now and again, if, depending on the changes in the time of day, the weather, his work schedule, and the like, he suddenly wishes to see an arm, any arm, to cling to—that person will not get by for long without a window facing the street. And if he is in no mood to look for anything and, being tired, merely steps over to his windowsill, his eyes darting up and down between the public and the sky, and wants none of it, and tilts his head back slightly, then the horses down below will nevertheless yank him down into their retinue of vehicles and hubbub and thus finally toward human harmony.

THE WISH TO BE AN INDIAN

If only one were an Indian, ever alert, and, leaning
into the wind on a speeding horse, always jerkily
quivering over the quivering ground, until one
dropped one's spurs, for there would be no spurs,
until one hurled away one's reins, for there would be
no reins, and one barely saw the countryside before
one as a smoothly mown heath, but now without the
horse's neck and horse's head.

THE TREES

For we are like tree trunks in the snow. They seem to be resting smoothly as if one could push them away with a slight nudge. No, one cannot, for they are firmly attached to the ground. But lo and behold, this too is sheer semblance.

UNHAPPINESS

One evening, when I could endure it no longer—
it was in November—and I was dashing around the
narrow carpet of my room as if it were a racetrack,
and, startled by the sight of the illuminated street, I
turned away, yet found a new goal in the depth of the
room, in the chasm of the mirror, and I shrieked
merely in order to hear the shriek to which nothing
responds, which nothing can deprive of the power of
shrieking, and which, consequently, rises unhampered and cannot stop even if it fades out—the door
flew open out of the wall, and so hastily because haste
was necessary, and even the cart horses down below
on the roadway reared like horses maddened in a
battle, baring their throats.

Like a small ghost, a child swept in from the pitch-
dark corridor, where the lamp was not yet burning,
and he remained on tiptoe, on an imperceptibly swaying floorboard. Instantly blinded by the twilight in the
room, he was about to quickly cover his face with his
hands, but then unexpectedly calmed down at the
sight of the window, where, beyond the crossbars, the
high-swept vapor of the streetlight had finally settled

beneath the darkness. Propping his right elbow against the wall of the room, he held himself upright in the open doorway, letting the draft from outside play around his ankles, and also his neck, and also his temples.

Eyeing him briefly, I then said, "Good day," and removed my robe from the stove screen because I didn't care to stand there half naked. For a short while I kept my lips open, to release my agitation through my mouth. I had a sour taste in my mouth, my eyelashes fluttered in my face; in short, that visit, although expected, was simply the last straw.

The child was still standing in the same place, by the wall, he had pressed his right hand against its surface and, with red cheeks, he simply couldn't get enough of the fact that the whitewashed plaster had a coarse grain, which chafed his fingertips. I said: "Are you sure it is I you are looking for? Could you be mistaken? There's nothing easier than making a mistake in this large building. My name is So-and-so, I live on the third landing. Am I the person you wish to visit?"

"Quiet, quiet!" said the child over his shoulder. "It's all correct."

"Then come further into the room, I'd like to close the door."

"I've just closed the door. Don't bother. Just calm down."

"It's no bother. But a lot of people live along this corridor, and naturally we're all acquainted. Most of them are coming home from their jobs now. If they hear someone talking in a room, they simply feel they have the right to open their doors and check what's

going on. That's just the way it is. These people have
their daily work behind them, and they won't knuckle
under to anybody in their provisional evening freedom! Besides, you're quite aware of that. Let me close
the door."

"Why, what's wrong? What's the matter with you?
The whole building can come for all I care. And let
me repeat: I've already closed the door. Do you believe you're the only person who can close it? I've
even turned the key."

"Well, fine. That's all I want. You didn't need to
turn the key. And now that you're here, do make
yourself comfortable. You are my guest. You must
trust me completely. Make yourself at home, don't be
shy. I won't force you to stay or to leave. Need I say
so? Don't you know me by now?"

"No. You really didn't need to say so. In fact, you
shouldn't have said so. I'm a child; why all this fuss
and bother?"

"It's not as bad as all that. Of course, a child. But
you're not that little. You're quite grown up. If you
were a girl, you couldn't just simply lock yourself up
in a room with me."

"We don't have to worry about that. I only wanted
to say that my knowing you so well offers me little
protection, it merely relieves you of the effort to tell
me lies. Nevertheless, you are paying me compli-
ments. Do stop, I demand that you stop. Besides, I
can't recognize you everywhere and every time, least
of all in this darkness. It would be much better if you
made some light. No, never mind. In any case, I'll
remember that you've already threatened me."

"What? I threatened you? Now look here. I'm so

glad you're finally here. I say 'finally' because it's already so late. I simply don't understand why you've come so late. Perhaps I was so overjoyed that I inadvertently said things I shouldn't have said, and you took them amiss. I'll admit ten times over that I did say those things—indeed, I threatened you with anything you like. Just let's not argue, for goodness' sake! But how could you believe it? How could you insult me like that? Why do you want to devote all your strength to spoiling this brief moment of your presence? A stranger would be more accommodating than you are."

"That I believe; it was no great insight. By nature, I'm as close and as accommodating to you as any stranger could get. And you know it, then why so wistful? If all you want to do is put on an act, I'll leave momentarily."

"Really? You have the nerve to tell me that too? You're a bit too bold. After all, you *are* in my room. You're rubbing your fingers like crazy on my wall. My room, my wall! And besides, the things you're saying are ridiculous and not just impudent. You say your nature forces you to speak to me like that. Really? Your nature forces you? That's so nice of your nature. Your nature is the same as mine, and if I act friendly to you by nature, then you should behave no differently."

"Is that friendly?"

"I'm talking about before."

"Do you know what I'll be like later on?"

"I know nothing."

And going over to the nightstand, I lit the candle on it. In those days, I had neither gas nor electric light in my room. Then I sat at the table for a while until I grew tired of that too, I put on my overcoat, took my hat from the sofa, and blew out the candle. As I walked out, my foot got caught in a chair leg.

On the stairs, I ran into a tenant from my floor.

"Are you going out again, you rascal?" he asked, resting on his legs, which were straddling two steps.

"What should I do?" I said, "I've just had a ghost in my room."

"You sound as dissatisfied as if you had found a hair in your soup."

"You're making fun of it. But I can assure you, a ghost is a ghost."

"How true. But what if someone doesn't believe in ghosts?"

"Why, do you think I believe in ghosts? But what good does it do not to believe?"

"It's quite simple. You don't have to be afraid when a ghost actually comes to you."

"Yes, but that's only an incidental fear. The real fear is the fear of what caused the apparition. And that fear remains. I've got a whole lot of it in me." I was so nervous that I began rummaging through all my pockets.

"Since you're not afraid of the apparition itself, you could easily have asked what caused it!"

"It's obvious you've never conversed with ghosts. One can never get precise information out of them. It's like pulling teeth. These ghosts seem to be more skeptical about their existence than we are—which, by the by, comes as no surprise, considering how frail they are."

"But I've heard they can be nursed back to health."

"My, you're well informed. It's true. But is anyone going to do it?"

"Why not? If, say, it's a female ghost?" he said, and swung his leg to the top step.

"I see," I said, "but even then it's not worth the trouble."

I thought of something else. My acquaintance was already so high up that in order to see me he had to bend under the well of the staircase. "But nevertheless," I exclaimed, "if you take away my ghost up there, then I'll never speak to you again."

"Oh, I was only joking," he said, pulling his head back.

"Well then, that's fine," I said, and indeed I could just as easily have gone for a walk. But, feeling so forlorn as I did, I preferred going back up and getting to bed.

THE JUDGMENT

A story by Franz Kafka
for Fräulein Felice B. [Bauer]

It was on a Sunday morning during the most beautiful time of spring. Georg Bendemann, a young businessman, was sitting in his private room on the first landing of one of the low, frail houses, which, differing almost only in height and coloring, stretched in a lengthy row along the river. Having just finished writing a letter to a boyhood friend in a foreign country, he sealed the envelope with playful slowness and then, propping his elbow on the desk, he gazed out the window at the river, the bridge, and the sparsely green rises on the opposite bank.

He was musing about his friend, who, dissatisfied with his progress at home, had virtually fled to Russia many years ago. Now, in St. Petersburg, he was running a business, which, although initially very promising, appeared to have been stagnating for quite a while, as the friend complained during his increasingly rarer visits. And so he was drudging uselessly in a foreign country, a full exotic beard poorly concealing the face with which Georg had been so familiar since childhood and whose sallow complexion seemed to indicate a developing disease. As the friend explained: having no real ties with the local colony of his compatriots and almost no social dealings with native families, he was settling in to become a bachelor for good.

What could one write to such a man, who had obviously painted himself into a corner, who could be pitied, but could not be helped? Should he perhaps be advised to come back home, transfer his livelihood here, resume all the old friendships—to which, after all, no obstacle existed—and, generally, rely on help from his friends? Yet this would, in effect, mean telling him, tactfully indeed, but all the more offensively, that his previous efforts had failed, that he should finally abandon them, that he should return home and let himself be gaped at by all as someone who had returned forever, that only his friends had any understanding, and that he was a big child who simply had to listen to the successful friends who had remained at home. And was it even certain that all the torments to be inflicted on him had any purpose? Perhaps they would never even succeed in bringing him home— after all, he himself said he no longer understood the conditions in the homeland; and so, despite everything, he would remain in his foreign country, embittered by his friends' advice and somewhat more alienated from them. But if he did heed their advice and (naturally through no one's intention but because of the actual conditions) were frustrated here, unable to find his bearings either with his friends or without them, feeling humiliated, and now truly having no homeland and no friends, would it not be far better for him to remain abroad just as he was doing? Could one, all things considered, imagine him truly getting anywhere here?

For these reasons, if one wished merely to keep corresponding with the friend, one could not really communicate things that one would unabashedly reveal to even the most casual acquaintances. The friend had not been home for over three years now, and he rationalized this very lamely by citing the insecure political conditions in Russia, which supposedly prevented a small businessman from taking even the briefest trip, while hundreds of thousands of Russians were traveling peacefully throughout the world. Yet for Georg many things had changed precisely during these three years. His friend had most likely heard that Georg's mother had passed away some two years ago, since which time Georg had been sharing a household with his old father; and the friend had written, expressing his condolences with a dryness that could only be attributed to the fact that in a foreign country the grief caused by such an event is quite inconceivable. Now since that time, Georg had been more resolute in tackling his business as indeed everything else. Perhaps, during his mother's lifetime, his father, by insisting on doing everything *his* way in the business, had prevented Georg from pursuing any real activity of his own; perhaps, since his mother's death, his father, although still working in the business, had become more restrained; perhaps— and this was even highly probable—various strokes of luck had played a far more important role. In any case, however, the business had quite unexpectedly prospered during those two years, they had had to double the staff, sales had quintupled, and further growth was, no doubt, just around the corner.

The friend, however, had no inkling of this change. Earlier—perhaps the last time was in that letter of condolence—he had tried to talk Georg into emigrating to Russia, and he had enlarged upon the fine prospects that St. Petersburg offered precisely in Georg's line of business. The figures he quoted were infinitesimal compared with the current volume of Georg's business. But Georg had not felt like writing to his friend about his business triumphs, and were he to do so now, belatedly, it would truly look bizarre.

So Georg always limited himself to writing to his friend about trivial occurrences, such as clutter up the memory when one ruminates on a quiet Sunday. All he was after was to keep intact his friend's image of his hometown, an image that he must have shaped during this long interval, and with which he had made his peace. Thus, in three letters spaced rather far apart, Georg had actually informed his friend about an insignificant person who had gotten engaged to an equally insignificant girl, until, quite contrary to Georg's intention, the friend actually became interested in this noteworthy event.

But Georg preferred writing to him about such things rather than admitting that he himself had gotten engaged one month ago to a Fräulein Frieda Brandenfeld, a girl from a well-to-do family. He would often talk to his fiancée about his friend and the peculiar relationship that had evolved in their correspondence.

"Why, then he won't be coming to our wedding," she said, "but I do have the right to meet all your friends."

"I don't want to bother him," Georg replied. "Mind you, he would probably come—at least, I think he would; but he would feel pressured and put upon, he might envy me and, feeling dissatisfied and incapable of ever overcoming that dissatisfaction, he would most certainly return to Russia alone. Alone—do you know what that means?"

"Yes, but couldn't he hear about our marriage in some other way?"

"That's something I can't prevent, of course, but given his life-style it's unlikely."

"If you have such friends, Georg, you should never have gotten engaged in the first place."

"Well, we are both at fault; but I would not have it any other way now."

And when, breathing quickly under his kisses, she managed to say, "I really do feel offended," Georg decided there was truly no harm in disclosing everything to his friend. "That is how I am, and that is how he must take me," he told himself. "I cannot tailor myself into a person who might be more suitable for a friendship with him than I am."

And indeed, in the long letter he had written to his friend on this Sunday morning, he reported the engagement in the following words: "I have saved the best news for last. I have gotten engaged to a Fräulein Frieda Brandenfeld, a girl from a well-to-do family that settled here a long time after your departure, so that you most likely don't know them. Later on there will be time enough for me to give you more details about my fiancée, but at present, it should be enough for you to know that I am very happy, and that my relationship with you has changed only to the extent that now, instead of a quite ordinary friend, you will have a happy friend in me. Furthermore, in my fiancée, who sends you her very best wishes, and who will soon be writing to you herself, you will have a sincere friend, which is not altogether unimportant for a bachelor. I realize that any number of things are preventing you from visiting us, but might not my wedding provide just the right occasion for throwing all obstacles aside? Still, be that as it may, do not concern yourself about anyone else and do only as you think best."

With this letter in his hand, Georg had been sitting at his desk for a long time, facing the window. An acquaintance passing in the street had waved to him, but Georg had barely responded with an absent smile.

Finally, he put the letter in his pocket, left his room, cut across a small hallway, and stepped into his father's room, which he had not entered for months. Nor was there ever any need for him to do so, since he dealt with his father constantly at the office, and they always had lunch together at a restaurant. True, for the evening meal each fended for himself; but normally, unless Georg, as was most often the case, was seeing friends or, nowadays, visiting his fiancée, he and his father would sit for a little while, each with his newspaper, in the common living room.

Georg was astonished at how dark his father's room was even on this sunny morning. So then the high wall looming on the other side of the narrow courtyard really cast this huge a shadow. His father was sitting by the window in a corner decorated with various mementos of the deceased mother, and he was reading the newspaper, holding it in front of his eyes but at an angle in order to compensate for some weakness in his vision. The table bore the remains of his breakfast, not much of which seemed to have been eaten.

"Ah, Georg!" his father said, promptly going toward him. His heavy robe swung open as he walked, and the skirts flapped around his legs. "My father is still a giant," Georg thought to himself.

"Why, it's unbearably dark here," he then said.

"Yes, it *is* dark," his father replied.

"And you've closed the window?"

"I prefer it like this."

"But it's quite warm outside," said Georg, virtually continuing his previous comment, and sat down.

The father cleared away the breakfast dishes, depositing them on a chest.

"I just wanted to tell you," Georg went on, quite somberly following the old man's movements, "that I've written to St. Petersburg about my engagement." He drew a bit of the letter from his pocket, then let it drop back in again.

"St. Petersburg?" his father asked.

"To my friend, of course," said Georg, seeking his father's eyes. "He's so different at the office," thought Georg, "sitting here so broadly, with his arms crossed."

"Yes. Your friend," his father said pointedly.

"But, Father, you know that at first I didn't want to tell him I was engaged. To spare his feelings, for no other reason. You know yourself that he's a difficult person. I told myself that he could hear about my engagement from someone else, although that would be quite unlikely, given his solitary life-style—that is something I cannot prevent—but he was simply not to hear about it from me."

"And now you've changed your mind?" asked his father, placing the large newspaper on the windowsill and, on top of the newspaper, his spectacles, which he covered with his hand.

"Yes, now I've changed my mind. If he is my good friend, I told myself, then my happy engagement will make him happy too. And that was why I no longer had qualms about notifying him. But before mailing the letter, I wanted to let you know."

"Georg," said the father, widening out his toothless mouth, "listen! You have come to me about this matter in order to discuss it. This is certainly to your credit. But it is useless, it is worse than useless if you refuse to tell me the whole truth. I do not wish to stir up things that are inappropriate here. Since the death of our dear mother, certain disagreeable things have occurred. Perhaps their time will come too, and perhaps it will come sooner than we think. At the office, many things elude me, perhaps they are not being held back from me—I by no means wish to assume that they are being held back from me—but I am not strong enough now, my memory is failing, I can no longer keep track of so many things. First of all, such is the course of nature, and secondly, I was struck a lot harder than you by our dear mother's death. . . . However, since we happen to be talking about this subject, about this letter, then I must beg you, Georg: Do not deceive me. It is a trivial matter, it is not worth wasting one's breath on, so do not hoodwink me. Do you really have that friend in St. Petersburg?"

Georg stood up, embarrassed. "Never mind my friends. A thousand friends won't replace my father. Do you know what I think? You're not really taking care of yourself. But old age demands its due. You are indispensable to me in the business, you know that very well; but if the business is going to threaten your health, then I'll shut it down for good tomorrow. That won't do, however. We have to establish a different life-style for you. A radically different one. You sit here in the dark, though you would have excellent light in the living room. You nibble at breakfast instead of eating properly. You sit with the window closed, and yet the fresh air would do you so much good. No, Father! I'm going to call the doctor, and we will follow his advice. We'll switch rooms, you'll move into the front room, I'll take this one. It will not be disruptive for you, all your things will be moved along with you. But all in good time, just lie down a bit for now, you absolutely need to rest. Come, I'll help you undress, you'll see that I know how. Or would you rather go to the front room right away? Then you can lie down in my bed for the time being. That would really be very sensible."

Georg was standing right next to his father, whose head, with its disheveled white hair, had dropped to his chest.

"Georg," his father said in a low, unemotional voice.

Georg instantly knelt down beside him, in his father's weary face he saw the enormous pupils ogling him from the corners of his eyes.

"You have no friend in St. Petersburg. You've always been a prankster, and you've never spared me either. How could you have a friend there of all places! I simply can't believe it."

"Just think about it, Father," said Georg, lifting him up from the chair and slipping off his robe while his father now stood there rather feebly. "Why, it's been almost three years since my friend visited us. I can still remember that you weren't particularly fond of him. At least twice I pretended he wasn't here, even though he was sitting with me in my room. I could certainly understand your aversion to him, my friend has his peculiarities. But then afterwards you did have a good talk with him after all. And I was so proud that you listened to him, nodding and asking him questions. If you think about it, you're sure to remember. He was telling us incredible stories about the Russian Revolution. For example, about the time he had gone to Kiev on business, and during a riot, he had seen a priest on a balcony, and after cutting a broad bloody cross into his palm, the priest had raised his hand and appealed to the mob. Why, you've even repeated that story yourself now and then."

Meanwhile Georg had managed to reseat his father, carefully taking off his socks as well as the knitted drawers he wore over his linen underpants. Upon seeing the not especially clean underwear, Georg reproached himself for neglecting his father. It would certainly have been his duty to make sure his father changed his linen. So far, Georg had not explicitly talked to his fiancée about what arrangements they would make regarding his father's future, for they had tacitly assumed that he would stay on alone in the old house. But now Georg quickly and firmly resolved to take his father along into his future household. Indeed, it almost seemed, on closer inspection, as if the care his father would receive there might come too late.

He carried his father to bed in his arms. He had a terrible feeling when he noticed, during the few steps to the bed, that his father, who was on his chest, was playing with Georg's watch chain. His father clung so tightly to this watch chain that Georg could not lay him down on the bed immediately.

But no sooner was his father in bed than everything seemed fine. He covered himself on his own and then pulled the blanket way over his shoulders. He looked up at Georg with eyes that were not unfriendly.

"You *are* starting to remember him, aren't you?" Georg asked, giving him an encouraging nod.

"Am I properly covered up now?" his father asked as if unable to see whether his feet were sufficiently covered.

"So you do like being in bed," said Georg, tucking the blanket in more snugly.

"Am I properly covered up?" his father asked once again and seemed particularly intent on hearing the answer.

"Don't worry, you're properly covered up."

"No!" cried his father so loudly that his reply banged against the question; he hurled the blanket away so violently that for an instant it unfolded completely in the air, and he stood upright in the bed. However, he held one hand lightly on the ceiling. "You wanted to cover me up, I know you did, my young pup, but I am not yet covered up. And even my final ounce of strength is enough for you, too much for you. I certainly do know your friend. He would be a son after my own heart. That's why you've been deceiving him all these years. Why else? Do you believe I haven't wept for him? After all, that's why you lock yourself up in your office, no one is to bother you, the boss is busy—just so you can write your dishonest little letters to Russia. But fortunately, no one has to teach your father how to see through his son. And now you thought you had wrestled him down, wrestled him down so thoroughly that you could sit on him with your behind, and he wouldn't budge, and so my fine son decided to up and marry!"

Georg looked up at the horrifying image of his father. His friend in St. Petersburg, whom his father suddenly knew so well, stirred Georg's feelings as never before. He pictured him lost in the vastness of Russia. He pictured him at the door of the empty, looted shop. He could barely keep standing amid the wreckage of the shelves, the tattered wares, the falling gas brackets. Why had he needed to move so far away?

"Look at me!" his father shouted, and Georg, almost distracted, dashed toward the bed in order to grasp everything, but stopped halfway there.

"Because she pulled her skirts up," his father began to simper, "because she pulled her skirts up like this, the nasty goose," and acting out the words, he pulled his shirt up so high that the wartime scar on his thigh could be seen. "Because she pulled her skirts up like this and this and this, you accosted her, and, in order to satisfy your lust with her unhampered, you disgraced our mother's memory, betrayed your friend, and put your father to bed so that he can't move. But can he move or can't he?"

And he stood entirely on his own and kicked out his legs. He was radiant with insight.

Georg stood in a corner, as far away as possible from his father. A long while ago, he had firmly resolved to keep a sharp eye on his every movement so as to avoid being deviously pounced on in some way, from behind, from above. Now he recalled his long-forgotten resolve and forgot it again, like someone drawing a short length of thread through a needle's eye.

"But now your friend has not been betrayed after all!" his father cried, underscoring his words by poking his forefinger to and fro. "I've been his local representative here."

"You actor!" Georg couldn't help shouting, then instantly realized the harm he had done, and with gaping eyes, he—too late—bit his tongue so hard that he curled up in pain.

"Yes, of course I've been acting! Acting! A good word! What other comfort was left for your old widowed father? Tell me—and while you're answering me, be my living son still—what else was left for me in my back room, bullied by the disloyal staff, old to the marrow of my bones? And my son strutted jubilantly through the world, closing deals that I had prepared, turning cartwheels in sheer delight, and walking away from his father with the poker face of an honorable man! Do you believe I didn't love you— I who fathered you?"

"Now he's going to lean forward," Georg thought to himself. "What if he keels over and shatters!" This word hissed through his mind.

His father leaned forward, but did not keel over. Since Georg did not approach him as he had expected, his father straightened up again.

"Stay where you are, I don't need you! You think you still have the strength to come here and are merely holding back because you want to. Don't fool yourself! I'm still a lot stronger than you. On my own, I might have had to yield, but Mother gave me her strength, I formed a marvelous alliance with your friend, and I've got your customers here in my pocket!"

"He has pockets even in his shirt!" Georg said to himself, believing that this remark could make his father look ridiculous to all the world. His thought lasted only an instant, for he always forgot everything.

"Just take your fiancée on your arm and come to me! I'll sweep her from your side, before you even know it!"

Georg grimaced in disbelief. His father merely nodded toward Georg's corner, clinching the truth of what he said.

"Oh, how you amused me today when you came and asked me if you should write your friend about the engagement. Why, he knows everything, you stupid boy, he knows everything! I've been writing to him because you forgot to take away my writing things. That's why he hasn't visited here for years, he knows everything a hundred times better than you do yourself, he crumples up your letters in his left hand without reading them while he holds up my letters in his right hand to read them!"

He enthusiastically swung his arm over his head. "He knows everything a thousand times better!" he cried.

"Ten thousand times!" said Georg, to ridicule his father; but in his mouth, the words sounded deadly earnest.

"For years now I've been expecting you to come with this question! Do you think I care about anything else? Do you believe I read newspapers? Look!" and he threw Georg a newspaper page which had somehow been carried along into the bed. An old newspaper, its name entirely unknown to Georg.

"How long you hesitated before you matured! Mother had to die, she could not live to see the joyful day, your friend is going to the dogs in his Russia, three years ago he was already yellow enough to be dumped out, and as for me, you can see what condition I'm in. You do have eyes in your head!"

"So you've been lying in ambush for me!" cried Georg.

In a pitying tone, his father casually said: "You probably wanted to say that before. But now it's no longer suitable."

And more loudly: "So now you know what else there was in the world besides you, previously you only knew about yourself! You were truly an innocent child, but you were even more truly a diabolical man! And therefore know: I hereby condemn you to death by drowning!"

Georg felt hounded from the room, his ears still rang with the crash of his father behind him, falling on the bed. Hurrying down the steps as if they were a sloping plane, he ran into his housekeeper, who was

71

about to go upstairs and clean the apartment after the night. "Jesus!" she cried, covering her face with her apron, but he was already outside. He leaped from the front door and dashed across the roadway, driven toward the water. He was already clutching the railing the way a hungry man clutches food. He swung himself over, like the outstanding gymnast he had been in his youth, the pride of his parents. He was still clutching tight with weakening hands when he spied a bus between the railing bars: it would easily drown out the sound of his fall. He softly cried, "Dear parents, I have always loved you," and let himself drop.

At that moment, a simply endless stream of traffic was passing across the bridge.

THE STOKER

A Fragment

Sixteen-year-old Karl Rossmann had been sent to America by his poor parents because a maid had seduced him, giving birth to his child, and as his ship, which was already slowing down, sailed into the harbor of New York, he viewed the statue of the goddess of freedom, which he had already observed long ago, but now saw as if in a suddenly more intense sunlight. Her arm with its sword towered as if for the first time, and the free breezes wafted around her figure.

"So high!" he said to himself and, not really giving any thought to disembarking, he was gradually pushed further and further, all the way to the railing, by the constantly swelling throng of porters trudging past him.

A young man with whom he had become casually acquainted during the voyage said as he walked by: "Hey, don't you feel like going ashore yet?"

"Oh, I'm quite ready," said Karl, smiling at him; and in his exuberance, Karl, being a strong boy, heaved his valise upon his shoulder. However, looking beyond his acquaintance, who, lightly swinging his cane, was already moving off with the others, Karl realized, to his dismay, that he had forgotten his umbrella down below. After hastily asking his acquaintance, who did not seem very happy about the prospect, to be kind enough to watch his valise for an instant, Karl checked his surroundings in order to regain his bearings when returning and then hurried off. Down below, he found to his regret that a corridor that would have considerably shortened his path was barred for the first time, probably because all the passengers were disembarking, so that he arduously had to seek his way through countless small rooms, over endless series of short staircases, along ever-twisting corridors, across an empty room with a deserted desk, until he was thoroughly lost, for he had taken this route only once or twice before and always in a large group. Bewildered as he was, encountering no one, hearing only the endless shuffling of the thousands of human feet overhead, noticing from afar, like a puff of air, the final wheeze of the engines, which had already been turned off, he began to knock, without reflecting, on a small door, where he had happened to pause in his wanderings.

"It's unlocked," someone called from inside, and Karl, with a genuine sigh of relief, opened the door. "Why are you banging so wildly on the door?" a gigantic man asked, barely glancing at Karl. Through some sort of hatch, a dim light, which had been used up long since on the upper decks of the ship, oozed into the miserable cabin, where a bed, a closet, a chair, and the man were jammed in side by side, as if in storage.

"I've lost my way," said Karl, "I didn't realize it during the crossing, but this is an awfully huge ship."

"Right you are," said the man somewhat proudly, but he did not stop fiddling with the lock of a small satchel, which he kept squeezing shut with both hands in order to hear the bolt snap into place. "Oh, why don't you come in!" the man went on. "You don't want to stand outside, do you?"

"Am I intruding?" asked Karl.

"Why, how could you intrude!"

"Are you German?" Karl tried to reassure himself further, for he had heard a great deal about the dangers threatening newcomers in America, especially from Irishmen.

"Yes, indeed, yes, indeed," said the man.

Karl still hesitated. Whereupon the man unexpectedly grabbed the doorknob and quickly shut the door, sweeping Karl inside. "I can't stand having people peer in from the corridor," said the man, fiddling with his trunk again. "They all hurry by and peer in. There are few people who can stand that!"

"But the corridor's totally deserted," said Karl, uncomfortably squashed against the bedpost.

"Yes, now," said the man.

"But this *is* now," thought Karl. "This man is hard to talk to."

"Why don't you lie down on the bed," said the man, "you'll have more room."

Karl crawled in as well as he could, guffawing at his first useless effort to swing into the bed. But no sooner was he in it than he cried, "Good Lord, I've forgotten all about my valise!"

"Where is it?"

"Up on deck, an acquaintance is watching it. Now just what was his name?" And from a secret pocket that his mother had sewn into his coat lining specifically for his voyage, he fished out a visiting card. "Butterbaum. Franz Butterbaum."

"Do you really need your valise?"

"Of course."

"Well, then why did you hand it over to a complete stranger?"

"I'd forgotten my umbrella below and I hurried to get it, but I didn't want to drag along my valise. Then to top it all off, I lost my way."

"Are you alone? No one accompanying you?"

"Yes, alone."

"Maybe I should stick with this man," Karl pondered, "where could I find a better friend?"

"And now you've lost your valise in the bargain. Not to mention your umbrella." And the man sat down on the chair as if he were developing some interest in Karl's problem.

"But I don't believe my valise is lost."

"Faith can move mountains," said the man, vigorously scratching his short, dark, thick hair. "On a ship, morals change with ports of call. In Hamburg, Butterbaum might have guarded your valise, but here there's most likely no trace of either him or it."

"Then I'll have to take a look right now," said Karl, peering around to see how he could leave.

"Stay where you are," said the man and pushed Karl's chest with one hand, roughly shoving him back into the bed.

"But why?" asked Karl in annoyance.

"Because it makes no sense," said the man. "I'm
leaving very soon and then we can go together. Either
the valise has been stolen, then there's nothing you
can do, or the man's still guarding it, in which case
he's a fool and should keep on guarding it, or he's
simply an honest person and has left the valise there,
and it will be easier to find once the ship has emptied
out. And the same goes for your umbrella."

"Do you know your way around the ship?" asked
Karl distrustfully, feeling as if there were some hidden
catch to the otherwise persuasive idea that things
could best be found when the ship was empty.

"Well, I am a stoker," said the man.

"You're a stoker!" cried Karl in delight, as if this
news were beyond all expectation, and propping himself on his elbow, he took a closer look at the man.

"Why, outside the room where I was sleeping with
the Slovak, there was a porthole through which you
could see into the engine room."

"Yes, that's where I worked," said the stoker.

"I've always been interested in technology," said
Karl, hewing to a specific train of thought, "and I'm
certain I would have eventually become an engineer
if I hadn't had to leave for America."

"But why did you have to leave?"

"Oh, well!" said Karl, waving off the whole business, whereby he smiled at the stoker as if asking his
indulgence even for the things he had not confessed.

"I'm sure you had your reason," said the stoker,
and there was no telling whether he was demanding
or dismissing the story behind that reason.

"Now I could be a stoker too," said Karl, "my parents don't care what becomes of me."

"My job is free," said the stoker, and in full awareness of that circumstance he put his hands into the pockets of his creased, leatherlike, iron-gray trousers and flung his legs across the bed in order to stretch them. Karl had to squeeze closer to the wall.

"You're leaving the ship?"

"Yes, we're marching off today."

"But why? Don't you like it?"

"Well, that's how things have worked out, it's not always a matter of liking or not liking something. Besides, you're right, I don't like it. You're probably not seriously thinking of becoming a stoker, but that's precisely the easiest way to become one. So I would strongly advise you against it. If you wanted to study in Europe, why not do it here? The American universities are incomparably better than the European ones."

"It's certainly possible," said Karl, "but I have almost no money to go to school. I did read about someone who worked in a shop during the day and studied at night, until he got a doctorate and I think he became a mayor, but that takes a lot of perseverance, don't you think? I'm afraid that's something I lack. Anyway, I was never a particularly good student, it wasn't really hard for me to leave high school. And the high schools here may be more demanding. I hardly speak a word of English. And anyway, I think people here are so prejudiced against foreigners."

"Have you come up against such prejudice? Well, that's good. Then you're my man. Look, we're on a German ship, it belongs to the Hamburg-America Line: so why aren't we all Germans here? Why is the chief engineer a Rumanian? His name is Schubal. Why, it's beyond belief. And that scoundrel makes us Germans work like dogs on a German ship! You mustn't think . . ."—he was out of breath and waving his hand—"that I'm complaining just to complain. I know you have no influence, you're a poor little fellow yourself. But it's really awful!" And he banged his fist on the table several times, never removing his eyes from his fist while banging. "Why, I've worked on so many ships"—and he reeled off twenty names as if they were a single word, totally confusing Karl, "and I've always done an excellent job, I was praised, all the captains were pleased with my work, and I even spent several years on one cargo ship"—he stood up as if that had been the high point of his life—"and here on this tub, where everything is done strictly by the book, where no intelligence is required, here I'm worthless, I'm always in Schubal's way, I'm a lazy good-for-nothing, I deserve to be tossed out on my ear, and they're doing me a big favor by paying me. Do you understand? I don't."

"You shouldn't put up with that," said Karl, all worked up. He felt so much at home here, on the stoker's bed, that he had practically lost all sense of being on the precarious bottom of a ship, off the coast of an unknown continent. "Have you gone to the captain? Have you tried to obtain justice from him?"

"Oh, come on, you'd better leave. I don't want you here, you don't listen to what I say and then you dish out advice. How can I go to the captain!" And the stoker wearily sat down again, burying his face in his hands.

"I can't give him any better advice," Karl thought

81

to himself. And on the whole he felt he should have gone after his valise rather than stay here and give advice that was simply considered stupid. When his father had handed him the valise for good, he had jokingly asked, "How long will you hold on to it?" and now this precious valise might seriously be lost. Karl's only comfort was that his father could scarcely find out about his current situation even if he made inquiries. The shipping line would only be able to report that Karl had sailed as far as New York. However, he was sorry that he had barely used the articles in the valise even though he ought to have, say, changed his shirt long ago. Thus, he had economized in the wrong place; now, at the very start of his career, when he would have needed to wear clean clothes, he would have to appear in a dirty shirt. Otherwise, the loss of the valise would not have been so bad, for the suit he had on was actually better than the one in the valise, which was just an emergency suit that his mother had hastily mended right before his departure. Now he also remembered that the valise contained a piece of Verona salami, which his mother had packed as an extra treat, of which, however, he had managed to eat only the smallest scrap, since he had had absolutely no appetite during the voyage, and the soup distributed in steerage had been quite enough for him. But now he would have been glad to have the salami at hand so he could present it to the stoker. For such people are easily won over if you slip them some trifle or other: Karl had learned that from his father, who, by handing out cigars, won over all the lower-level employees with whom he dealt in business. Now the

only thing that Karl could give away was his money,
but he did not care to touch it for the time being,
since he might have already lost his valise. Again his
thoughts turned back to the valise, and he really could
not see why he had guarded it so vigilantly during the
passage that it had practically cost him his sleep, if
he had now let this selfsame valise be taken away
from him so easily. He recalled the five nights during
which he had unabatingly suspected a short Slovak,
who lay two bunks to his left, of being after his valise.
This Slovak had merely been lying in wait for Karl to
be overcome with drowsiness and finally nod off for a
moment, so that he, the Slovak, could pull the valise
over with a long pole with which he kept playing or
practicing throughout the day. In the daytime, this
Slovak looked innocent enough; but once the night
had come, he would get up from his bed from time to
time and peer sadly at Karl's valise. Karl could make
him out quite clearly, for every so often someone, with
the uneasiness of an emigrant, would light a small
candle, although thereby flouting the shipboard rules,
and try to decipher the unintelligible brochures of the
emigration companies. If such a candle was burning
nearby, then Karl could doze off a little, but if the
light was far away or the hold was dark, then he had
to keep his eyes open. The strain had thoroughly
exhausted him, and now it may have been all for
nothing. Oh, that Butterbaum—if ever he ran into
him somewhere!

At that instant, brief thuds could be heard in the
distance, breaking into the utter hush, like the footsteps of children, coming closer and growing louder,

until they sounded like the quiet marching of men. They were apparently walking in single file, which was natural in the narrow corridor, and a rattling, as if of weapons, could be heard. Karl, who had been on the verge of stretching out in bed and drifting into a sleep that would be free of all worries about valises and Slovaks, jumped up and nudged the stoker, in order to warn him finally, for the head of the procession seemed to have just reached the door.

"That's the ship's band," said the stoker, "they've played on deck and now they're coming to pack up. Everything is clear now, and we can go. Come on!"

He grabbed Karl's hand; at the last moment, he took a framed picture of the Madonna from the wall over the bed, stuffed the image into his breast pocket, grabbed his suitcase, and hurried out of the cabin with Karl.

"I'm heading straight for the office now and I'm going to give those gentlemen a piece of my mind. There are no passengers left, so I don't have to pull any punches."

The stoker kept repeating this in various ways, and while walking along, he kicked out sideways, trying to stamp down on a rat that scurried across his path, but he merely drove it faster into the hole, which it managed to reach in the nick of time. He was generally slow in his movements, for while his legs were long, they were also very clumsy.

Karl and the stoker walked through a section of the kitchen, where several girls in dirty aprons—they were deliberately splashing them—were washing dishes in huge tubs. The stoker called over a girl named Lina, put his arm around her waist, and pulled her along for a bit, while she snuggled coquettishly against his arm.

"We're going for our pay, wouldn't you like to come along?" he asked.

"Why bother, just bring me the money," she replied, squirming out from under his arm and hurrying off. "Where did you pick up that handsome boy?" she called back, but without waiting for an answer. They heard the laughter of all the other girls, who had paused in their work.

However, Karl and the stoker kept walking until they came to a door under a small pediment resting on small, gilded caryatids. It looked quite lavish for a decor on a ship. Karl realized he had never been in this area, which had probably been reserved for first- and second-class passengers during the voyage, while now, right before the major overhauling of the ship, the dividing doors had been unhinged. They had also run into several men, who, carrying brooms on their shoulders, had greeted the stoker. Karl was astonished at the vast workings of the ship; in steerage, he had, of course, witnessed little of that. Furthermore, the wires of electric lines ran along the corridors, and a small bell kept ringing incessantly.

The stoker knocked respectfully on the door, and when a voice called, "Come in," he motioned to Karl not to be afraid and to go on in. Karl did go in, but remained standing at the door. Through the three windows of the room, he saw the ocean waves, and as he watched their cheerful movements, his heart pounded as though he had not been looking at the ocean uninterruptedly for five long days. Huge ships were passing one another, yielding to the breakers only to the extent that their weight permitted. If you squinted, those ships seemed to be staggering under their own weight. Their masts sported narrow but lengthy pennants that, while stiffened by the ship's motion, kept flapping to and fro. Salutes boomed, probably from men-of-war; one such battleship was sailing by not too far away, and the reflections shone on the steel gun barrels, which were virtually coddled by the sure, smooth, and yet not level gliding of the ship. From the door, the small skiffs and boats could be seen only in the distance as swarms of them nosed into the gaps between the huge vessels. But beyond all that loomed New York, peering at Karl with the hundred thousand windows of its skyscrapers. Yes indeed, in this room you knew where you were.

Three gentlemen were sitting at a round table: one of them a ship's officer in a blue maritime uniform; the two others, officials of the port authority, in black American uniforms. On the table lay high stacks of various documents, which the officer first skimmed, pen in hand, then passed on to the two others, who read them, made excerpts, and then stowed them away in their briefcases, unless the one official, almost perpetually clicking his teeth, dictated something to his colleague, who recorded it.

By one window, a small man sat at a desk, keeping his back to the door while fiddling with huge, ponderous ledgers that were lined up on a sturdy shelf in front of his head. Next to him lay an open strongbox, which looked empty, at least at first glance.

The second window, being vacant, offered the best view. But at the third window stood two gentlemen, conversing in low voices. One of them, leaning against the window, was likewise wearing a maritime uniform and playing with the hilt of the sword. The man he was speaking with was facing the window, and occasionally his movements exposed a portion of the row of decorations on the other man's chest. Dressed in civilian attire, he was holding a thin bamboo cane, which, since both his hands were on his hips, likewise stuck out like a sword.

Karl did not have much time to take in everything, for an attendant promptly came over to them, and with a glance that told the stoker he did not belong here, the attendant asked him what he wanted. Answering as softly as he had been asked, the stoker said he wished to speak to the purser. The attendant, for his part, waved off this request, but nevertheless, giving wide berth to the round table, he tiptoed over to the man with the ledgers. This man—it was plain to see— simply froze at the attendant's words, but finally turned toward the man who wished to speak to him, and vehemently warding him off, he gesticulated toward the stoker and also, to make sure, toward the attendant. The latter thereupon returned to the stoker and said as if confiding something: "Get out of this room at once!"

At this response, the stoker looked down at Karl as if the boy were his heart, to which he was mutely bewailing his woe. Not giving it a second thought, Karl lunged forward and charged straight across the room, brushing against the officer's chair; the attendant dashed after him, hulking forward with outspread arms, ready to tackle, as if chasing some sort of vermin; but Karl beat him to the purser's desk, which he gripped hard in case the attendant tried to pull him away.

Naturally, the entire room burst into life. The ship's officer at the table leaped up, the port officials watched calmly but attentively, the two gentlemen at the window moved close together, the attendant, feeling it was not his place to interfere now that his superiors were showing interest, stepped back. The stoker, at the door, waited nervously for the moment when his help would be needed. The purser, in his armchair, finally made a broad turn to the right.

Reaching into his secret pocket, which he had no qualms about exposing to these people, Karl pulled out his passport, opened it, and placed it upon the desk in lieu of further introduction. The purser seemed to regard the passport as irrelevant, for he flicked it aside with two fingers, whereupon Karl repocketed it as if this formality had been concluded satisfactorily.

"Permit me to say," he then began, "that in my opinion the stoker has been treated unjustly. There is a man named Schubal here who has it in for him. The stoker himself has worked on many ships, all of which he can list for you, and his performance has always been completely satisfactory, he is diligent, has a good attitude toward his job, and it is hard to see why he should fall short on this particular ship, where the work is not so exceedingly difficult as, say, on merchant vessels. It can therefore only be slander that interferes with his advancement, depriving him of the recognition that would otherwise quite certainly be his. I am outlining this matter in only the most general terms, he will submit his specific grievances to you himself."

Karl had addressed his statements to all the gentlemen because all of them were, in fact, listening, and it seemed far likelier that a just man could be found among them rather than that this just man would turn out to be the purser. Moreover, Karl had been artful enough not to mention that he had first met the stoker only a very short while ago. On the whole, he would have spoken far more effectively had he not been disconcerted by the red face of the man with the bamboo cane upon first seeing that face from his present vantage point.

"Every single word is correct," said the stoker before anyone had so much as asked—indeed, before anyone had so much as glanced in his direction. The stoker's overeagerness would have been a great mistake if the man with the decorations—who, as it now dawned on Karl, was obviously the captain—had not clearly made up his mind to hear what the stoker had to say. For the captain held out his hand and called to the stoker, "Come here!" in a voice that was so solid it could have been hit with a hammer. Now everything hung on the stoker's conduct, for Karl did not doubt that his grievance was just.

Fortunately, the stoker, as it turned out, was not born yesterday. With exemplary composure, he reached into his satchel and, at the first try, produced a small bundle of papers and a notebook; then, as if

Franz Kafka

it were the most natural thing in the world, he walked
over to the captain, thoroughly ignoring the purser,
and spread out his evidence on the windowsill. The
purser had no choice, he had to go to the bother of
joining him there.

"This man is a known grumbler," the purser said
by way of explanation, "he spends more time in the
teller's office than in the engine room. Schubal is a
very peaceable man, but he has driven him to utter
distraction. Now listen!" he turned to the stoker. "You
are really getting much too pushy. How often have
you been thrown out of the teller's offices, and it
served you right with your demands, which are completely, entirely, and consistently unjustified! How
often have you gone running from there to the purser's
office! How often have you been patiently informed
that Schubal is your immediate superior, with whom
you must find some way of coming to terms yourself!
And now you actually have the nerve to come here,
when the captain himself is present, and you do not
even think twice about pestering him. Indeed, you
actually have the effrontery to bring along this boy,
whom you have trained as the mouthpiece of your
nonsensical accusations, and yet this is the first time
I have ever seen him on this ship!"

Karl mustered all his self-control to keep from
jumping forward. However, the captain was already
intervening: "Why don't we hear what the man has to
say. Besides, Schubal's becoming far too independent
for my taste, which, however, does not mean that I
am taking your part." Those latter words were addressed to the stoker; it was quite natural that the

90

captain could not instantly side with him, but everything seemed to be moving in the right direction. The
stoker launched into his explanations, pulling himself
together at the very start by referring to Schubal as
"Mr. Schubal." How delighted Karl was, standing at
the purser's vacant desk, where he took such pleasure
in repeatedly pressing down on a postal scale.—Mr.
Schubal was unfair! Mr. Schubal gave preference to
foreigners! Mr. Schubal had ordered the stoker out of
the engine room and made him clean toilets, which
was certainly not part of his job. At one point, Mr.
Schubal's capabilities were challenged as supposedly
more bogus than real. At this juncture, Karl stared at
the captain with all his might, unabashedly, as if the
two of them were colleagues, simply so the captain
would not be unfavorably influenced by the stoker's
awkward way of expressing himself. Still, nothing sub-
stantial was gleaned from the stoker's outpourings,
and even though the captain kept gazing straight
ahead, his eyes revealing his determination to hear
the stoker out this time, the other gentlemen were
growing impatient, and soon the stoker's voice no
longer unrestrictedly dominated the room, which was
a cause of some concern for Karl. First, the gentleman
in civilian attire began wielding his bamboo cane,
tapping it, albeit softly, on the floor. The other gentlemen, of course, glanced over now and then; but the
two port officials, who were obviously in a hurry,
reached for their files again and started going through
them, if still somewhat absently; the ship's officer
moved closer to his desk; and the purser, believing
he had carried the day, heaved a deep, ironic sigh.

Only the attendant seemed to be free of the generally developing indifference; sympathetic to the sufferings of the poor man confronting the great, he earnestly nodded at Karl as if trying to explain something.

Meanwhile the hubbub in the harbor continued outside the windows; a barge glided by, almost darkening the room with a mountain of barrels, which must have been marvelously stowed since none of them rolled about; small motorboats, which Karl, had he now had time, could have carefully scrutinized, roared by dead straight, obeying the jerking hands of a man standing erect at the wheel; now and then, some peculiar piece of flotsam surfaced on its own from the restless water and was promptly swallowed up, sinking before Karl's astonished eyes; crowded boats belonging to the ocean liners were being rowed along by fiercely working sailors and were full of passengers who sat there exactly as they had been squeezed in, quiet and expectant, although some could not help turning their heads to look at the changing scenery. A ceaseless movement, an agitation transmitted from the agitated element to helpless human beings and their works!

But everything urged haste, clarity, very precise description; yet what did the stoker do? He was talking himself into a sweat, his trembling hands had long since been unable to hold the papers on the windowsill; complaints about Schubal came pouring into his mind from all directions, and in his opinion any one of them would have sufficed to bury that Schubal completely; yet all he could offer the captain was a dismal hodgepodge. For a long time now, the man with the bamboo cane had been faintly whistling toward the ceiling, the port officials were already keeping the officer at their desk and showing no sign of ever letting him go, the purser was visibly held back from horning in only by the captain's calm demeanor, the attendant, standing at attention, expected the captain to issue an order about the stoker at any moment.

Karl could no longer remain inactive. He walked slowly toward the group and, while walking, reflected all the more quickly on how to handle this business as deftly as possible. It was certainly high time—a bit longer and both of them could very well be tossed out of the office. The captain might be a good man and might also, at this very moment, as it seemed to Karl, have some special reason for acting as a fair superior; but ultimately, he was no instrument that one could play into the ground—and that was precisely how the stoker was treating him, although out of a profound sense of utter indignation.

So Karl said to the stoker: "You have to express yourself more simply, more clearly, the captain can't appreciate what you say if you talk to him like that. Does he know all the mechanics and cabin boys by their last names, much less Christian names, so that if you just mention a name he instantly realizes whom you're talking about? Sort your grievances out clearly, give him the most important ones first, and then the others in descending order. Perhaps then you won't even need to articulate most of them. You've always presented everything to me so lucidly!" If people can steal a valise in America, then you can also lie now and then, he thought to himself by way of excuse.

If only it could help! Might it not be too late by

now? The stoker did instantly break off upon hearing
that familiar voice, but his eyes were so blinded with
tears of wounded manly honor, terrible memories,
and extreme current distress that he could not even
properly recognize Karl. How should he now—and
Karl silently realized this upon seeing the now silent
stoker—how should he now abruptly change his style
of speaking, since he did feel that he had said everything there was to say, but without receiving the slightest acknowledgment, and that he had, on the other
hand, said nothing as yet and could not expect these
gentlemen to hear him out. At this point, Karl, his
sole champion, had stepped in, trying to give him
some sound advice, yet instead had shown him that
everything, absolutely everything, was lost.

"If only I had come forward sooner instead of looking out the window," Karl thought to himself, lowering
his head in front of the stoker and folding his hands
on the seam of his trousers, to signal the end of all
hope.

But the stoker misunderstood, thinking most likely
that Karl was secretly reproaching him, and with the
good intention of disabusing him, the stoker crowned
all his previous actions by starting to argue with Karl.
Now that the gentlemen at the round table had long
since grown indignant at the senseless racket that was
disrupting their important work, now that the purser,
gradually at a loss to comprehend the captain's patience, was about to explode, now that the attendant,
fully back within the sphere of his superiors, was
glowering savagely at the stoker, and now that the
man with the bamboo cane, at whom even the captain

was occasionally darting friendly glances, was completely indifferent to, even repelled by, the stoker and, pulling out a small notebook and apparently occupied with entirely different matters, kept glancing back and forth between the notebook and Karl.

"I know, I know," said Karl, who had trouble warding off the stoker's torrent, yet managed to keep up a friendly smile for him through all the arguing. "You're right, you're right, I've never once doubted it." For fear of getting hit, Karl would have liked to hold the stoker's gesticulating hands, or even, to be sure, urge him into a corner and whisper a few quiet, soothing words that no one else need hear. But the stoker was beside himself. Karl now began drawing some measure of comfort from the thought that if push came to shove, the stoker would overwhelm all the seven men present with the sheer strength of his despair. However, as a glance instructed Karl, the desk had a panel with far too many buttons for the electric line; and if a hand simply pressed down on it, the entire ship, with its corridors full of hostile men, could turn rebellious.

Now the so uninterested gentleman with the bamboo cane stepped over to Karl and asked, not too loudly, yet audibly enough through all the stoker's ravings: "Just what is your name?" At that moment, someone knocked as if he had been waiting behind the door for the man to say those very words. The attendant looked at the captain, who nodded. And so the attendant went over to the door and opened it. Outside, wearing an old military coat, stood a man of medium height, who, to judge by his appearance, did not really seem suitable for working on the engines, and yet this was—Schubal. If Karl had not understood this from everyone's eyes—which all expressed a certain satisfaction, of which not even the captain was free—then he, to his horror, would have inferred it by looking at the stoker, who clenched his fists so vehemently on his rigid arms as if this clenching were the most important thing in the world, something to which he was willing to sacrifice his last ounce of life. All his strength was concentrated in his fists, including the strength that kept him on his feet.

And so here was the enemy, free and fresh, in festive garb, with a ledger under his arm, probably the stoker's payroll information and work papers, and with the fearless intention of trying above all to determine each individual's mood, he peered one by one into every person's eyes. All seven gentlemen were already his friends, for while the captain may once have had or perhaps merely pretended to have certain qualms about him, he now could probably find absolutely no fault with Schubal after the harm done to him by the stoker. One could not deal severely enough with a man like the stoker, and if Schubal could be reproached for anything, it was for failing to subdue the stoker's recalcitrance in the course of time— enough to keep him from daring to face the captain today.

Now one could perhaps assume that the confrontation between the stoker and Schubal would fail to have its effect on human beings such as it would appropriately have before a higher tribunal, for even if Schubal managed to put on an act, he might not necessarily go through with it all the way. A brief flare-up would be enough to make his nasty character obvious to these gentlemen—Karl wanted to make sure of that. By now, he was already casually acquainted with the shrewdness, the weaknesses, the whims of these individual gentlemen, and in this respect the time already spent here had not been wasted. If only the stoker had done a better job of standing his ground, but he seemed utterly incapable of putting up a fight. Had Schubal now been thrust out to him, the stoker would no doubt have pummeled that hated skull with his fists. Yet he was probably unable to take the few steps separating them. Why had not Karl managed to foresee something that could be foreseen so easily—namely, that Schubal was bound to show up eventually, if not of his own accord, then at the captain's orders. Why had not Karl and the stoker come up with a precise plan of action on the way over here instead of doing what they had actually done: arriving hopelessly unprepared and simply entering a door that happened to be there? Was the stoker even able to speak now, say yes or no, as would be necessary in the cross-examination, which, however, would take place only if things worked out fully to their advantage? The stoker stood there, his legs wide apart, his knees slightly bent, his head tilting back, and the air flowed through his open mouth as if he had no lungs inside him for dealing with it.

Karl, to be sure, felt stronger and more lucid than he may ever have been at home. If only his parents could have seen him now, battling for justice in a foreign country, in front of highly prestigious men, and, although not yet triumphant, utterly determined to fight on until the ultimate victory! Would his parents revise their opinion of him? Have him sit down between them and praise him? Look just once, just once into his so devoted eyes? Puzzling questions and the most inappropriate moment for asking them!

"I have come here because I believe that the stoker is accusing me of some sort of dishonesty. A girl in the kitchen told me she had seen him heading here. Captain, and the rest of you gentlemen, I am prepared to refute any charges with the aid of my documents and, if necessary, with statements from unbiased and disinterested witnesses, who are standing outside the door."

That was what Schubal said. His declaration was certainly manly and to the point, and judging by the changes in the listeners' faces, one might have thought that these were the first human sounds they had heard in a long while. Of course, they failed to notice that even this eloquent speech had holes in it. Why was the first pertinent word that occurred to him "dishonesty"? Should the accusations have begun here instead of with his national prejudices? A girl in the kitchen had seen the stoker heading toward this office, and Schubal had instantly guessed his purpose? Was it not a sense of guilt that sharpened his wits? And he had promptly brought witnesses along, and what was more, he described them as unbiased and disinterested. A swindle, nothing but a swindle. And these gentlemen were tolerating it and even acknowledging it as correct behavior? Why had Schubal presumably allowed so much time to elapse between the kitchen maid's report and his arrival here?—obviously for no other reason than to let the stoker wear the gentlemen out so thoroughly that they would gradually lose their capacity for clear judgment, which Schubal had to fear most of all. Had not he, after probably standing behind the door for such a long time, knocked only when he could hope that the stoker was dispatched after the unimportant question asked by that man?

Schubal's intentions were quite plain and they were inadvertently confirmed by him, but they had to be pointed out to these gentlemen in a different, a more concrete manner. These gentlemen needed to be shaken up. So Karl, hurry, take advantage of the scant time that's left before the witnesses come in and overwhelm everything!

However, the captain was already waving off Schubal, who, since his case seemed to be briefly postponed, instantly stepped aside and, promptly joined by the attendant, began conversing quietly with him, while both men kept darting sidelong glances at the stoker and Karl and making gestures of utmost conviction. Schubal seemed to be rehearsing his next grand speech.

"Didn't you wish to ask the young man something, Mr. Jacob?" said the captain, amid general silence, to the gentleman with the thin bamboo cane.

"Indeed I would," he said, with a slight bow to thank the captain for his attentiveness. And then he asked Karl again: "Just what is your name?"

Karl, believing it would be helpful to the important main issue if this interference by the stubborn questioner were quickly disposed of, answered tersely, without his usual response of presenting his passport, which he would have had to rummage for anyway: "Karl Rossmann."

"Why," the man addressed as Mr. Jacob repeated, at first stepping back with a well-nigh incredulous smile. The captain, the purser, the ship's officer, and even the attendant were likewise extremely astonished upon hearing Karl's name. Only the port officials and Schubal remained indifferent.

"Why," Mr. Jacob repeated, striding toward Karl rather stiffly, "then I am your Uncle Jacob and you are my dear nephew. I suspected it all the time!" he said to the captain before hugging and kissing Karl, who mutely put up with everything.

"What is your name?" asked Karl, very polite, yet utterly unmoved, after feeling himself released, and he tried very hard to assess the consequences that this turn of events might have for the stoker. At the moment, nothing indicated that Schubal could derive any benefit from it.

"Don't you understand how lucky you are, young man?" said the captain, believing that Mr. Jacob's personal dignity had been wounded by Karl's question, for his uncle was now standing at the window to avoid showing his agitated face, which, moreover, he was dabbing with a handkerchief. "It is Senator Edward Jacob who has identified himself to you as your uncle. A brilliant future lies ahead of you, no doubt quite contrary to your previous expectations. Try to grasp this as well as you can for now and pull yourself together!"

"I do have an Uncle Jacob in America," said Karl,

turning to the captain, "but if I understand you correctly, 'Jacob' is the senator's *last* name."

"Very true," said the captain expectantly.

"Well, my Uncle Jacob is my mother's brother, but 'Jacob' is his Christian name, while his last name, naturally, must be the same as my mother's maiden name, which was Bendelmeyer."

"Gentlemen!" cried the senator, referring to Karl's statement as he cheerfully came back from his recuperative retreat at the window. All of them, except for the port officials, burst out laughing, some as if deeply moved, others for no apparent reason.

"What I said wasn't the least bit funny," thought Karl.

"Gentlemen," the senator repeated. "With no intention on your part or mine, you are participating in a small family scene, and I therefore have no choice but to provide you with an explanation, since I believe that only the captain" (this mention led to mutual bows) "is fully informed of the circumstances."

"Now I really have to pay attention to every word," Karl said to himself, and looking sideways, he was delighted to see that the stoker was livening up.

"Through all the long years of my American sojourn—to be sure, the word 'sojourn' does not fit in with the American citizen that I am with all my heart and soul—well, through all these long years, I have been living completely cut off from my European relatives, for reasons that, first of all, are irrelevant here and, secondly, would be too upsetting for me to go into now. I actually dread the moment when I will have to explain them to my dear nephew, whereby

frank words about his parents and their near and dear
will, alas, be unavoidable."

"He *is* my uncle, no doubt about it," Karl told
himself as he listened, "he probably changed his
name."

"My dear nephew has been—let us use the word
that most aptly describes what happened—simply
thrust aside by his parents, the way one tosses out a
cat when it gets annoying. By no means do I wish to
gloss over what my nephew has done to merit so severe
a punishment, but his transgression was such that the
mere mention of it is enough of an exculpation."

"I like that," thought Karl, "but I don't want him
to tell the story to everybody. Besides, he can't possibly know about it. Who could have told him?"

"He was, you see," the uncle went on, supporting
himself with brief bows on the bamboo cane propped
up in front of him, whereby he actually succeeded in
forestalling the unnecessary solemnity that his words
were bound to assume. "You see, he was seduced by
a housemaid, Johanna Brummer, a woman of thirty-
five. I do not mean to offend my nephew by using the
word 'seduce,' but it *is* difficult to find another word
that is equally befitting."

At this point, Karl, who had moved fairly close to
his uncle, turned around to read the faces of those
present and see what impact the story had made.
Nobody was laughing, everybody was listening patiently and earnestly. After all, one does not laugh at
a senator's nephew at the very first opportunity that
presents itself. Rather, it could be said that the stoker
was smiling at Karl, albeit quite faintly, which was,

first of all, agreeable as a sign of reviving life and, secondly, excusable, since Karl, in the stoker's cabin, had wanted to hush up his great secret, which was now being made public.

"Well, that Brummer woman," the uncle went on, "had a baby by my nephew, a healthy boy, who was christened Jacob—no doubt in honor of your humble servant, who, although, no doubt, mentioned only casually by my nephew, must have succeeded in making a profound impression on her. Fortunately, let me add. For the boy's parents, in order to avoid paying child support or enduring any other scandal involving them (I am not acquainted, I must emphasize, with either the laws over there or the situation of his parents)—in order to avoid child-support payments and scandal, they shipped off their son, my dear nephew, to America with irresponsibly inadequate baggage, as we can see; and he would be left entirely to his own devices but for the signs and wonders that are still just barely alive in America if anywhere; and the boy would have gone to the dogs in some alley by the wharves of New York if that maid had not written me a letter, which, after many twists and turns, came into my possession the day before yesterday, providing me with the entire background of the matter plus a personal description of my nephew and, sensibly enough, the name of the ship. If my purpose were to entertain you, gentlemen, I could read you a few passages from this letter" (he produced and flourished two gigantic, densely written pages from his pocket). "The letter would certainly have its effect, for it was written with a somewhat simple, albeit well-intentioned cunning and with a great deal of love for the father of the child. But I neither wish to entertain you any more than is necessary for your information, nor, in receiving my nephew, offend any feelings he may still nurture; indeed, he can, if he likes, read the letter for his own instruction in the privacy of the room that is already awaiting him."

But Karl had no feelings for that girl. In the thronging memories of a past that was waning further and further, she sat in her kitchen, at the kitchen cabinet, propping her elbows upon it. She would be looking at him when he occasionally came to get a glass of water for his father or convey some instructions from his mother. Sometimes, sitting awkwardly at the side of the cabinet, the girl would be writing a letter, drawing her inspiration from Karl's face. Sometimes she would cover her eyes with her hand, then no words would get through to her. Sometimes she would kneel in her tiny room next to the kitchen, praying to a wooden cross; Karl, passing by, would observe her timidly through the crack of the slightly open door. Sometimes she would dash around the kitchen and, cackling like a witch, recoil whenever Karl crossed her path. Sometimes, after Karl came in, she would shut the kitchen door, clutching its knob until he said he wanted to leave. Sometimes she would bring him things he did not even want, and she would press them silently into his hands. But one day, she said, "Karl," and amid his astonishment at the unexpected familiarity, she led him into her tiny room, sighing and grimacing, and locked the door. She then almost choked him in her embrace, and even while telling him to undress her, she actually undressed him and put him in her bed as if wanting to let no one else have him from now on and to caress him and take care of him until the end of the world. "Karl, oh my Karl!" she cried as if clinching her possession of him by looking at him, while he saw nothing whatsoever and felt uncomfortable in the mass of warm bedclothes, which she seemed to have piled up specifically for him. Then she lay down next to him and wanted to learn some secrets from him, but he could not tell her any, and she was annoyed in jest or in earnest, she shook him, listened to his heart, offered her breast for him to listen in return, but could not get Karl to do so; she squeezed her naked belly against his body, groped about between his legs and so repulsively that Karl shook his head and his neck out of the pillows; then she thrust her belly against him several times, he felt as if she were a part of him, and perhaps that was the reason he was overwhelmed with a dreadful distress. Weeping, he at last got back to his own bed after she repeatedly begged him to see her again. That was all that had happened, and yet his uncle succeeded in making a mountain out of it. And apparently the cook had been thinking about Karl and had notified his uncle about his arrival. That was nice of her, and he would no doubt reward her eventually.

"And now," exclaimed the senator, "I want you to tell me straight out whether or not I am your uncle."

"You are my uncle," said Karl, kissing his hand and receiving a kiss on the forehead. "I am very glad that I have met you, but you are mistaken if you believe that my parents only speak ill of you. Aside from that, you have said a number of other things that are not so—that is, I do not think that it all really happened like that. You cannot really judge things so accurately from here, and I also believe that it will do no harm if these gentlemen have been slightly misinformed in regard to details of a matter that they cannot really care so much about."

"Well put," said the senator, leading Karl to the visibly sympathetic captain and asking, "Don't I have a splendid nephew?"

"I am delighted," said the captain with a bow that only men with military training are capable of executing, "to have made your nephew's acquaintance, Senator. It is a special honor for my ship to have provided the setting for such a meeting. However, the crossing in steerage must have been very unpleasant—why, who can say who else was there. Now we do everything possible to make the voyage as pleasant as possible for the people in steerage—far more, say, than the American lines do—but of course we still have not succeeded in making it a pleasure cruise."

"It did me no harm," said Karl.

"It did him no harm!" the senator repeated, guffawing.

"Only I am afraid I have lost my valise"—and with that he remembered everything that had happened and everything that still had to be done, he looked around and saw all those present in the same places, gaping at him, mute with awe and amazement. Only the port officials, so far as their smug and severe faces permitted the slightest access, displayed regret at having come at such an inopportune moment, and the watch now lying in front of them was probably more important to them than anything that was happening or might still happen in the room.

The first person to express his sympathy after the captain was, oddly enough, the stoker. "My heartiest congratulations," he said, shaking Karl's hand, whereby he partly wanted to express something like appreciation. When he then tried to turn to the senator with the same words, the senator drew back as if the stoker were overstepping his bounds; and the stoker instantly retreated.

However, the others now saw what was to be done, and they promptly formed a chaotic throng around Karl and the senator. Indeed, Karl received congratulations even from Schubal, accepting them and thanking him. The last to join them in the restored peace and quiet were the port officials, who uttered two English words, which made a ludicrous impression.

The senator was fully in the mood to completely relish the pleasure of reminding himself and the others of less significant details, which, of course, were not only tolerated by all of them, but welcomed with great interest. Thus he pointed out that he had taken Karl's most salient features, as listed in the cook's letter, and had recorded them in his notebook should unexpected use of them prove necessary. Now during the stoker's unendurable prattling, the senator had pulled out the notebook for no other reason than to distract himself and, purely for his own amusement, had compared the cook's observations with Karl's appearance, for they were correct if not exactly up to a detective's standards. "And that's how one finds one's nephew!"

he concluded, sounding as if he wanted to be congrat-
ulated once again.

"What is going to happen to the stoker now?" asked
Karl, ignoring his uncle's latest story. He believed
that in his new circumstances he could say whatever
was on his mind.

"The stoker will get what he deserves," said the
senator, "and what the captain considers appropriate.
I believe we have had enough and more than enough
of the stoker, and I am sure that each of the gentlemen
present here will concur."

"But that is not the issue in a matter of justice,"
said Karl. He stood between his uncle and the captain
and, perhaps influenced by that position, he believed
he could force a decision.

And yet the stoker himself appeared to have given
up all hope. His hands were half inside his trouser
belt, which, because of his agitated movements, had
been exposed along with the strip of a checkered shirt.
This did not trouble him in the least; he had bewailed
his entire woe, now let them see the few rags he had
on his body, and then they could carry him away. He
figured that the attendant and Schubal, as the two
lowest in rank here, should do him that final favor.
Schubal would then have his peace and no longer be
driven to distraction, as the purser had phrased it.
The captain would be able to hire whole crowds of
Rumanians, Rumanian would be spoken everywhere,
and perhaps everything might then indeed run more
smoothly. No stoker would prattle away in the cashier's office, they would have a rather fond memory
of only his last prattling, which as the senator had

explicitly stated, had indirectly led to his recognizing his nephew. Incidentally, this nephew had tried to be of service to the stoker several times and had long since repaid him more than amply for his help with the recognition; it did not even cross the stoker's mind to ask anything of him now. Besides, while he might be the senator's nephew, Karl was a long way from being the captain, and after all, the unpleasant verdict would be issuing from the captain's lips. Consistent with these thoughts, the stoker tried not to look at Karl, but, unfortunately, in this roomful of enemies, there was no other place for his eyes to linger.

"Do not misunderstand the situation," the senator told Karl, "this may be a matter of justice, but at the same time it is a matter of discipline. On shipboard, both and especially the latter are subject to the captain's decision."

"So they are," murmured the stoker. Anyone who heard him and caught his drift smiled queasily.

"Moreover, the captain's official duties undoubtedly accumulate to an unbelievable degree precisely during the arrival in New York, and we have already hindered him so greatly in performing them that it is high time we left the ship rather than make matters worse by permitting any utterly unwelcome interference to turn this petty bickering between two enginemen into an incident. By the by, I perfectly understand what you are doing, my dear nephew, but that is precisely what gives me the right to lead you away from here as swiftly as possible."

"I will have a rowboat lowered for you immediately," said the captain, who, to Karl's astonishment, did not utter even the slightest protest against the senator's words, which, after all, could undoubtedly be viewed as self-abasement on his uncle's part. The purser scurried over to the desk and telephoned the captain's order to the bosun.

"Time is running out," Karl said to himself, "but I can't do anything without offending everyone. I can't just desert my uncle now, right after he's found me again. The captain is certainly polite, but that's all. His politeness stops at discipline, and my uncle has probably expressed the captain's innermost thoughts. I don't want to talk to Schubal, I even regret shaking his hand. And the rest of the people here are worthless."

And thinking those thoughts, Karl slowly walked over to the stoker, pulled the man's right hand out of his belt, and held it playfully in his hand. "Why don't you say something?" he asked. "Why do you put up with everything?"

The stoker merely knitted his brow as if searching for the right words for what he had to say. Meanwhile he peered down at Karl's hand and his own.

"You have suffered an injustice like no one else on this ship, I know it for a fact." And Karl drew his fingers to and fro between those of the stoker, who looked around with glistening eyes as if experiencing a delight that no one ought to begrudge him.

"But you have to defend yourself, reply yes or no, otherwise no one will have the least inkling of the truth. You must promise to do as I say, for I have every reason to fear that I will no longer be able to help you." And now Karl wept as he kissed the stoker's hand, taking that chapped, almost lifeless hand and pressing it to his cheek like a treasure that must be given up. But his uncle, the senator, was already at his side, pulling him away, albeit with only the gentlest pressure.

"The stoker seems to have bewitched you," he said and gazed knowingly over Karl's head at the captain. "You felt abandoned, then you found the stoker, and you are now grateful to him—that is quite praiseworthy. But do not, if only for my sake, go too far and please try to understand your position."

Outside the door there were noises, shouts were heard, and it even sounded as if someone were being shoved brutally against the door. A sailor walked in, rather seedy looking and wearing a girl's apron. "There's a crowd of people outside," he yelled, thrusting out his elbows as if he were still in the throng. He finally pulled himself together and was about to salute the captain when he noticed his apron, yanked it off, threw it on the floor, and shouted, "This is disgusting, they've tied a girl's apron on me." But then he clicked his heels and saluted. Someone was about to laugh, but the captain snapped: "This is what I call a cheerful state of affairs. Just who is outside?"

"Those are my witnesses," said Schubal, stepping forward, "please accept my humblest apologies for their unseemly behavior. When people have a voyage behind them, they sometimes go crazy."

"Call them in immediately!" the captain ordered, and promptly turning to the senator, he said courteously, but quickly, "Please be so kind, my dear Senator, as to take your nephew and follow this sailor, who will conduct you to the rowboat. I need hardly tell you, Senator, how pleased and honored I am to have made your personal acquaintance. I only hope that I will soon have the opportunity, Senator, to resume our interrupted conversation about American naval conditions and that it will then perhaps again be interrupted in as agreeable a manner as today."

"At present, this one nephew is quite enough for me," said Karl's uncle, laughing. "And now please accept my sincerest gratitude for your kindness, and let me bid you farewell. Incidentally, it is by no means unlikely that we," and he hugged Karl ardently, "might be with you for a lengthy spell on our next voyage to Europe."

"The pleasure would be all mine," said the captain. The two gentlemen shook hands, Karl could only graze the captain's hand mutely and hurriedly, for the captain was already preoccupied with the perhaps fifteen men who, with Schubal at their head, were entering the room, somewhat perplexed, but very noisy. The sailor asked the senator if he himself could take the lead and he then opened a path through the crowd for the senator and Karl, who easily made their way through the bowing people. It appeared as if these actually good-natured souls regarded Schubal's quarrel with the stoker as a joke, which not even the captain's presence could induce them to take seriously. Karl also noticed Lina, the kitchen maid, who, winking merrily at him, put on the apron that the man had thrown down, for it was hers.

Still following the sailor, Karl and his uncle left the office and turned into a short corridor, which, after a

couple of steps, brought them to a small door, behind
which a short staircase led down to the rowboat that
had been rigged up for them. Their guide leaped
straight into it at one swoop while the sailors in the
boat stood up and saluted. The senator was warning
Karl to exert caution in climbing down—when Karl,
still on the top step, burst into violent sobs. The
senator put his right hand under Karl's chin, held him
tight, and stroked him with his left hand. In this way,
closely entwined, they climbed down gingerly, step
by step, and trod into the boat, where the senator
chose a comfortable seat for Karl right across from
himself. At a signal from the senator, the sailors
pushed off from the ship and were instantly rowing
hard. No sooner had they moved a few yards than Karl
unexpectedly discovered that they were on the same
side of the ship as the windows of the office. All three
windows were crowded with Schubal's witnesses, who
greeted them with friendly waves. Karl's uncle waved
back, and a sailor accomplished the feat of blowing
them a kiss without so much as interrupting the even
rhythm of the oars. It was truly as if the stoker no
longer existed. Karl peered more sharply at his uncle,
whose knees were almost touching his, and he wondered whether this man could ever replace the stoker
for him. Indeed, his uncle, avoiding his gaze, kept
staring at the waves that were lolloping around their
boat.

THE
METAMORPHOSIS

I

One morning, upon awakening from agitated dreams, Gregor Samsa found himself, in his bed, transformed into a monstrous vermin. He lay on his hard, armorlike back, and when lifting his head slightly, he could view his brown, vaulted belly partitioned by arching ridges, while on top of it, the blanket, about to slide off altogether, could barely hold. His many legs, wretchedly thin compared with his overall girth, danced helplessly before his eyes.

"What's happened to me?" he wondered. It was no dream. His room, a normal if somewhat tiny human room, lay quietly between the four familiar walls. Above the table, on which a line of fabric samples had been unpacked and spread out (Samsa was a traveling salesman), hung the picture that he had recently clipped from an illustrated magazine and inserted in a pretty gilt frame. The picture showed a lady sitting there upright, bedizened in a fur hat and fur boa, with her entire forearm vanishing inside a heavy fur muff that she held out toward the viewer.

Gregor's eyes then focused on the window, and the dismal weather—raindrops could be heard splattering on the metal ledge—made him feel quite melancholy.

"What if I slept a little more and forgot all about this nonsense," he thought. But his idea was impossible to carry out, for while he was accustomed to sleeping on his right side, his current state prevented him from getting into that position. No matter how forcefully he attempted to wrench himself over on his right side, he kept rocking back into his supine state. He must have tried it a hundred times, closing his eyes to avoid having to look at those wriggling legs, and he gave up only when he started feeling a mild, dull ache in his side such as he had never felt before.

"Oh, God," he thought, "what a strenuous profession I've picked! Day in, day out on the road. It's a lot more stressful than the work in the home office, and along with everything else I also have to put up with these agonies of traveling—worrying about making trains, having bad, irregular meals, meeting new people all the time, but never forming any lasting friendships that mellow into anything intimate. To hell with it all!"

Feeling a slight itch on his belly, he slowly squirmed along on his back toward the bedpost in order to raise his head more easily. Upon locating the itchy place, which was dotted with lots of tiny white specks that he could not fathom, he tried to touch the area with one of his legs, but promptly withdrew it, for the contact sent icy shudders through his body.

He slipped back into his former position.

"Getting up so early all the time," he thought,

"makes you totally stupid. A man has to have his sleep. Other traveling salesmen live like harem women. For instance, whenever I return to the hotel during the morning to write up my orders, those men are still having breakfast. Just let me try that with my boss; I'd be kicked out on the spot. And anyway, who knows, that might be very good for me. If I weren't holding back because of my parents, I would have given notice long ago, I would have marched straight up to the boss and told him off from the bottom of my heart. He would have toppled from his desk! Besides, it's so peculiar the way he seats himself on it and talks down to the employees from his great height, and we also have to get right up close because he's so hard of hearing. Well, I haven't abandoned all hope; once I've saved enough to pay off my parents' debt to him— that should take another five or six years—I'll go through with it no matter what. I'll make a big, clean break! But for now, I've got to get up, my train is leaving at five A.M."

And he glanced at the alarm clock ticking on the wardrobe. "God Almighty!" he thought. It was six-thirty, and the hands of the clock were calmly inching forward, it was even past the half hour, it was almost a quarter to. Could the alarm have failed to go off? From the bed, you could see that it was correctly set at four o'clock; it must have gone off. Yes, but was it possible to sleep peacefully through that furniture-quaking jangle? Well, fine, he had not slept peacefully, though probably all the more soundly. But what should he do now? The next train would be leaving at seven; and to catch it, he would have to rush like mad, and the samples weren't packed up yet, and he felt anything but fresh or sprightly. And even if he did catch the train, there would be no avoiding the boss's fulminations, for the errand boy must have waited at the five A.M. train and long since reported Gregor's failure to show up. The boy was the director's creature, spineless and mindless. Now what if Gregor reported sick? But that would be extremely embarrassing and suspect, for throughout his five years with the firm he had never been sick even once. The boss was bound to come over with the medical-plan doctor, upbraid the parents about their lazy son, and cut off all objections by referring to the doctor, for whom everybody in the world was in the best of health but work-shy. And besides, would the doctor be all that wrong in this case? Aside from his drowsiness, which was really superfluous after his long sleep, Gregor actually felt fine and was even ravenous.

As he speedily turned all these things over in his mind, but could not resolve to get out of bed—the alarm clock was just striking a quarter to seven—there was a cautious rap on the door near the top end of his bed.

"Gregor," a voice called—it was his mother—"it's a quarter to seven. Didn't you have a train to catch?" The gentle voice! Gregor was shocked to hear his own response; it was unmistakably his earlier voice, but with a painful and insuppressible squeal blending in as if from below, virtually leaving words in their full clarity for just a moment, only to garble them in their resonance, so that you could not tell whether you had heard right. Gregor had meant to reply in detail and explain everything, but, under the circumstances, he limited himself to saying, "Yes, yes, thank you, Mother, I'm getting up."

Because of the wooden door, the change in Gregor's voice was probably not audible on the other side, for the mother was put at ease by his reassurance and she shuffled away. However, their brief exchange had made the rest of the family realize that Gregor, unexpectedly, was still at home, and the father was already at one side door, knocking weakly though with his fist: "Gregor, Gregor," he called, "what's wrong?" And after a short pause, he admonished him again, though in a deeper voice, "Gregor! Gregor!"

At the other side door, however, the sister plaintively murmured, "Gregor? Aren't you well? Do you need anything?"

Gregor replied to both sides, "I'm ready now," and by enunciating fastidiously with drawn-out pauses between words, he tried to eliminate anything abnormal from his voice. Indeed, the father returned to his breakfast; but the sister whispered, "Gregor, open up, I beg you." However, Gregor had absolutely no intention of opening up; instead, he praised the cautious habit he had developed during his travels of locking all doors at night, even in his home.

For now, he wanted to get up calmly and without being nagged, put on his clothes, above all have breakfast, and only then think about what to do next; for he realized he would come to no sensible conclusion by pondering in bed. He remembered that often, perhaps from lying awkwardly, he had felt a slight ache, which, upon his getting up, had turned out to be purely imaginary, and he looked forward to seeing today's fancies gradually fading away. He had no doubt whatsoever that the change in his voice was nothing but the harbinger of a severe cold, an occupational hazard of traveling salesmen.

Throwing off the blanket was quite simple; all he had to do was puff himself up a little, and it dropped away by itself. Doing anything else, however, was difficult, especially since he was so uncommonly broad. He would have needed arms and hands to prop himself up, and all he had was the numerous tiny legs that kept perpetually moving every which way but without his managing to control them. If he tried to bend a leg, it first straightened out; and if he finally succeeded in taking charge of it, the other legs meanwhile all kept carrying on, as if emancipated, in extreme and painful agitation. "Just don't dawdle in bed," Gregor told himself.

To start with, he wanted to get out of bed with the lower part of his body; but this portion, which, incidentally, he had not yet seen and could not properly visualize, proved too cumbersome to move—it went so slowly. And when eventually, having grown almost frantic, he gathered all his strength and recklessly thrust forward, he chose the wrong direction and slammed violently into the lower bedpost, whereupon the burning pain he then felt made him realize that the lower part of his body might be precisely the most sensitive, at least for now.

He therefore first tried to get his upper portion out of the bed, and to do so he cautiously turned his head toward the side of the mattress. This actually proved easy; and eventually, despite its breadth and weight, his body bulk slowly followed the twisting of his head. But when his head was finally looming over the edge of the bed, in the free air, he was scared of advancing any further in this manner; for if he ultimately let himself plunge down like this, only an outright miracle would prevent injury to his head. And no matter what, he must not lose consciousness now of all times; he would be better off remaining in bed.

But when, sighing after repeating this exertion, he still lay there as before, watching his tiny legs battle each other perhaps even more fiercely and finding no way to bring peace and order to this idiosyncratic condition, he again mused that he could not possibly stay there. The most logical recourse would be to make any sacrifice whatsoever if there was even the slightest hope of his freeing himself from the bed. Yet at the same time, he did not neglect to keep reminding himself that a calm, indeed the calmest reflection was far superior to desperate resolves. In such moments, he fixed his eyes as sharply as he could on the window; but unfortunately, little comfort or encouragement could be drawn from the sight of the morning fog, which shrouded even the other side of the narrow street. "Already seven o'clock," he said to himself when the alarm clock struck again, "already seven o'clock and still such a thick fog." And for a short while, he lay quietly, breathing faintly, as if perhaps expecting the silence to restore real and normal circumstances.

But then he told himself, "I absolutely must be out of bed completely before the clock strikes seven-fifteen. Besides, by then someone from work will come to inquire about me, since the office opens before seven." And he now began seesawing the full length of his body at an altogether even rhythm in order to rock it from the bed. If he could get himself to tumble from the bed in this way, then he would no doubt prevent injury to his head by lifting it sharply while falling. His back seemed hard; nothing was likely to happen to it during the landing on the carpet. His greatest misgiving was about the loud crash that was sure to ensue, probably causing anxiety if not terror behind all the doors. Still, this risk had to be run.

By the time Gregor was already sticking halfway out of the bed (this new method was more of a game than a struggle, all he had to do was keep seesawing and wrenching himself along), it occurred to him how easy everything would be if someone lent him a hand. It would take only two strong people (he thought of his father and the maid); they would only have to slip their arms under his vaulted back, slide him out of the bed, crouch down with their burden, and then just wait patiently and cautiously as he flipped over to the floor, where he hoped his tiny legs would have some purpose. Now quite aside from the fact that the doors were locked, should he really call for assistance? Despite his misery, he could not help smiling at the very idea.

By now he was already seesawing so intensely that he barely managed to keep his balance, and so he would have to make up his mind very soon, for it was already ten after seven—when the doorbell rang. "It's someone from the office," he told himself, almost pet-

rified, while his tiny legs only danced all the more
hastily. For an instant, there was total hush. "They're
not answering," Gregor said to himself, prey to some
absurd hope. But then of course, the maid, as usual,
strode firmly to the door and opened it. Gregor only
had to hear the visitor's first word of greeting and he
knew who it was—the office manager himself. Why oh
why was Gregor condemned to working for a company
where the slightest tardiness aroused the murkiest
suspicions? Was every last employee a scoundrel,
wasn't there a single loyal and dedicated person
among them, a man who, if he failed to devote even
a few morning hours to the firm, would go crazy with
remorse, becoming absolutely incapable of leaving
his bed? Wouldn't it suffice to send an office boy to
inquire—if indeed this snooping were at all necessary? Did the office manager himself have to come,
did the entire innocent family have to be shown that
this was the only person who had enough brains to
be entrusted with investigating this suspicious affair?
And more because of these agitating reflections than
because of any concrete decision, Gregor swung himself out of bed with all his might. There was a loud
thud, but not really a crash. His fall was slightly
cushioned by the carpet; and also, his back was more
pliable than he had thought. Hence the dull thud was
not so blatant. However, by not holding his head
carefully enough, he had banged it; now he twisted
it, rubbing it on the carpet in annoyance and pain.

"Something fell in there," said the office manager
in the left-hand room. Gregor tried to imagine whether
something similar to what had happened to him today

might not someday happen to the office manager. After all, the possibility had to be granted. However, as if in brusque response to this question, the office manager now took a few resolute steps in the next room, causing his patent-leather boots to creak.

From the right-hand room, the sister informed Gregor in a whisper, "Gregor, the office manager is here."

"I know," said Gregor to himself, not daring to speak loudly enough for the sister to hear.

"Gregor," the father now said from the left-hand room, "the office manager has come to inquire why you didn't catch the early train. We have no idea what to tell him. Besides, he would like to speak to you personally. So please open the door. I'm sure he will be kind enough to overlook the disorder in the room."

"Good morning, Mr. Samsa," the office manager was calling amiably.

"He's not well," the mother said to the office manager while the father kept talking through the door, "he's not well, believe me, sir. Why else would Gregor miss a train! I mean, the boy thinks of nothing but his job. I'm almost annoyed that he never goes out in the evening; goodness, he's been back in town for a whole week now, but he's stayed in every single night. He just sits here at the table, quietly reading the newspaper or poring over timetables. The only fun he has is when he does some fretsawing. For instance, he spent two or three evenings carving out a small picture frame; you'd be amazed how pretty it is. It's hanging inside, in his room; you'll see it in a moment when Gregor opens the door. By the way, sir, I'm delighted that you're here; we could never have gotten Gregor to unlock the door by ourselves—he's so stubborn; and he must be under the weather, even though he denied it this morning."

"I'll be right there," said Gregor slowly and deliberately, but not stirring so as not to miss one word of the conversation.

"I can think of no other explanation either, Mrs. Samsa," said the manager, "I do hope it is nothing serious. Though still and all, I must say that for business reasons we businessmen—unfortunately or fortunately, as you will—very often must simply overcome a minor indisposition."

"Well, can the manager come into your room now?" asked the impatient father, knocking on the door again.

"No," said Gregor. In the left-hand room there was an embarrassed silence, in the right-hand room the sister began sobbing.

Why didn't she join the others? She had probably only just gotten out of bed and not yet started dressing. And what was she crying about? Because Gregor wouldn't get up and let the manager in, because he was in danger of losing his job, and because the boss would then go back to dunning Gregor's parents with his old claims? For the time being, those were most likely pointless worries. Gregor was still here and had no intention whatsoever of running out on his family. True, at this moment he was simply lying on the carpet, and no one aware of his condition would have seriously expected him to let in the manager. Indeed, Gregor could hardly be dismissed on the spot for this petty discourtesy, for which he would easily hit on an appropriate excuse later on. He felt it would make far more sense if they left him alone for now instead of pestering him with tears and coaxing. However, the others were in a state of suspense, which justified their behavior.

"Mr. Samsa," the manager now called out, raising his voice, "what is wrong? You are barricading yourself in your room, answering only 'yes' or 'no,' causing your parents serious and unnecessary anxieties, and—I only mention this in passing—neglecting your professional duties in a truly outrageous manner. I am speaking on behalf of your parents and the director of the firm and I am quite earnestly requesting an immediate and cogent explanation. I am dumbfounded, dumbfounded. I believed you to be a quiet, reasonable person, and now you suddenly seem intent on flaunting bizarre moods. This morning the director hinted at a possible explanation for your tardiness—it pertained to the cash collections that you were recently entrusted with—but in fact I practically gave him my word of honor that this explanation could not be valid. Now, however, I am witnessing your incomprehensible stubbornness, which makes me lose any and all desire to speak up for you in any way whatsoever. And your job is by no means rock solid. My original intention was to tell you all this in private, but since you are forcing me to waste my time here needlessly, I see no reason why your parents should not find out as well. Frankly, your recent work has been highly unsatisfactory. We do appreciate that this is not the season for doing a lot of business; still, there is no season whatsoever, there can be no season for doing no business at all, Mr. Samsa."

"But, sir," Gregor exclaimed, beside himself, forgetting everything else in his agitation, "I'll open the door immediately, this very instant. A slight indisposition, a dizzy spell have prevented me from getting up. I am still lying in bed. But now I am quite fresh again. I am getting out of bed this very second. Please be patient for another moment or two! It is not going as well as I expected. But I do feel fine. How suddenly it can overcome a person! Just last night I was quite well, my parents know I was—or rather, last night I did have a slight foreboding. It must have been obvious to anyone else. Just why didn't I report it at the office!? But one always thinks one can get over an illness without staying home. Sir! Please spare my parents! There are no grounds for any of the things you are accusing me of—in fact, no one has ever so much as breathed a word to me. Perhaps you have not seen the latest orders that I sent in. Anyhow, I *will* be catching the eight A.M. train, these several hours of rest have revitalized me. Do not waste any more of your time, sir; I'll be in the office myself instantly— please be kind enough to inform them of this and to give my best to the director!"

And while hastily blurting out all these things, barely knowing what he was saying, Gregor, most likely because of his practice in bed, had managed to get closer to the wardrobe and was now trying to pull himself up against it. He truly wanted to open the door, truly show himself and speak to the office manager; he was eager to learn what the others, who were so keen on his presence now, would say upon seeing him. If they were shocked, then Gregor would bear no further responsibility and could hold his peace.

But if they accepted everything calmly, then he likewise had no reason to get upset, and could, if he
stepped on it, actually be in the station by eight. At
first, he kept sliding down the smooth side of the
wardrobe, but eventually he gave himself a final swing
and stood there ignoring the burning pains in his
abdomen, distressful as they were. Next he let himself
keel over against the back of a nearby chair, his tiny
legs clinging to the edges. In this way, he gained
control of himself and he kept silent, for now he could
listen to the office manager.

"Did you understand a single word of that?" the
office manager asked the parents. "He's not trying to
make fools of us, is he?!"

"For goodness' sake," the mother exclaimed, already weeping, "he may be seriously ill and we're
torturing him. Grete! Grete!" she then shouted.

"Mother?" the sister called from the other side.
They were communicating across Gregor's room. "You
have to go to the doctor immediately. Gregor is sick.
Hurry, get the doctor. Did you hear Gregor talking
just now?"

"That was an animal's voice," said the manager,
his tone noticeably soft compared with the mother's
shouting.

"Anna! Anna!" the father called through the vestibule into the kitchen, clapping his hands, "Get a
locksmith immediately!" And the two girls, their skirts
rustling, were already dashing through the vestibule
(how could the sister have dressed so quickly?) and
tearing the apartment door open. No one heard it
slamming; they must have left it open, as is common
in homes that are struck by disaster.

Gregor, however, had grown much calmer. True, the others no longer understood what he said even though it sounded clear enough to him, clearer than before, perhaps because his ears had gotten used to it. But nevertheless, the others now believed there was something not quite right about him, and they were willing to help. His spirits were brightened by the aplomb and assurance with which their first few instructions had been carried out. He felt included once again in human society and, without really drawing a sharp distinction between the doctor and the locksmith, he expected magnificent and astonishing feats from both. Trying to make his voice as audible as he could for the crucial discussions about to take place, he coughed up a little, though taking pains to do so quite softly, since this noise too might sound different from human coughing, which he no longer felt capable of judging for himself. Meanwhile, the next room had become utterly hushed. Perhaps the parents and the office manager were sitting and whispering at the table, perhaps they were all leaning against the doors and eavesdropping.

Gregor slowly lumbered toward the door, shoving the chair along, let go of it upon arriving, tackled the door, held himself erect against it—the pads on his tiny feet were a bit sticky—and for a moment he rested from the strain. But then, using his mouth, he began twisting the key in the lock. Unfortunately he appeared to have no real teeth—now with what should he grasp the key?—but to make up for it his jaws were, of course, very powerful. They actually enabled him to get the key moving, whereby he ignored the likelihood of his harming himself in some way, for a brown liquid oozed from his mouth, flowing over the key and dripping to the floor.

"Listen," said the office manager in the next room, "he's turning the key." This was very encouraging for Gregor; but everyone should have cheered him on, including the father and the mother. "Attaboy, Gregor!" they should have shouted. "Don't let go, get that lock!" And imagining them all as suspensefully following his efforts, he obliviously bit into the key with all the strength he could muster. In tune with his progress in turning the key, he kept dancing around the lock, holding himself upright purely by his mouth and, as need be, either dangling from the key or pushing it down again with the full heft of his body. It was the sharper click of the lock finally snapping back that literally brought Gregor to. Sighing in relief, he told himself, "So I didn't need the locksmith after all," and he put his head on the handle in order to pull one wing of the double door all the way in.

Since he had to stay on the same side as the key, the door actually swung back quite far without his becoming visible. He had to twist slowly around the one wing, and very gingerly at that, to avoid plopping over on his back before entering the next room. He was still busy performing this tricky maneuver, with no time to heed anything else, when he heard the office manager blurt out a loud "Oh!"—it sounded like a whoosh of wind—and now he also saw him, the person nearest to the door, pressing his hand to his open mouth and slowly shrinking back as if he were being ousted by some unseeable but relentless force. The mother, who, despite the office manager's presence, stood there with her hair still undone and bristling, first gaped at the father, clasping her hands, then took two steps toward Gregor and collapsed, her petticoats flouncing out all around her and her face sinking quite undetectably into her breasts. The father clenched his fist, glaring at Gregor as if trying to shove him back into his room, then peered unsteadily around the parlor before covering his eyes with his hands and weeping so hard that his powerful chest began to quake.

Gregor did not step into the parlor after all; instead he leaned against his side of the firmly bolted second wing of the door, so that only half his body could be seen along with his head, which tilted sideways above it, peeping out at the others. Meanwhile the day had grown much lighter. Across the street, a portion of the endless, grayish black building (it was a hospital) stood out clearly with its regular windows harshly disrupting the façade. The rain was still falling, but only in large, visibly separate drops that were also literally hurled separately to the ground. The breakfast dishes still abundantly covered the table because breakfast was the most important meal of the day for Gregor's father; and he would draw it out for hours on end by reading various newspapers. The opposite wall sported a photograph of Gregor from his military days: it showed him as a lieutenant, hand on sword, with a carefree smile, demanding respect for his bearing and his uniform. The vestibule door was open, and since the apartment door was open too, one could see all the way out to the landing and the top of the descending stairs.

"Well," said Gregor, quite aware of being the only one who had kept calm, "I'll be dressed in a minute, pack up my samples, and catch my train. Would you all, would you all let me go on the road? Well, sir, you can see I am not stubborn and I enjoy working. Traveling is arduous, but I could not live without it. Why, where are you going, sir? To the office? Right? Will you report all this accurately? A man may be temporarily incapacitated, but that is precisely the proper time to remember his past achievements and to bear in mind that later on, once the obstacle is eliminated, he is sure to work all the harder and more intently. After all, I am so deeply obligated to the director, you know that very well. And then, I have to take care of my parents and my sister. I'm in a tight spot, but still I'll work my way out again. So please don't make things more difficult for me than they already are. Put in a good word for me at the office! People don't like a traveling salesman, I know. They think he makes barrels of money and has a wonderful life. They simply have no special reason to examine their prejudice. But you, sir, you have a better notion of what it's all about than the rest of the staff, why, than even—this is strictly between us—a better notion than even the director, who, as owner of the firm, is easily swayed against an employee. You also know very well that a traveling salesman, being away from the office most of the year, can so easily fall victim to gossip, coincidences, and unwarranted complaints, and he cannot possibly defend himself since he almost never finds out about them, except perhaps when he returns from a trip, exhausted, and personally suffers their awful consequences at home without fathoming their inscrutable causes. Sir, please do not leave without saying something to show that you agree with me at least to some small extent!"

But the office manager had already turned away at Gregor's very first words, and he only looked back at him over his twitching shoulder and with gaping lips. Indeed during Gregor's speech, the manager did not halt for even an instant. Rather, without losing sight of Gregor, he retreated toward the door, but only very gradually, as if there were some secret ban on leaving the room. He was already in the vestibule, and to judge by his abrupt movement when he finally pulled his leg out of the parlor, one might have thought he had just burned the sole of his foot. In the vestibule, however, he stretched out his right hand very far, toward the staircase, as if some unearthly redemption were awaiting him there.

Gregor realized he must on no account allow the office manager to leave in this frame of mind; if he did, Gregor's position at the office would be thoroughly compromised. The parents did not quite understand this. During these long years, they had become convinced that he was set up for life at this firm, and besides they were so preoccupied with their immediate problems as to have lost all sense of foresight. Gregor, however, did possess such foresight. The office manager had to be held back, calmed down, cajoled, and finally won over; Gregor's future and that of his family hinged on it! If only the sister had been here! She was intelligent; she had already started to cry when Gregor was still lying calmly on his back. And the office manager, that ladies' man, would certainly have let her take him in hand: she would have shut the apartment door, kept him in the vestibule, and talked him out of his terror. But the sister was not there, so Gregor had to act on his own. Forgetting that he was as yet unacquainted with his current powers of movement and also that once again his words had possibly, indeed probably, not been understood, he left the wing of the door and lumbered through the opening. He intended to head toward the office manager, who was ludicrously clutching the banister on the landing with both hands. But Gregor, fumbling for support, yelped as he flopped down upon his many tiny legs. The instant this happened, he felt a physical ease and comfort for the first time that morning. His tiny legs had solid ground underneath, and he was delighted to note that they were utterly obedient— they even strove to carry him off to wherever he wished; and he already believed that the final recovery from all sufferings was at hand. He lay on the floor, wobbling because of his checked movement, not that far from his mother, who seemed altogether self-absorbed. But at that same moment, she unexpectedly leaped up, stretched her arms far apart, splayed her fingers, and cried, "Help! For God's sake, help!" Next she lowered her head as if to see Gregor more clearly, but then, in self-contradiction, she senselessly backed away, forgetting the covered table behind her, hurriedly sat down upon it without thinking, and apparently failed to notice that next to her the large coffeepot had been knocked over and was discharging a torrent of coffee full force upon the carpet.

"Mother, Mother," Gregor murmured, looking up at her. For an instant, the office manager had entirely slipped his mind; on the other hand, Gregor could not help snapping his jaws a few times at the sight of the flowing coffee. This prompted the mother to scream again, flee from the table, and collapse into the father's arms as he came dashing up to her. But Gregor had no time for his parents: the office manager was already on the stairs; with his chin on the banister, he took one final look back. Gregor broke into a run, doing his best to catch up with him. The office manager must have had an inkling of this, for he jumped down several steps at a time and disappeared. However, he did shout, "Ugh!" and his shout rang through the entire stairwell.

Unfortunately, the father, who so far had stayed relatively composed, seemed thoroughly bewildered by the office manager's flight. For, instead of rushing after him or at least not preventing Gregor from pursuing him, the father, with his right hand, grabbed the cane that the office manager, together with a hat and overcoat, had forgotten on a chair and, with his left hand, took a large newspaper from the table. Stamping his feet, he brandished the cane and the newspaper at Gregor in order to drive him back into his room. No pleading from Gregor helped, indeed no pleading was understood; no matter how humbly Gregor turned his head, the father merely stamped his feet all the more forcefully. Across the room, the mother had flung open a window despite the cool weather, and leaning way out, she buried her face in her hands. A strong draft arose between the street and the stairwell, the window curtains flew up, the newspapers rustled on the table, stray pages wafted across the floor. The father charged pitilessly, spewing hisses like a savage. Since Gregor as yet had no practice in moving backwards, it was really slow going. Had he only been permitted to wheel around, he would have been inside his room at once. But he was afraid it would take too long, trying the father's patience even more—and at any moment now the cane in the father's hand threatened to deal the lethal blow to Gregor's back or head. Ultimately, however, Gregor had no choice, for he realized with dismay that he did not even know how to stay the course when backing up. And so, while constantly darting fearful side glances at his father, he began rotating as swiftly as he could, though he was actually very slow. Perhaps the father sensed Gregor's good intention, for he did not interfere—instead, he occasionally even steered the pivoting motion from a distance with the tip of his cane. If only the father would stop that unbearable hissing! It made Gregor lose his head altogether. He had swung around almost fully when, constantly distracted by those hisses, he actually miscalculated and briefly shifted the wrong way. And then, as soon as he finally managed to get his head to the doorway, his body proved too broad to squeeze through all that readily. Naturally, in the father's present mood, it never even remotely crossed his mind to push back the other wing of the door and create a passage wide enough for Gregor. He was obsessed simply with forcing Gregor back into his room as fast as possible. Nor would he ever have stood for the intricate preparations that

Gregor needed for hoisting himself on end and perhaps passing through the doorway in that posture. Instead, as if there were no hindrance, the father drove Gregor forward with a great uproar: behind Gregor the yelling no longer sounded like the voice of merely one father. Now it was do or die, and Gregor—come what might—jammed into the doorway. With one side of his body heaving up, he sprawled lopsided in the opening. His one flank was bruised raw, ugly splotches remained on the white door, and he was soon wedged in and unable to budge on his own. The tiny legs on his one side were dangling and trembling in midair and the tiny legs on his other side were painfully crushed against the floor. But now the father gave him a powerful shove from behind—a true deliverance. And Gregor, bleeding heavily, flew far into his room. The door was slammed shut with the cane, and then the apartment was still at last.

II

It was almost dusk by the time Gregor emerged from his comatose sleep. He would certainly have awoken not much later even without being disturbed, for he felt sufficiently well rested; yet it seemed to him as if he had been aroused by fleeting steps and a cautious shutting of the vestibule door. The glow from the electric streetlamps produced pallid spots on the ceiling and the higher parts of the furniture, but down by Gregor it was dark. Slowly, still clumsily groping with his feelers, which he was just learning to appreciate, he lumbered toward the door to see what had been going on. His left side appeared to be one long, unpleasantly tightening scar, and he actually had to limp on his two rows of legs. One tiny leg, moreover, had been badly hurt during that morning's events (it was almost miraculous that only one had been hurt) and it dragged along lifelessly.

Only upon reaching the door did Gregor discover what had actually enticed him: it was the smell of something edible. For there stood a bowl full of fresh milk with tiny slices of white bread floating in it. He practically chortled for joy, being even hungrier now than in the morning, and he promptly dunked his head into the milk until it was nearly over his eyes. Soon, however, he withdrew his head in disappointment. Not only did the bruises on his left side make it difficult for him to eat—he could eat only if his entire wheezing body joined in—but he did not care for the milk, even though it had always been his favorite beverage, which was no doubt why his sister had placed it in his room. As a matter of fact, he turned away from the bowl almost with loathing and crawled back to the middle of the room.

In the parlor, as Gregor could see through the door crack, the gaslight was lit. But while at this time of day his father would usually take up his newspaper, an afternoon daily, and read it in a raised voice to the mother and sometimes also to the sister, not a sound was to be heard. Well, perhaps this practice of reading aloud, which the sister had always told Gregor about and written him about, had recently been discarded altogether. Yet while the entire apartment was hushed, it was anything but deserted.

"My, what a quiet life the family used to lead," Gregor thought to himself, and as he peered into the darkness, he felt a certain pride that he had managed to provide his parents and his sister with such a life in such a beautiful apartment. What if now all calm, all prosperity, all contentment should come to a horrifying end? Rather than lose himself in such ruminations, Gregor preferred to start moving, and so he crept up and down the room.

Once, during the long evening, one side door and then the other was opened a tiny crack and quickly shut again: somebody had apparently felt an urge to come in, but had then thought the better of it. Gregor halted right at the parlor door, determined to somehow bring in the hesitant visitor or at least find out who it was. But the door was not reopened, and Gregor waited in vain. That morning, when the doors had been locked, everybody had wanted to come in; but now that he had opened one door, and the rest had clearly been opened during the day, nobody came, and the keys were on the other side.

It was not until late at night that the light in the parlor was put out. Gregor could easily tell that the parents and the sister had stayed up this long, for, as he could clearly discern, all three of them were tiptoeing off. Since nobody would be visiting Gregor until morning, he had lots of time to reflect undisturbed and to figure out how to restructure his life. But the free, high-ceilinged room where he was forced to lie flat on the floor terrified him without his being able to pinpoint the cause; after all, it was his room and he had been living there for the last five years. Turning half involuntarily and not without a faint sense of embarrassment, he scurried under the settee, where, even though his back was a bit squashed and he could not lift his head, he instantly felt very cozy, regretting only that his body was too broad to squeeze in all the way.

There he remained for the rest of the night, either drowsing and repeatedly yanked awake by his hunger, or else fretting amid vague hopes, all of which, how-

ever, led to his concluding that for now he would have
to lie low and, by being patient and utterly considerate, help the family endure the inconveniences that,
as it happened, he was forced to cause them in his
present state.

By early morning—it was still almost night—Gregor had a chance to test the strength of the resolutions
he had just made, for the sister, almost fully dressed,
opened the vestibule door and suspensefully peered
in. She did not find him right away, but when she
noticed him under the settee (goodness, he had to be
somewhere, he couldn't just have flown away), she
was so startled that unable to control herself she
slammed the door from the outside. But, apparently
regretting her behavior, she instantly reopened the
door and tiptoed in as if visiting a very sick patient
or even a stranger. Gregor, having pushed his head
forward to the very edge of the settee, was watching
her. Would she notice that he had barely touched the
milk, though by no means for lack of hunger, and
would she bring in some other kind of food more to
his taste? If she did not do so on her own, he would
rather starve to death than point it out to her, even
while he felt a tremendous urge to scoot out from
under the settee, throw himself at her feet, and beg
her for some good food. But the sister, with some
surprise, instantly noticed the full bowl, from which
only a little milk had splattered all around. She
promptly picked up the bowl, though not with her bare
hands, but with a rag, and carried it away. Gregor
was extremely curious as to what she would replace it
with, and all sorts of conjectures ran through his mind.

But he would never have hit on what the sister actually did in the goodness of her heart. Hoping to check his likes and dislikes, she brought him a whole array of food, all spread out on an old newspaper. There were old, half-rotten vegetables, some bones left over from supper and coated with a solidified white sauce, a few raisins and almonds, some cheese that Gregor had declared inedible two days ago, dry bread, bread and butter, and salted bread and butter. Furthermore, along with all those things, she brought some water in the bowl, which had probably been assigned to Gregor for good. And sensing that Gregor would not eat in front of her, she discreetly hurried away, even turning the key, just to show him that he could make himself as comfortable as he wished. Gregor's tiny legs whirred as he charged toward the food. His wounds, incidentally, must have healed up by now, he felt no handicap anymore, which was astonishing; for, as he recalled, after he had nicked his finger with a knife over a month ago, the injury had still been hurting the day before yesterday. "Am I less sensitive now?" he wondered, greedily sucking at the cheese, which had promptly exerted a more emphatic attraction on him than any of the other food. His eyes watered with contentment as he gulped down the cheese, the vegetables, and the sauce in rapid succession. By contrast, he did not relish the fresh foods, he could not even stand their smells, and he actually dragged the things he wanted to eat a short distance away. He was already done long since and was simply lazing in the same spot when the sister, to signal that he should withdraw, slowly turned the key. Startled, he jumped up though he was almost dozing, and scuttered back under the settee. However, it took a lot of self-control to remain there even during the few short moments that the sister spent in the room, for his body was slightly bloated from the ample food and he could scarcely breathe in that cramped space. Amid short fits of suffocation, he stared with somewhat bulging eyes while the unsuspecting sister, wielding a broom, swept up not only the leftovers but also the untouched food, as if this too were now unusable; she then hastily dumped everything into a pail, shutting its wooden lid and carrying everything out. No sooner had she turned her back than he skulked out from under the settee and began stretching and puffing up.

That was how Gregor received his food every day: once in the morning, when the parents and the maid were still asleep, and the second time after the family lunch, for the parents would then take a brief nap while the sister would send the maid out on some errand. While the parents certainly did not want Gregor to starve either, they may not have endured knowing more about his eating than from hearsay, or the sister may have wished to spare them some—perhaps only slight—grief, for they were really suffering enough as it was.

Gregor could not find out what excuses they had come up with to get the doctor and the locksmith out of the apartment; for since he was not understood, no one, including the sister, assumed that he could understand them. And so, whenever she was in his room, he had to content himself with occasionally hearing her sighs and her appeals to the saints. It was only later, when she had gotten a bit accustomed to everything (naturally there could be no question of her ever becoming fully accustomed), Gregor sometimes caught a remark that was meant to be friendly or might be interpreted as such. "He certainly enjoyed it today," she would say when Gregor had polished off a good portion of the food; while in the opposite event, which was gradually becoming more and more frequent, she would say almost sadly: "Now once again nothing's been touched."

But while Gregor could learn no news directly, he would eavesdrop, picking up a few things from the adjacent rooms, and the instant he heard voices, he would promptly scuttle over to the appropriate door, squeezing his entire body against it. During the early period in particular, no conversation took place that was not somehow about him, even if only in secret. For two whole days, every single meal was filled with discussions about what they ought to do; but even between meals, they kept harping on the same theme, for there were always at least two family members in the apartment, since plainly nobody wished to stay home alone and they could by no means all go out at the same time. Furthermore, on the very first day, the maid—it was not quite clear how much she knew about what had occurred—had implored the mother on bended knees to dismiss her immediately. Then, saying goodbye a quarter hour later, she had tearfully thanked them for the dismissal as if it were the most benevolent deed that they had ever done for her; and without being asked, she had sworn a dreadful oath that she would never breathe a single word to anyone.

So now the sister, together with the mother, also had to do the cooking; but this was not much of a bother, for they ate next to nothing. Over and over, Gregor heard them urging one another to eat, though in vain, receiving no other answer than, "Thanks, I've had enough," or something similar. They may not have drunk anything either. The sister would often ask the father if he would like some beer and she warmly offered to go and get it herself; when he failed to respond, she anticipated any misgivings on his part by saying she could also send the janitor's wife. But then the father would finally utter an emphatic "No," and the subject was no longer broached.

In the course of the very first day, the father laid out their overall financial circumstances and prospects to both the mother and the sister. From time to time, he rose from the table to fetch some document or notebook from his small strongbox, which he had salvaged after the collapse of his business five years earlier. They heard him opening the complicated lock and then shutting it again after removing whatever he had been looking for. The father's explanations were to some extent the first pleasant news that Gregor got to hear since his imprisonment. He had been under the impression that the father had failed to rescue anything from his business—at least, the father had told him nothing to the contrary, nor, admittedly, had Gregor ever asked him. Gregor's sole concern at that time had been to do whatever he could to make the family forget as quickly as possible the business catastrophe that had plunged them all into utter despair. And so he had thrown himself into his job with tremendous fervor, working his way up, almost overnight, from minor clerk to traveling salesman, who, naturally, had an altogether different earning potential and whose professional triumphs were instantly translated, by way of commissions, into cash, which could be placed on the table at home for the astonished and delighted family. Those had been lovely times, and they had never recurred, at least not with that same luster, even though Gregor was eventually earning so much money that he was able to cover and indeed did cover all the expenditures of the family. They had simply grown accustomed to this, both the family and Gregor; they accepted the money gratefully, he was glad to hand it over, but no great warmth came of it. Only the sister had remained close to Gregor; and since she, unlike Gregor, loved music and could play the violin poignantly, he was secretly planning to send her to the conservatory next year regardless of the great expense that it was bound to entail and that would certainly be made up for in some other way. During Gregor's brief stays in the city, the conservatory was often mentioned in his talks with the sister, but only as a lovely dream that could never possibly be realized; nor did the parents care to hear these innocent references. But Gregor's ideas on the subject were very definite and he intended to make the solemn announcement on Christmas Eve.

Such were the thoughts, quite futile in his present condition, that ran through his mind as he clung upright to the door, eavesdropping. Sometimes he was so thoroughly exhausted that he could no longer listen. His head would then inadvertently bump against the

Franz Kafka

door, but he promptly pulled it erect again; for even that slight tap had been heard in the next room, causing everyone to stop talking. "What's he up to now!?" the father would say after a while, obviously turning toward the door, and only then did the interrupted conversation gradually resume.

Gregor now learned precisely enough (for the father would often repeat his explanations, partly because he himself had not dealt with these matters in a long time and partly because the mother did not always understand everything right off) that despite the disaster, some assets, albeit a very tiny sum, had survived from the old days, growing bit by bit because of the untouched interest. Furthermore, since the money that Gregor had brought home every month (keeping only a little for himself) had never been fully spent, it had accumulated into a small principal. Gregor, behind his door, nodded eagerly, delighted at this unexpected thrift and prudence. Actually, he could have applied this surplus toward settling the father's debt to the director, thereby bringing the day when he could have been rid of that job a lot closer; but now, the way the father had arranged things was better, no doubt.

Of course this sum was by no means large enough for the family to live off the interest; it might suffice to keep them going for one, at most two years, and that was all. It was simply money that really should not be drawn on and that ought to be put aside for emergencies, while the money to live on had to be earned. But the father, though still healthy, was an old man, who had not done a lick of work in five years

150

and in any case could not be expected to take on very much. During those five years, his first vacation in an arduous and yet unsuccessful life, he had grown very fat, becoming rather clumsy. And should perhaps the old mother go to work—she, who suffered from asthma, who found it strenuous just walking through the apartment, and who spent every other day on the sofa, gasping for air by the open window? Or should the sister go to work—she, who was still a child at seventeen and should certainly keep enjoying her lifestyle, which consisted of dressing nicely, sleeping late, lending a hand with the housekeeping, going out to a few modest amusements, and above all, playing the violin? At first, whenever the conversation turned to this need to earn money, Gregor would always let go of the door and throw himself on the cool leather sofa nearby, for he felt quite hot with shame and grief.

Often he would lie there all through the long night, not getting a wink of sleep and merely scrabbling on the leather for hours on end. Or else, undaunted by the great effort, he would shove a chair over to the window, clamber up to the sill, and, propped on the chair, lean against the panes, obviously indulging in some vague memory of the freedom he had once found by gazing out the window. For actually, from day to day, even the things that were rather close were growing hazier and hazier; he could no longer even make out the hospital across the street, the all-too-frequent sight of which he used to curse. And if he had not known for sure that he lived on Charlotte Street, a quiet but entirely urban thoroughfare, he might have believed that he was staring at a wasteland in which

gray sky and gray earth blurred together indistinguish-
ably. Only twice had the observant sister needed to
see the chair standing by the window; now, whenever
she tidied up the room she would push the chair back
to the window—indeed, from then on she would even
leave the inside casement ajar.

If only Gregor could have spoken to her and
thanked her for everything she had to do for him, he
would have endured her kind actions more readily;
but instead they caused him great suffering. Of
course, she tried to surmount the overall embarrassment as much as possible, and naturally, as time
wore by, she succeeded more and more. However,
Gregor too eventually gained a sharper sense of things.
Her very entrance was already terrible for him. No
sooner had she stepped in than, without even taking
time to close the door—careful as she usually was to
protect everyone else from seeing Gregor's room—
she charged straight over to the window and, as if
almost suffocating, yanked it open with hasty hands,
lingering there briefly no matter how chilly the weather
and inhaling deeply. This din and dashing terrified
Gregor twice a day. Throughout her visits he would
cower under the settee, fully realizing that she would
certainly have preferred to spare him this disturbance
if only she had been able to keep the window shut
while staying in the same room with him.

Once—something like a month had passed since
Gregor's metamorphosis, and there was truly no special reason why the sister should still be alarmed by
his appearance—she turned up a bit earlier than
usual and caught Gregor staring out the window, mo-

tionless and terrifyingly erect. He would not have been surprised if she had refused to come in since his position prevented her from opening the window immediately. But not only did she not come in, she actually recoiled and closed the door; an outsider might have honestly thought that Gregor had meant to ambush her and bite her. Naturally he hid under the settee at once, but then had to wait until noon for his sister to return, and she seemed far more upset than usual. It thus dawned on him that his looks were still unbearable to her and were bound to remain unbearable, which meant that it must have taken a lot of self-control for her not to run away upon glimpsing even the tiny scrap of his body that protruded from under the settee. So one day, hoping to spare her even this sight—the job took him four hours—he got the sheet on his back and lugged it over to the settee, arranging it in such a way that it concealed him entirely, thereby preventing the sister from seeing him even when she stooped down. After all, if she considered the sheet unnecessary, she could have removed it, for it was plain that Gregor could not possibly enjoy cutting himself off so thoroughly. But she left the sheet just as it was, and once, he even believed he caught a grateful glance when he cautiously lifted it a smidgen with his head to see how his sister was taking this innovation.

During the first two weeks, the parents could not get themselves to come into his room, and he often heard them expressing their great appreciation of the sister's efforts, whereas earlier they had often been cross with her for being, they felt, a somewhat useless girl. But now both the father and the mother would frequently wait outside Gregor's door while the sister tidied up inside, and upon reemerging, she promptly had to render a detailed account of what the room looked like, what Gregor had eaten, how he had behaved this time, and whether he was perhaps showing some slight improvement. The mother, incidentally, wanted to visit Gregor relatively soon. At first, the father and the sister tried to reason with her, and Gregor paid very close attention to their arguments, approving of them wholeheartedly. Later, however, the mother had to be held back forcibly, and when she then cried out, "Let me go to Gregor, he's my unhappy son! Don't you understand I have to go to him?" Gregor felt it might be a good idea if she did come in after all—not every day, naturally, but perhaps once a week: she was much better at everything than the sister, who, for all her courage, was still a child and might ultimately have taken on such a demanding task purely out of teenage capriciousness.

Gregor's wish to see his mother came true shortly. During the day, if only out of consideration for his parents, he did not want to appear at the window. On the other hand, he could not creep very far around the few square meters of the floor, he found it hard to lie still even at night, and eating soon gave him no pleasure whatsoever. So, for amusement, he got into the habit of prowling crisscross over the walls and ceiling. He particularly liked hanging from the ceiling. It was quite different from lying on the floor: he could breathe more freely and a faint tingle quivered through his body. In his almost blissful woolgathering up there, Gregor might, to his own surprise, let go and crash down on the floor. But since he naturally now controlled his body far more effectively than before, he was never harmed by that great plunge. The sister instantly noticed the new entertainment that Gregor had found for himself—after all, when creeping, he occasionally left traces of his sticky substance behind. And so, taking it into her head to enable Gregor to crawl over the widest possible area, she decided to remove the obstructive furniture—especially the wardrobe and the desk. However, there was no way she could manage this alone. She did not dare ask her father for help, and the maid would most certainly not have pitched in; for while this girl, who was about sixteen, had been valiantly sticking it out since the cook's departure, she had asked for special favor of keeping the kitchen door locked all the time and opening it only when specifically called. As a result, the sister had no choice but to approach the mother one day during the father's absence. And indeed, with cries of joyful excitement, the mother came over, although falling silent at the door to Gregor's room. First, naturally, the sister checked inside to make sure everything was in order; only then did she let the mother enter. Gregor had hurriedly pulled the sheet lower and in tighter folds, truly making it look as if it had been tossed casually over the settee. This time, Gregor also refrained from peeping out from under the sheet: he would go without seeing the mother for now and was simply glad that she had come despite everything.

"Come on, he's out of sight," said the sister, evidently leading the mother by the hand. Gregor now heard the two delicate women pushing the very heavy old wardrobe from its place and the sister constantly insisting on doing the major share of the work, ignoring the warnings from the mother, who was afraid she would overexert herself. It took a very long time. After probably just a quarter hour of drudging, the mother said it would be better if they left the wardrobe here. For one thing, it was too heavy—they would not be done before the father's arrival; and if the wardrobe stood in the middle of the room, it would block Gregor's movements in all directions. Secondly, it was not at all certain that they were doing Gregor a favor by removing the furniture. She said that the opposite seemed to be the case, the sight of the bare wall literally made her heart bleed. And why wouldn't Gregor respond in the same way since he was long accustomed to the furniture and would therefore feel desolate in the empty room? "And isn't that," the mother concluded very softly (in fact, she persistently almost whispered, as if, not knowing Gregor's precise whereabouts, she wanted to keep him from hearing the very sound of her voice, convinced as she was that he did not understand the words), "and if we remove the furniture, isn't that like showing him that we've given up all hope of his improvement and that we're callously leaving him to his own devices? I believe it would be best if we tried to keep the room just as it was, so that when Gregor comes back to us he will find that nothing's been changed and it will be much easier for him to forget what happened."

Upon hearing the mother's words, Gregor realized

that in the course of these two months the lack of having anyone to converse with, plus the monotonous life in the midst of the family, must have befuddled his mind, for there was no other way to account for how he could have seriously longed to have his room emptied out. Did he really want the warm room, so cozily appointed with heirlooms, transformed into a lair, where he might, of course, be able to creep, unimpeded, in any direction, though forgetting his human past swiftly and totally? By now, he was already on the verge of forgetting, and had been brought up sharply only by the mother's voice after not hearing it for a long time. Nothing should be removed, everything had to remain: he could not do without the positive effects of the furniture on his state of mind. And if the furniture interfered with his senselessly crawling about, then it was a great asset and no loss.

Unfortunately, the sister was of a different mind; in the discussions concerning Gregor, she had gotten into the habit—not without some justification, to be sure—of acting the great expert in front of the parents. So now the mother's advice was again reason enough for the sister to demand that they remove not only the wardrobe and the desk, in line with her original plan, but all the furniture except for the indispensable settee. Her resoluteness was, naturally, prompted not just by childish defiance and the unexpected self-confidence she had recently gained at such great cost. After all, she had observed that while he needed a lot of space to creep around in, Gregor, so far as could be seen, made no use whatsoever of the furniture. Perhaps, however, the enthusiasm of girls her age also played its part—an exuberance that they try to indulge every chance they get. It now inveigled Grete into making Gregor's situation even more terrifying, so she could do even more for him than previously. For most likely no one but Grete would ever dare venture into a room where Gregor ruled the bare walls all alone.

And so she dug in her heels, refusing to give in to the mother, who, apparently quite anxious and uncertain of herself in this room, soon held her tongue and, to the best of her ability, helped the sister push out the wardrobe. Well, Gregor could, if necessary, do without the wardrobe, but the desk had to remain. And no sooner had the squeezing, groaning women shoved the wardrobe through the doorway than Gregor poked his head out from under the settee to judge how he could intervene as cautiously and considerately as possible. But alas, it was precisely the mother who was the first to return while Grete was still in the next room, holding her arms around the wardrobe and rocking it back and forth by herself without, of course, getting it to budge from the spot. The mother, however, was not used to the sight of Gregor—it might sicken her. And so Gregor, terrified, scuttered backwards to the other end of the settee, but was unable to prevent the front of the sheet from stirring slightly. That was enough to catch the mother's eye. She halted, stood still for an instant, then went back to Grete.

Gregor kept telling himself that nothing out of the ordinary was happening, it was just some furniture being moved. But these comings and goings of the women, their soft calls to one another, the scraping of the furniture along the floor was, as he soon had to admit, like a huge rumpus pouring in on all sides. And no matter how snugly he pulled in his head and legs and pressed his body against the floor, he inevitably had to own up that he would not endure the hubbub much longer. They were clearing out his room, stripping him of everything he loved. They had already dragged away the wardrobe, which contained the fretsaw and other tools, and they were now unprying the solidly embedded desk, where he had done his assignments for business college, high school, why, even elementary school—and he really had no time to delve into the good intentions of the two women, whom, incidentally, he had almost forgotten about, for they were so exhausted that they were already laboring in silence, and all that could be heard was the heavy plodding of their feet.

And so, while the women were in the next room, leaning against the desk to catch their breath, he broke out, changing direction four times, for he was truly at a loss about what to rescue first—when he saw the picture of the woman clad in nothing but furs hanging blatantly on the otherwise empty wall. He quickly scrambled up to it and squeezed against the glass, which held him fast, soothing his hot belly. At least, with Gregor now covering it up, this picture would certainly not be carried off by anyone. He turned his head toward the parlor door, hoping to observe the women upon their return.

After granting themselves little rest, they were already coming back; Grete had put her arm around her mother, almost carrying her. "Well, what should we take next?" said Grete, looking around. At this point, her eyes met those of Gregor on the wall. It was no doubt only because of the mother's presence that she maintained her composure. Bending her face toward the mother to keep her from peering about, she said, although trembling and without thinking: "Come on, why don't we go back to the parlor for a moment?" It was obvious to Gregor that she wanted to get the mother to safety and then chase him down from the wall. Well, just let her try! He clung to his picture, refusing to surrender it. He would rather jump into Grete's face.

But Grete's words had truly unnerved the mother, who stepped aside, glimpsed the huge brown splotch on the flowered wallpaper, and cried out in a harsh, shrieking voice before actually realizing that this was Gregor, "Oh God, oh God!" With outspread arms as if giving up everything, she collapsed across the settee and remained motionless.

"Hey, Gregor!" the sister shouted with a raised fist and a penetrating glare. These were her first direct words to him since his metamorphosis. She ran into the next room to get some sort of essence for reviving the mother from her faint. Gregor also wanted to help (there was time enough to salvage the picture later), but he was stuck fast to the glass and had to wrench himself loose. He then also scurried into the next room as if he could give the sister some kind of advice as in earlier times, but then had to stand idly behind her while she rummaged through an array of vials. Upon spinning around, she was startled by the sight of him. A vial fell on the floor and shattered. A sliver of glass injured Gregor's face, and some corrosive

medicine oozed from the sliver. Grete, without further
delay, grabbed as many vials as she could hold and
dashed over to the mother, slamming the door with
her foot. Gregor was thus cut off from the mother, who
might have been dying because of him; he had to
refrain from opening the door lest he frighten away
the sister, who had to remain with the mother. There
was nothing he could do but wait, and so, tortured by
self-rebukes and worries, he began to creep about—
he crept over everything, walls, furniture, and ceiling,
and finally, in his despair, when the entire room began
whirling around him, he plunged down to the middle
of the large table.

A short while passed, with Gregor lying there worn
out. The entire apartment was still, which was possibly a good sign. Then the doorbell rang. The maid
was, naturally, locked up in her kitchen, and so Grete
had to go and answer the door. The father had come.

"What's happened?" were his first words; Grete's
face must have revealed everything. She replied in a
muffled voice, obviously pressing her face into his
chest: "Mother fainted, but she's feeling better now.
Gregor broke out."

"I expected it," said the father, "I kept telling you
both, but you women refuse to listen."

It was clear to Gregor that the father had misinter-
preted Grete's all-too-brief statement and leaped to
the conclusion that Gregor had perpetrated some kind
of violence. That was why he now had to try and
placate the father, for he had neither the time nor the
chance to enlighten him. He therefore fled to the door
of his room, squeezing against it, so that the father,

upon entering from the vestibule, could instantly see
that Gregor had every intention of promptly returning
to his room and that there was no need to force him
back. All they had to do was open the door and he
would vanish on the spot.

But the father was in no mood to catch such nice-
ties. "Ah!" he roared upon entering, and his tone
sounded both furious and elated. Gregor drew his
head back from the door and raised it toward the
father. He had really not pictured him as he was
standing there now; naturally, because of his new
habit of creeping around, Gregor had lately failed to
concern himself with anything else going on in the
apartment and he should actually have been prepared
for some changes. And yet, and yet, was this still his
father? The same man who used to lie buried in bed,
exhausted, whenever Gregor started out on a business
trip; who, whenever Gregor came home in the evening,
would greet him, wearing a robe, in the armchair;
who, being quite incapable of standing up, would only
raise his arms as a sign of joy; and who, bundled up
in his old overcoat, laboriously shuffled along during
rare family strolls on a few Sundays during the year
and on the highest holidays, always cautiously plant-
ing his cane, trudging a bit more slowly between Gregor and the mother (they were walking slowly as it
was), and who, whenever he was about to say anything, nearly always halted and gathered the others
around him? But now the father stood quite steady,
in a snug blue uniform with gold buttons, such as
attendants in banks wear; his heavy double chin un-
furled over the high stiff collar of the jacket. From
under his bushy eyebrows, the black eyes gazed fresh

and alert; the once disheveled hair was now glossy, combed down, and meticulously parted. Removing his cap with its gold monogram, probably that of a bank, and pitching it in an arc the full length of the room over to the settee, he lunged toward Gregor, his face grim, his hands in his trouser pockets, the tails of his long uniform jacket swinging back. He himself most likely did not know what he had in mind; nevertheless he lifted his feet unusually high, and Gregor marveled at the gigantic size of his boot soles. But he did not dwell on this; after all, from the very first day of his new life, he had known that the father viewed only the utmost severity as appropriate for dealing with him. And so now Gregor scooted away, stopping only when the father halted, and skittering forward again the instant the father moved. In this way, they circled the room several times with nothing decisive happening; in fact, because of its slow tempo, the whole business did not even resemble a chase. That was why Gregor kept to the floor for now, especially since he feared that the father might view an escape to the walls or the ceiling as particularly wicked. Nevertheless, Gregor had to admit that he could not endure even this scurrying much longer, because for every step the father took, Gregor had to carry out an endless string of movements. He was already panting noticeably, just as his lungs had never been altogether reliable even in his earlier days. He was just barely staggering along, trying to focus all his strength on running, scarcely keeping his eyes open, feeling so numb that he could think of no other possible recourse than running, and almost forgetting that he was free to use the walls, which, however, were blocked here by intricately carved furniture bristling with sharp points and notches—when all at once a lightly tossed something flew down right next to him, barely missing him, and rolled on ahead of him. It was an apple. Instantly a second one flew after the first. Gregor halted, petrified. Any more running would be useless, for the father was dead set on bombarding him. He had filled his pockets with fruit from the bowl on the sideboard and, not taking sharp aim for the moment, was hurling apple after apple. Those small red apples ricocheted around the floor as if galvanized, colliding with one another. A weakly thrown apple grazed Gregor's back, sliding off harmlessly. Another one, however, promptly following it, actually dug right into his back. Gregor wanted to keep dragging himself along as though this startling and incredible pain would vanish with a change of location, yet he felt nailed to the spot and so he stretched out with all his senses in utter derangement. It was only with his final glance that he saw the door to his room burst open. The mother, wearing only a chemise (for the sister had undressed her to let her breathe more freely while unconscious), hurried out in front of the screaming sister and dashed toward the father. Stumbling over her unfastened petticoats as they glided to the floor one by one, she pressed against the father, flung her arms around his neck in total union with him—but now Gregor's eyesight failed entirely—and, with her hands clutching the back of the father's head, she begged him to spare Gregor's life.

III

Gregor's serious injury, from which he suffered for over a month (since no one had the nerve to remove the apple, it stayed lodged in his flesh as a visible memento), apparently reminded even the father that Gregor, despite his now dismal and disgusting shape, was a member of the family and could not be treated like an enemy. Instead, familial obligations dictated that they swallow their repulsion and endure, simply endure.

Now Gregor's injury may have cost him some mobility, no doubt for good, impelling him to take long, long minutes to shuffle across his room like an old war invalid (there was no question of his creeping up the walls). Still, this worsening of his condition was, to his mind, more than made up for by the fact that every evening the parlor door, which he would watch sharply for one or two hours in advance, was opened, so that he, lying in the darkness of his room and invisible from the parlor, was allowed to see the entire family at the illuminated table and, by general consent

165

as it were, listen to their talks—rather, that is, than eavesdropping as before.

Of course, these were no longer the lively exchanges of earlier days, which Gregor had always somewhat wistfully mused about in the tiny hotel rooms whenever he had wearily collapsed into the damp bedding. Now, the evenings were usually very hushed. The father would doze off in his armchair shortly after supper; the mother and the sister would urge one another to keep still. The mother, hunched way over beneath the light, would be sewing fine lingerie for a fashion boutique; the sister, having found a job as salesgirl, was studying shorthand and French every evening in hopes of perhaps eventually obtaining a better position. Sometimes the father would wake up and, as if unaware that he had been sleeping, would say to the mother: "How long you've been sewing again today!" and doze off again while mother and sister smiled wearily at each other.

In a kind of obstinacy, the father refused to take off his attendant's uniform at home; and while his robe dangled uselessly on the clothes hook, he would slumber in his chair, fully dressed, as if always on duty and at his superior's beck and call even here. And so, despite all the painstaking efforts of mother and sister, the uniform, which had not been brand-new in the first place, grew less and less tidy, and Gregor would often spend entire evenings gazing at this soiled and spotted garment, which shone with its always polished gold buttons, while the old man slept a very uncomfortable and yet peaceful sleep.

The instant the clock struck ten, the mother, by

speaking softly to the father, tried to awaken him and talk him into going to bed, for after all, this was no way to get proper sleep, which the father, who had to start work at six A.M., badly needed. But with the obstinacy that had gotten hold of him upon his becoming a bank attendant, he would always insist on remaining at the table a bit longer even though he invariably nodded out and, moreover, could then be coaxed only with the greatest difficulty to trade the chair for the bed. No matter how much the mother and the sister cajoled and gently admonished him, he would shake his head slowly for a quarter of an hour, keeping his eyes shut and refusing to stand up. The mother would tug at his sleeve, whispering honeyed words into his ear, and the sister would leave her homework to help the mother; but none of this had any effect on the father. He would merely sink deeper into his chair. It was only when the women lifted him under his armpits that he would open his eyes, glance to and fro between mother and sister, and say: "What a life. This is my rest in my old days." And supporting himself on the two women, he would ponderously struggle to his feet as if being the greatest burden on himself, let the two women steer him to the door, wave them off upon arriving and trudge on unaided, while the mother hastily discarded her sewing and the daughter her pen in order to run after him and continue being helpful.

Who in this overworked and exhausted family had time to look after Gregor any more than was absolutely necessary? The household was reduced further; the maid was now dismissed after all, and a gigantic bony

Franz Kafka

charwoman with white hair fluttering around her head would come every morning and evening to do the heaviest chores. Everything else was taken care of by the mother along with her great amount of needlework. It even happened that various items of family jewelry, which mother and sister had once blissfully sported at celebrations and festivities, were now being sold off, as Gregor learned in the evenings from the general discussions of the prices they had obtained. Their greatest persistent complaint, though, was that since they could hit on no way of moving Gregor, they could not give up this apartment, which was much too large for their present circumstances. Gregor, however, realized it was not just their consideration for him that held them back, for they could have easily transported him in a suitable crate with a couple of air holes in it. The main obstacle to the family's relocation was their utter despair and their sense of being struck by a misfortune like no one else among their friends and relatives. Whatever the world demands of poor people, they carried out to an extreme: the father fetched breakfast for the minor bank tellers, the mother sacrificed herself to underwear for strangers, the sister, ordered around by customers, ran back and forth behind the counter. But those were the limits of the family's strength. And the injury in Gregor's back started hurting again whenever mother and sister, having returned from getting the father to bed, ignored their work as they huddled together cheek to cheek, and the mother, pointing toward Gregor's room, now said: "Close that door, Grete," so that Gregor was back in the dark, while the women in the next room mingled their tears or peered dry-eyed at the table.

168

Gregor spent his nights and days almost entirely
without sleep. Occasionally he decided that the next
time the door opened, he would take over the family's
affairs as in the past. Now, after a long absence,
the director and the office manager reappeared in his
thoughts, the clerks and the trainees, the dim-witted
errand boy, two or three friends from other companies,
a chambermaid in a provincial hotel, a dear, fleeting
memory, a milliner's cashier whom he had courted
earnestly but too slowly—they all reappeared, min-
gling with strangers or forgotten people. Yet rather
than helping him and his family, they were all unapproachable, and he was glad when they dwindled
away. At other moments, he was in no mood to worry
about his family—he was filled with sheer rage at
being poorly looked after; and although unable to picture anything that might tempt his appetite, he did try
to devise ways of getting into the pantry and, while
not hungry, taking what was ultimately his due. No
longer paying any heed to what might be a special
treat for Gregor, the sister, before hurrying off to work
in the morning and after lunch, would use her foot to
shove some random food into Gregor's room. Then, in
the evening, indifferent as to whether the food had
been merely tasted or—most often the case—left entirely untouched, she would sweep it out with a swing
of the broom. She would now tidy up the room in the
evening, and she could not have done it any faster.
Grimy streaks lined the walls, knots of dust and filth
littered the floor. In the beginning, when the sister
arrived, Gregor would station himself in such particularly offensive corners as if to chide her. But he could
have waited there for weeks on end without her making

any improvement; she certainly saw the dirt as clearly as he did, but she had simply made up her mind to leave it there. Nevertheless, with a touchiness that aside from being quite novel for her had actually seized hold of the entire family, she made sure that this tidying-up remained her bailiwick. Once, the mother had subjected Gregor's room to a major cleansing, which had required several buckets of water (the great dampness, of course, made Gregor ill, and afterwards he sprawled on the settee, embittered and immobile). But the mother's punishment was not long in coming. For that evening, the instant the sister noticed the change in Gregor's room, she ran, deeply offended, into the parlor, and even though the mother raised her hands beseechingly, the sister had a crying fit. The father was, naturally, startled out of his armchair, and both parents gaped, at first in helpless astonishment, until they too started in: the father upbraided the mother, on his right, for not leaving the cleaning to the sister and he yelled at the sister, on his left, warning her that she would never again be allowed to clean Gregor's room. The mother tried to drag the father, who was beside himself with rage, into the bedroom; the sister, quaking with sobs, kept hammering the table with her little fists; and Gregor hissed loudly in his fury because no one thought of closing his door to shield him from this spectacle and commotion.

But even if the sister, exhausted from her work at the shop, was fed up with looking after Gregor as before, by no means did the mother have to step in to keep Gregor from being neglected. For now the charwoman was here. This old widow, who, with the help of her strong bone structure, must have managed to overcome the worst things in her long life, felt no actual repugnance toward Gregor. While not really snooping, she had once happened to open the door to his room and, at the sight of Gregor, who, completely caught off guard, began scrambling every which way even though no one was chasing him, she had halted in astonishment with her hands folded on her abdomen. Since then, she had never failed to quickly open the door a crack every morning and evening and peep in on him. Initially, she would even summon him with phrases that she must have considered friendly, like "C'mon over, you old dung beetle!" or "Just look at the old dung beetle!" But Gregor refused to respond to such overtures; he stayed motionless in his place as though the door had not been opened. If only they had ordered this charwoman to clean his room daily instead of letting her gratuitously disturb him whenever the mood struck her! Early one morning, when a violent rain, perhaps a sign of the coming spring, was pelting against the windowpanes, the charwoman launched into her phrases again. Gregor felt so bitterly provoked that he charged toward her as if to attack, albeit slowly and feebly. But the charwoman, undaunted, merely heaved up a chair by the door and stood there with her mouth wide open, obviously intending to close it only when the chair in her hand smashed down into Gregor's back. "So that's as far as you're going?" she asked when he shifted away, and she calmly returned the chair to the corner.

Gregor was now eating next to nothing. It was only

when he happened to pass the food left for him that he would playfully take a morsel into his mouth, keep it in for hours and hours, and then usually spit it out again. At first, he thought that his anguish about the condition of his room was what kept him from eating, but he very soon came to terms with those very changes. The family had gotten used to storing things here that could not be put anywhere else, and now there were many such items here, for they had rented out one room of the apartment to three boarders. These earnest gentlemen—all three had full beards, as Gregor once ascertained through the crack of the door— were sticklers for order, not only in their room, but also, since they were lodging here, throughout the apartment, especially the kitchen. They could not endure useless, much less dirty refuse. Moreover, they had largely brought in their own household goods. For this reason, many of the family's belongings had become superfluous; but while they had no prospects of selling them, they did not want to throw them out either. All these items wound up in Gregor's room— as did the ash bucket and the garbage can from the kitchen. If anything was unusable at the moment, the charwoman, who was always in a mad rush, would simply toss it into Gregor's room; luckily, he mostly saw only the object in question and the hand that held it. She may have intended to come for these things in her own good time or dump them all out in one fell swoop; but instead, they remained wherever they happened to land, unless Gregor twisted his way through the clutter, making it shift. At first, he had no choice, there being nowhere else for him to crawl; but later on it got to be more and more fun, even if, dead-tired and mournful after such treks, he would lie unstirring for hours on end.

Since the boarders sometimes also ate their supper at home in the common parlor, the door between that room and Gregor's would remain shut on those evenings. But Gregor easily did without the open door—after all, there had been evenings when he had not even taken advantage of it; instead, unnoticed by the family, he had crouched in the darkest nook of his room. Once, however, the charwoman had left the parlor door ajar, and it remained ajar even when the boarders came in that evening and the light was turned on. Settling down at the head of the table, where the father, the mother, and Gregor had eaten in earlier times, they unfolded their napkins and took hold of their knives and forks. Instantly the mother appeared in the kitchen doorway with a platter of meat and, right behind her, the sister with a heaping platter of potatoes. The steaming food gave off thick fumes. The platters were set down in front of the boarders, who bent over them as if to test the food before eating it; and indeed the man sitting in the middle, and apparently looked up to as an authority by the two others, cut up a piece of meat on the platter, clearly in order to determine whether it was tender enough or should perhaps be sent back to the kitchen. He was satisfied, and so mother and sister, who had been watching in suspense, began to smile with sighs of relief.

The family itself ate in the kitchen. Nevertheless, before heading there, the father would stop off in the

parlor, bowing once, with his cap in his hand, and
circle the table. The boarders would all rise and mum-
ble something into their beards. Then, by themselves
again, they would eat in almost total silence. It struck
Gregor as bizarre that amid all the various and sundry
noises of eating, he kept making out the noise of their
chewing as if he were being shown that one needed
teeth for eating and that one could accomplish nothing
with even the most wonderful toothless jaws. "I do
have an appetite," Gregor told himself, "but not for
these foods. How well these boarders eat, and I'm
starving to death!"

That very evening (Gregor could not recall hearing
it all this time), the sound of the violin came from
the kitchen. The boarders had already finished their
supper. The middle one had pulled out a newspaper,
giving the other two one page each; and now they were
leaning back, reading and smoking. When the violin
began to play, the boarders pricked up their ears, got
to their feet, and tiptoed over to the vestibule doorway,
crowding into it and remaining there.

They must have been overheard from the kitchen,
for the father called: "Do you gentlemen mind the
violin? We can stop it immediately."

"Quite the contrary," said the middle gentleman,
"would the young lady care to come and play in this
room, which is far more convenient and comfortable?"

"Oh, thank you," called the father as if he were the
violinist. The gentlemen came back into the parlor
and waited. Soon the father arrived with the music
stand, the mother with the sheet music, and the sister
with the violin. The sister calmly prepared everything

for the playing. The parents, having never rented out rooms before, which was why they were being so overly courteous to the boarders, did not dare sit in their own chairs. The father leaned against the door, slipping his right hand between two buttons of his buttoned-up uniform jacket; the mother, however, was offered a chair by one gentleman and, leaving it where he happened to place it, she sat off to the side, in a corner.

The sister began to play; the father and the mother, on either side, closely followed the motions of her hands. Gregor, drawn to the playing, had ventured a bit further out, so that his head was already sticking into the parlor. He was hardly aware of his recent lack of consideration toward the others, although earlier he had prided himself on being considerate. For now more than ever he had reason to hide, thoroughly coated as he was with the dust that shrouded everything in his room, flurrying about at the vaguest movement. Furthermore, threads, hairs, and scraps of leftover food were sticking to his back and his sides, for he had become much too apathetic to turn over and scour his back on the carpet as he used to do several times a day. And so, despite his present state, he had no qualms about advancing a bit across the spotless parlor floor.

Nor, to be sure, did anyone take any notice of him. The family was engrossed in the violin playing; the boarders, in contrast, their hands in their trouser pockets, had initially placed themselves much too close to the sister's music stand so they could all read the score, which was bound to fluster her. As a result,

half muttering with lowered heads, they soon retreated
to the window, where they remained, with the father
eyeing them uneasily. It now truly seemed more than
obvious that their hope of listening to a lovely or
entertaining violin recital had been dashed, that they
had had enough of the performance, and that it was
only out of sheer courtesy that they were allowing
themselves to be put upon in their leisure. It was
especially the manner in which they all blew their
cigar smoke aloft through their mouths and noses that
hinted at how fidgety they were. And yet the sister
was playing so beautifully. Her face was leaning to
the side, her sad, probing eyes were following the
lines of notes. Gregor crawled a bit farther out, keeping his head close to the floor, so that their eyes might
possibly meet. Was he a beast to be so moved by
music? He felt as if he were being shown the path
to the unknown food he was yearning for. He was
determined to creep all the way over to the sister, tug
at her skirt to suggest that she take her violin and
come into his room, for no one here would reward her
playing as he intended to reward it. He wanted to
keep her there and never let her out, at least not in
his lifetime. For once, his terrifying shape would be
useful to him; he would be at all the doors of his room
simultaneously, hissing at the attackers. His sister,
however, should remain with him not by force, but of
her own free will. She should sit next to him on the
settee, leaning down to him and listening to him con-
fide that he had been intent on sending her to the
conservatory, and that if the misfortune had not interfered, he would have announced his plan to everyone

last Christmas (Christmas was already past, wasn't it?), absolutely refusing to take "no" for an answer. After his declaration, the sister would burst into tears of emotion, and Gregor would lift himself all the way up to her shoulder and kiss her throat, which she had been keeping free of any ribbon or collar since she had first started working.

"Mr. Samsa!" the middle gentleman called to the father and, not wasting another word, pointed his index finger at Gregor, who was slowly edging forward. The violin broke off, the middle gentleman first smiled at his friends, shaking his head, and then looked back at Gregor. The father, instead of driving Gregor out, evidently considered it imperative first to calm the boarders, even though they were not the least bit upset and appeared to find Gregor more entertaining than the violin playing. The father hurried over to them and, with outspread arms, tried to push them into their room while simultaneously blocking their view of Gregor with his body. They now in fact began to grow a bit irate, though there was no telling whether it was due to the father's behavior or to their gradual realization that they had unknowingly had a neighbor like Gregor in the next room. They demanded explanations from the father, raised their arms like him, plucked at their beards, and only very slowly backed away toward their room. Meanwhile the sister had managed to overcome her bewilderment, caused by the abrupt end to her playing, and after a time of holding the violin and the bow in her slackly dangling hands and gazing at the score as if still playing, she suddenly pulled herself together, left the instrument in the mother's lap (she was still in her chair, her lungs heaving violently), and rushed into the next room, toward which the father was more and more forcefully herding the boarders. One could see the blankets and pillows in the beds flying aloft, then being neatly arranged under the sister's practiced hands. Before the gentlemen ever reached the room, she had finished making up the beds and slipped out. The father seemed once again so thoroughly overcome by his obstinacy that he neglected to pay the tenants the respect nevertheless due them. He merely kept shoving until the middle gentleman, who was already in the doorway of the room, brought him to a halt by thunderously stamping his foot. "I hereby declare," said the middle gentleman, raising his hand and looking around for the mother and the sister as well, "that in consideration of the repulsive conditions" (here he abruptly spit on the floor) "prevailing in this apartment and in this family, I am giving immediate notice in regard to my room. Naturally, I will not pay a single penny for the days I have resided here; on the other hand, I will give serious thought to the eventuality of pursuing some sort of claims against you, for which—believe me—excellent grounds can easily be shown." He paused and peered straight ahead as if expecting something. And indeed, his two friends promptly chimed in, saying, "We are giving immediate notice too." Thereupon he grabbed the doorknob and slammed the door with a crash.

The father, groping and staggering along, collapsed into his chair; he looked as if he were stretching out for his usual evening nap, but his head, dangling as if unsupported, revealed that he was anything but asleep. All this while, Gregor had been lying right where the boarders had first spotted him. His frustration at the failure of his plan, and perhaps also the feebleness caused by his persistent hunger, made it impossible for him to move. Dreading with some certainty that at any moment now he would have to bear the blame for the overall disaster, he waited. He was not even startled when the violin, sliding away from the mother's trembling fingers, plunged from her lap with a reverberating thud.

"My dear parents," said the sister, pounding her hand on the table by way of introduction, "things cannot go on like this. You may not realize it, but I do. I will not pronounce my brother's name in front of this monstrosity, and so all I will say is: We must try to get rid of it. We have done everything humanly possible to look after it and put up with it; I do not believe there is anything we can be reproached for."

"She couldn't be more right," said the father to himself. The mother, still struggling to catch her breath and with an insane look in her eyes, began to cough into her muffling hand.

The sister hurried over to the mother and held her forehead. The father, apparently steered to more concrete thoughts by the sister's words, sat bolt upright now, toying with his attendant's cap, which lay on the table, among the borders' leftover supper dishes. Every so often he glanced at Gregor, who kept silent.

"We've got to get rid of it," the sister now said exclusively to the father, for the mother heard nothing through her coughing, "it will kill the both of you, I can see it coming. People who have to work as hard as we do can't also endure this nonstop torture at home. I can't stand it anymore either." And she began sobbing so violently that her tears flowed down to the mother's face, from which she wiped them with mechanical gestures.

"But, child," said the father with compassion and marked understanding, "what should we do?"

The sister merely shrugged her shoulders to convey the perplexity that, in contrast with her earlier self-assurance, had overcome her as she wept.

"If he understood us," said the father, half wondering. The sister, in the thick of her weeping, wildly flapped her hand to signal that this was inconceivable.

"If he understood us," the father repeated, closing his eyes in order to take in the sister's conviction that this was impossible, "then perhaps we might come to some sort of terms with him. But as things are now—"

"It has to go," exclaimed the sister, "that's the only way, Father. You simply have to try and get rid of the idea that it is Gregor. Our real misfortune is that we believed it for such a long time. Just how can that possibly be Gregor? If that were Gregor, he would have realized long ago that human beings can't possibly live with such an animal and he would have left of his own accord. We might have no brother then, but we could go on living and honor his memory. Instead, this animal harries us, it drives out the boarders, it obviously wants to take over the whole apartment and make us sleep in the gutter. Look, Father," she suddenly screamed, "he's starting again!" And in a panic that Gregor could not for the life of him fathom, the sister actually deserted the mother. Literally thrusting away from her chair as if she would rather sacrifice her mother than remain near Gregor, she dashed behind the father, who, made frantic only by the sister's behavior, stood up, half raising his hands to shield her.

Yet Gregor never even dreamed of scaring anyone, least of all his sister. He had merely started wheeling around in order to lumber back to his room, although because of his sickly condition his movements did look peculiar, for he had to execute the intricate turns by repeatedly raising his head and banging it against the floor. He paused and looked around. His good intention seemed to have been recognized; the panic had only been momentary. Now they all gazed at him in dismal silence. The mother, stretching out her legs and pressing them together, sprawled in her chair, her eyes almost shut in exhaustion; the father and the sister sat side by side, she with her arm around his neck.

"Now maybe I can turn around," Gregor thought, resuming his labor. He could not help panting from the strain and he also had to rest intermittently. At least, no one was bullying him, and he was left to his own devices. Upon completing the turn, he headed straight back. Amazed that his room was far away, he could not understand how, given his feebleness, he had come this great distance almost unwittingly. But, absorbed in creeping rapidly, he scarcely noticed that no interfering word or outcry came from his family. It was only upon reaching the door that he turned his head—not all the way for he felt his neck stiffening; nevertheless, he did see that nothing had changed behind him, except that the sister had gotten to her feet. His final look grazed the mother, who was fast asleep by now.

No sooner was he inside his room than the door was hastily slammed, bolted, and locked. Gregor was so terrified by the sudden racket behind him that his tiny legs buckled. It was the sister who had been in such a rush. She had been standing there, waiting, and had then nimbly jumped forward, before Gregor had even heard her coming. "Finally!" she yelled to the parents while turning the key in the lock.

"What now?" Gregor wondered, peering around in the dark. He soon discovered that he could no longer budge at all. He was not surprised, it even struck him as unnatural that he had ever succeeded in moving on these skinny little legs. Otherwise he felt relatively comfortable. His entire body was aching, but it seemed to him as if the pains were gradually fading and would ultimately vanish altogether. He could barely feel the rotting apple in his back or the inflamed area around it, which were thoroughly cloaked with soft dust. He recalled his family with tenderness and love. His conviction that he would have to disappear was, if possible, even firmer than his sister's. He lingered in this state of blank and peaceful musing until the tower clock struck three in the morning. He held on long enough to glimpse the start of the overall brightening outside the window. Then his head involuntarily sank to the floor, and his final breath came feebly from his nostrils.

When the charwoman showed up early that morning
(in her haste and sheer energy, and no matter how
often she had been asked not to do it, she slammed
all the doors so hard that once she walked in no
peaceful sleep was possible anywhere in the apartment), and peeked in on Gregor as usual, she at first
found nothing odd about him. Having credited him
with goodness knows what brain power, she thought
he was deliberately lying there so motionless, pretending to sulk. Since she happened to be clutching
the long broom, she tried to tickle him from the doorway. This had no effect, and so she grew annoyed and
began poking Gregor. It was only upon shoving him
from his place but meeting no resistance that she
became alert. When the true state of affairs now
dawned on the charwoman, her eyes bulged in amazement and she whistled to herself. But instead of daw-
dling there, she yanked the bedroom door open and
hollered into the darkness: "Go and look, it's croaked;
it's lying there, absolutely croaked!"

Mr. and Mrs. Samsa sat upright in their matrimonial
bed, trying to cope with the shock caused by the
charwoman. When they managed to grasp what she
meant, the two of them, one on either side, hastily
clambered out of bed. Mr. Samsa threw the blanket
over his shoulders, while Mrs. Samsa emerged in her
nightgown; that was how they entered Gregor's room.
Meanwhile, the door to the parlor, where Grete had
been sleeping since the arrival of the boarders, had
likewise opened; she was fully dressed and her face
was pale as if she had not slept.

"Dead?" said Mrs. Samsa, quizzically eyeing the

charwoman even though she could have gone to check everything for herself, or could have surmised it without checking.

"You bet," said the charwoman and by way of proof she thrust out the broom and pushed Gregor's corpse somewhat further to the side. Mrs. Samsa made as if to hold back the broom, but then let it be.

"Well," said Mr. Samsa, "now we can thank the Lord." He crossed himself and the three women imitated his example. Grete, her eyes glued to the corpse, said: "Just look how skinny he was. Well, he stopped eating such a long time ago. The food came back out exactly as it went in." And indeed, Gregor's body was utterly flat and dry; they realized this only now when it was no longer raised on its tiny legs and nothing else diverted their eyes.

"Grete, come into our room for a bit," said Mrs. Samsa, smiling wistfully, and Grete, not without looking back at the corpse, followed her parents into the bedroom. The charwoman closed the door to Gregor's room and opened the window all the way. Though it was still early morning, there was a touch of warmth in the fresh air. It was already late March, after all.

The three boarders stepped out of their room and, astonished, cast about for their breakfast; they had been forgotten. "Where is breakfast?" the middle gentleman peevishly asked the charwoman. But putting her finger on her lips, she hastily and silently beckoned for the gentlemen to come into Gregor's room. And come they did, and with their hands in the pockets of their somewhat threadbare jackets, they stood around Gregor's corpse in the now sunlit room.

Next, the bedroom door opened, and Mr. Samsa, in his livery, appeared with his wife on one arm and his daughter on the other. Their eyes were all slightly tearstained; now and then, Grete pressed her face into the father's arm.

"Leave my home at once!" Mr. Samsa told the three gentlemen, pointing at the door without releasing the women.

"What do you mean?" asked the middle gentleman, somewhat dismayed and with a sugary smile. The two other gentlemen held their hands behind their backs, incessantly rubbing them together as if gleefully looking forward to a grand argument that they were bound to win.

"I mean exactly what I said," replied Mr. Samsa, and with his two companions he made a beeline toward the tenant. The latter at first stood his ground, eyeing the floor as if his thoughts were being rearranged to form a new pattern in his head.

"Well, then we'll go," he said, looking up at Mr. Samsa as if, in a sudden burst of humility, he were requesting sanction even for this decision. Mr. Samsa, with bulging eyes, merely vouchsafed him a few brief nods. Thereupon the gentleman strode right into the vestibule. His two friends, who had been listening for a short while with utterly calm hands, now quite literally hopped after him as if fearing that Mr. Samsa might precede them into the vestibule and might thrust himself between them and their leader. Once in the vestibule, all three boarders pulled their hats from the coat rack, their canes from the umbrella stand, bowed wordlessly, and left the apartment. Impelled by a suspicion that proved to be thoroughly groundless, Mr. Samsa and the two women stepped out on the landing. As they leaned on the banister, they watched the three gentlemen marching down the long stairway slowly but steadily, vanishing on every floor in the regular twist of the staircase, and popping up again several moments later. The lower the gentlemen got, the more the Samsa family lost interest in them, and as a butcher's boy, proudly balancing a basket on his head, came toward the gentlemen and then mounted well beyond them, Mr. Samsa and the women left the banister, and as if relieved, they all returned to their apartment.

They decided to spend this day resting and strolling; not only had they earned this break from work, they absolutely needed it. And so they sat down at the table to write three letters of explanation: Mr. Samsa to his superiors, Mrs. Samsa to her customer, and Grete to her employer. As they were writing, the charwoman came in to tell them she was leaving, for her morning's work was done. The three letter writers at first merely nodded without glancing up; it was only when she kept hovering that they looked up in annoyance. "Well?" asked Mr. Samsa. The charwoman stood beaming in the doorway as if she were about to announce some great windfall for the family, but would do so only if they dragged it out of her. On her hat, the small, almost erect ostrich plume, which had annoyed Mr. Samsa throughout her service here, swayed lightly in all directions. "What can we do for you?" asked Mrs. Samsa, whom the charwoman respected the most.

"Well," the charwoman replied with such friendly chuckling that she had to break off, "listen, you don't have to worry about getting rid of that stuff in the next room. It's all been taken care of."

Mrs. Samsa and Grete huddled over their letters as if to keep writing; Mr. Samsa, aware that the charwoman was on the verge of launching into a blow-by-blow description, resolutely stretched out his arm to ward her off. Not being allowed to tell her story, she suddenly remembered that she was in an awful hurry, and clearly offended, she called out: "So long, everybody." She then vehemently whirled around and charged out of the apartment with a horrible slam of the door.

"She'll be dismissed tonight," said Mr. Samsa, receiving no answer from his wife or his daughter, for the charwoman had ruffled the peace and quiet that they had barely gained. Standing up, the two women went over to the window and remained there, clasped in each other's arms. Mr. Samsa looked back from his chair and silently watched them for a while. Then he exclaimed: "Come on, get over here. Forget about the past once and for all. And show me a little consideration." The women, promptly obeying him, hurried over, caressed him, and swiftly finished their letters.

Then all three of them left the apartment together, which they had not done in months, and took the trolley out to the countryside beyond the town. The streetcar, where they were the only passengers, was flooded with warm sunshine. Leaning back comfortably in their seats, they discussed their future prospects and concluded that, upon closer perusal, these

187

were anything but bad; for while they had never actually asked one another for any details, their jobs were all exceedingly advantageous and also promising. Naturally, the greatest immediate improvement in their situation could easily be brought about by their moving; they hoped to rent a smaller and cheaper apartment, but with a better location and altogether more practical than their current place, which had been found by Gregor. As they were conversing, both Mr. and Mrs. Samsa, upon seeing the daughter becoming more and more vivacious, realized almost in unison that lately, despite all the sorrows that had left her cheeks pale, she had blossomed into a lovely and shapely girl. Lapsing into silence and communicating almost unconsciously with their eyes, they reflected that it was high time they found a decent husband for her. And it was like a confirmation of their new dreams and good intentions that at the end of their ride the daughter was the first to get up, stretching her young body.

IN THE PENAL
COLONY

"It's a singular apparatus," the officer said to the explorer, running his somewhat admiring eyes over the apparatus, with which he was after all familiar. The traveler seemed to have accepted the invitation purely out of courtesy: the commander had asked him to attend the execution of a soldier, who had been condemned to death for insubordination and for insulting a superior. There probably wasn't all that much interest in this execution even within the penal colony. At least, here in this deep, sandy valley, which was closed in by naked slopes on all sides, the only people present, aside from the officer and the traveler, were the condemned man—an obtuse person with a broad mouth and seedy hair and face—and a soldier clutching the heavy shackle with the small, interconnected chains that fettered the condemned man's ankles, wrists, and neck. At any rate, the condemned man looked so doglike and cringing that they could, no doubt, have let him run free over the slopes and would have needed only to whistle for him to come at the beginning of the execution.

The traveler had little interest in the apparatus and

was almost visibly unconcerned as he walked up and down behind the condemned man, while the officer took care of the final adjustments, crawling underneath the apparatus, which was inserted deep in the ground, or scaling a ladder to examine the upper parts. These were chores that could have actually been left to a mechanic; but the officer performed them with great zeal either because he was a strong supporter of this apparatus or because there were other reasons why the job could not have been entrusted to anyone else.

"It's all set!" he finally called and climbed down the ladder. He was extremely worn out, breathed with his mouth wide open, and had two delicate ladies' handkerchiefs tucked in behind his uniform collar.

"These uniforms must be far too heavy for the tropics," the traveler said instead of inquiring about the apparatus, as the officer had expected.

"True enough," said the officer, washing his greasy, oily hands in a pail of water that stood ready, "but they represent our homeland, and we do not want to lose our homeland.

"But now look at this apparatus," he promptly added, drying his hands with a towel while simultaneously motioning toward the apparatus. "Up to this point, it requires manual labor, but from now on, the apparatus works automatically."

The traveler nodded and followed him. The officer, seeking to protect himself against all contingencies, then said, "Naturally, malfunctions do occur, but while I hope we won't have any today, they must be reckoned with. After all, the apparatus has to keep working uninterruptedly for twelve hours. If malfunctions do occur, however, they are very minor and they can be dealt with immediately.

"Won't you sit down?" he finally asked, pulling out a cane chair from a whole pile of them and offering it to the traveler; the latter could not refuse. He now sat at the edge of a pit, into which he fleetingly glanced. It wasn't very deep. On one side of the pit, the excavated soil was heaped up into an embankment; on the other side stood the apparatus.

"I don't know," said the officer, "whether the commander has already filled you in about the apparatus." The traveler gestured vaguely; the officer could ask for nothing better, since now he could explain the apparatus himself. "This apparatus," he said, grasping a crank handle and leaning against it, "was invented by our former commander. I assisted in the very first tests and I was involved in all the work until it was perfected. However, he alone deserves the credit for the invention. Have you heard about our former commander? No? Well, I'm not exaggerating when I say that the entire setup of the penal colony is his achievement. By the time he died, we, his friends, already knew that the colony, as he had organized it, was so self-contained that it would take his successor many years to change anything, even if he had a thousand plans in mind. And our prediction was correct; the new commander was forced to realize it. Too bad you never met the old commander! But," the officer interrupted himself, "I'm rattling on, and his apparatus is standing here in front of us. It consists, as you can see, of three parts. Over the years, a popular nickname has developed for each of these parts. The lower part is called the 'bed,' the upper one the 'draftsman,' and the middle one floating here is called the 'harrow.' "

"The 'harrow'?" asked the traveler. He hadn't been listening very closely, the sun was entangled all too deeply in the shadeless valley, it was hard to focus one's thoughts. Thus, the officer, in his tight, full-dress tunic, which was weighed down with epaulets and loaded with piping, struck him as all the more admirable, so eagerly explaining his subject and also, while speaking, applying a screwdriver to an occasional screw. The soldier appeared to be in the same frame of mind as the traveler. The chain attached to the condemned man was wound about both the soldier's wrists, his one hand was propped on his rifle, his head was drooping at the neck, and he was utterly indifferent. The traveler was not surprised, for the officer was speaking French, and presumably neither the soldier nor the condemned man understood French. It was therefore all the more striking that the condemned man nevertheless made an effort to follow the officer's explanations. With a kind of sleepy obstinacy, he kept peering at whatever the officer happened to be showing, and when the traveler now interrupted him with a question, the condemned man, just like the officer, looked at the traveler.

"Yes, the 'harrow,' " said the officer, "the name fits. The needles are arranged like the teeth in a harrow, and the whole thing is handled like a harrow, though it acts in only one place and far more skillfully. Anyhow, you'll understand it right away. The con-

demned man is laid out here on the bed. You see,
first I want to describe the apparatus and only then
set the procedure in motion. You'll be able to follow
it better. Besides, one cog in the draftsman is ground
down far too much—it screaks loudly when it's running, you can barely communicate. Unfortunately, it's
hard getting spare parts here. Well, here's the bed,
as I've pointed out. It's fully padded with a layer of
cotton; you'll soon find out why. The condemned man
is put belly-down on this cotton—naked, of course.
We have straps to tie him in—here for his hands,
here for his feet, here for his neck. And here at the
top of the bed, where the man, as I have said, lies
face down, we have this small felt stump, which can
be easily regulated so that it pushes precisely into
the man's mouth. Its purpose is to prevent him from
screaming and from chewing up his tongue. Naturally,
he has to take in the felt; otherwise the neck strap
will break his neck."

"This is cotton?" asked the traveler, bending forward.

"Yes, certainly," said the officer with a smile, "feel
it for yourself." He took the traveler's hand and guided
it across the bed. "It's a specially prepared cotton,
that's why it looks so unusual; I'll get back to its
purpose later on."

The traveler now felt a slight interest in the apparatus. Shading his eyes with one hand to protect them
from the sun, he peered up the side of the structure.
It was huge. The bed and the draftsman were of equal
size and looked like two dark chests. The draftsman
was installed almost seven feet above the bed; their

corners were linked by four brass rods that practically radiated in the sunlight. Between the chests, the harrow shuttled on a steel band.

The officer had barely noticed the traveler's earlier indifference, but he was alive to his now budding interest; that was why he broke off his explanations—to give the traveler time for undisturbed study. The condemned man imitated the traveler; since he couldn't shade his eyes with his hand, they squinted upward uncovered.

"So now the man is lying there," said the traveler, leaning back in his chair and crossing his legs.

"Yes," said the officer, pushing his cap back slightly and running his hand over his hot face, "now listen! Both the bed and the draftsman have an electric battery each; the bed needs one for itself, the draftsman needs one for the harrow. Once the man is strapped tight, the bed is set in motion. It quivers in tiny, very rapid twitches, both sideways and up and down. You must have seen similar apparatuses in sanitariums; except that in our bed all the movements are precisely calculated. You see, they have to be meticulously geared to the motions of the harrow. But this harrow has the job of actually carrying out the judgment."

"Just what is the judgment?" asked the traveler.

"You don't know even that?" said the astounded officer, then bit his lip. "Please forgive me if my explanations are unsystematic; I apologize from the bottom of my heart. You see, it was the commander who used to provide the explanations; but the new commander has backed out of this honorary obligation. Although his failure to inform such an important visitor—" (the traveler tried to ward off the tribute with both hands, but the officer insisted on his wording) "such an important visitor about even the form of our judgment is a further new development that . . ." He had some strong words on the tip of his tongue, but, checking himself, merely said: "I was not informed, I am not the guilty one. Still and all, I am the person most capable of explaining our modes of judgment, for I have on me"—he patted his breast pocket—"the pertinent designs hand-drawn by the former commander."

"The commander's own hand-drawn designs?" asked the traveler. "Did he wear all those hats? Was he a soldier, a judge, an engineer, a chemist, a draftsman?"

"Yes, indeed," said the officer, nodding, with a thoughtful, glassy stare. Then he scrutinized his hands: he didn't find them clean enough to touch the drawings; so he walked over to the pail and washed them again. Then he produced a small leather portfolio, saying: "Our judgment does not sound severe. The commandment that the condemned man has broken is written on his body by the harrow. For instance, on this condemned man's body," the officer pointed at him, "the harrow is to write: 'Honor Thy Superior!' "

The traveler glanced casually at the man, who, when pointed at by the officer, had kept his head lowered and now seemed to be all ears, trying to catch something. But the movements of his pressed, pouting lips made it obvious that he could understand nothing. The traveler had wanted to put various questions to the officer, but, at the sight of the condemned man, asked only: "Does he know his judgment?"

"No," said the officer, about to continue his explanations; but the traveler broke in: "He doesn't know his own judgment?"

"No," the officer repeated, pausing for an instant as if demanding a more detailed explanation of the question. The officer then said: "It would be no use informing him. He's going to experience it on his body anyway."

The traveler wanted to hold his tongue, but he felt the condemned man staring at him: he seemed to be asking whether the traveler could approve of the described procedure. That was why the traveler, who had already leaned back in his chair, now bent forward again and asked: "But he does know that he has been condemned?"

"No again," said the officer, smiling at the traveler as if expecting further bizarre revelations from him.

"No," said the traveler, rubbing his forehead. "Then the man doesn't yet know how his defense was received?"

"He had no opportunity to defend himself," said the officer, looking sideways as if talking to himself and not caring to embarrass the traveler by telling him about these self-evident matters.

"He must have had an opportunity to defend himself," said the traveler, rising from the chair.

The officer realized he was in danger of delaying his explanation of the apparatus for a long time; so he went over to the traveler, took him by the arm, and motioned toward the condemned man, who, now that he was so obviously the center of attention, pulled himself up rigidly—the soldier had also yanked on the chain.

"This is how things stand," said the officer. "I have been appointed judge here in the penal colony. Despite my youth. For I assisted the former commander in all criminal matters and I am also the person most familiar with the apparatus. The principle on which I base my decisions is: guilt is always beyond doubt. Other courts of law cannot follow this principle, for they consist of many people and they also have higher courts over them. But this is not the case here, or at least it wasn't the case under the former commander. The new one, to be sure, has shown some desire to interfere in my court; but so far, I have managed to hold him at bay, and I will keep managing to do so.

"You wanted an explanation of this case; it is as simple as any other case. This man was assigned to a captain as his orderly and slept outside his door; but this morning the captain brought charges against him for sleeping while on duty. You see, he has standing orders to get up at the stroke of each hour and salute outside the captain's door. Certainly not a hard task, but an important one, for he is to remain alert both as a sentry and as an orderly. Last night, the captain wanted to check whether the man was performing his duty. At the stroke of two, he opened the door and found him curled up asleep. He got his riding crop and lashed the man's face. Instead of standing up and asking his forgiveness, the man grabbed his superior's legs, shook him, and yelled,

'Throw away that crop or I'll eat you alive!' Those are the facts of the case. The captain came to see me one hour ago: I wrote down his statement and then appended the judgment. Next I had the man put in chains. It was all quite simple. Had I first summoned the man and questioned him, it would have brought nothing but confusion. He would have lied, and once I had exposed his lies, he would have piled on new lies, and so forth. But now I've got him and I'll never let him go.

"Is everything clarified? But we're wasting time, the execution should have started by now, and I still haven't finished explaining the apparatus."

He pressed the traveler back down on the chair, returned to the apparatus, and began: "As you can see, the harrows correspond to the human shape: this is the harrow for the upper body, these are the harrows for the legs. This tiny spike is all that's used for the head. Is that clear?" He leaned amiably toward the traveler, ready to launch into the most comprehensive explanations.

The traveler frowned at the harrow. He had not been satisfied with the information on the judicial procedure. Nevertheless he had to remind himself that this was a penal colony, that unusual measures were needed here, and that they had to resort to even the most stringent military discipline. However, he also pinned some hope on the new commander, who evidently planned to introduce, though gradually, a new procedure that was simply beyond the officer's narrow grasp. It was this train of thought that led the traveler to ask, "Will the commander be attending the execution?"

"It's not certain," said the officer, embarrassed by the abrupt question, and his friendly expression became distorted: "That's precisely why we have to hurry. Much as I regret it, I'll have to shorten my explanations. But tomorrow, of course, when the apparatus has been cleaned (its only failing is that it gets so dirty), I can go into greater detail. For now, just the bare gist.

"When the man lies on the bed, and the bed begins to quiver, the harrow is lowered upon the body. It automatically adjusts itself so that its points just barely graze the skin. Once it's in place, this steel cable instantly stiffens into a rigid band. And now the performance begins. An outsider won't notice any external difference between the punishments. The harrow seems to work identically. As it quivers, it sticks its points into the body, which, moreover, quivers with the bed. Now to enable anyone to check the progress of the judgment, the harrow is made of glass. Attaching the needles involved some technical difficulties, but we succeeded after a lot of trial and error. We simply spared no effort. And now everyone can see through the glass and watch the inscription emerging on the body. Won't you come closer and look at the needles?"

The traveler slowly rose, walked across, and bent over the harrow. "You can see," said the officer, "two kinds of needles in multiple patterns. Each long needle is accompanied by a short one. The long one does the writing, you know, and the short one spurts out water to wash away the blood and to keep the writing clear. The mixture of blood and water is then channeled into tiny runnels and eventually flows into the main gutter, from where the drain pipe leads to the pit." The officer pointed out the precise route that the mixture had to take. When, in order to make it as graphic as possible, he pretended to scoop up the liquid with both hands at the mouth of the drainpipe, the traveler raised his head and, groping backwards with one hand, tried to return to his chair. But then to his horror, he saw that the condemned man had likewise followed the officer's invitation to look closely at the way the harrow was set up. The condemned man had tugged the drowsy soldier slightly forward by his chain and was also bending over the glass. One could see that his uncertain eyes were seeking what the two gentlemen had just observed, but that he would fail since he hadn't heard the explanation. He kept bending every which way. His eyes kept scurrying over the glass. The traveler wanted to drive him away, for what he was doing must have been punishable. But with one hand the officer held on to the traveler and with the other hand he took a clod of soil from the embankment and threw it at the soldier. The soldier's head jolted up; upon seeing what the condemned man had dared to do, he dropped the rifle, dug his heels into the ground, and yanked the condemned man back so hard that he instantly fell down; the soldier then watched him writhing and rattling his chains.

"Get him on his feet!" the officer yelled, for he noticed that the traveler was being all too greatly distracted by the condemned man. The traveler even leaned across the harrow, paying it no heed, trying only to determine what was happening to the condemned man. "Treat him carefully!" the officer again yelled. He hurried around the apparatus, grabbed the condemned man under the shoulders, and, with the soldier's help, got him back on his feet, which, however, kept slipping.

"Now I know everything," said the traveler when the officer came back to him.

"Except the most important part," said the officer, grabbing the traveler's arm and pointing upward: "Up there in the draftsman you'll find the gear unit that controls the movements of the harrow; now this unit is regulated according to the design prescribed by the judgment. I still use the former commander's drawings. Here they are. . . ." He pulled a few pages from the leather portfolio. "Unfortunately, I can't let you handle them, they are my most precious possessions. Sit down, I'll hold them up to you from here: then you'll be able to see everything clearly."

He showed him the first sheet. The traveler would have liked to express his appreciation, but all he could see was a crisscross of labyrinthine lines covering the paper so densely that the blank gaps were barely discernible.

"Read it," said the officer.

"I can't," said the traveler.

"But it's quite legible," said the officer.

"It's very intricate," said the traveler evasively, "but I can't decipher it."

"Yes," said the officer, laughing and putting the portfolio away. "It's no calligraphy for schoolchildren. It has to be studied for a long time. Eventually, you'd be able to make it out too. It can't be a simple script, of course—after all, it's not supposed to kill right away, it's planned for an average of twelve hours; the climax is calculated for the sixth hour. So lots and lots of curlicues have to surround the actual script: the script itself forms only a narrow belt around the body, the rest of the skin is reserved for embellishments. Can you now appreciate the work of the harrow and the entire apparatus? Just look!" He bounded up the ladder, turned a wheel, called down, "Watch out, step aside!" and everything started moving. If the cog hadn't screaked, it would have been wonderful. As if surprised by this troublesome cog, the officer shook his fist, then, by way of apology, held out his arms to the traveler and hastily clambered down in order to observe the workings of the apparatus from below. Something was still amiss, which he alone noticed. He climbed up again, thrust both hands into the draftsman, then, in order to descend more quickly, he slid down the pole instead of using the ladder, and, trying to make himself heard above the racket, yelled into the traveler's ear at the top of his lungs: "Do you understand the procedure? The harrow starts writing. Once it's applied the first round of script to the man's back, the layer of cotton slowly rolls the man over on his side to offer the harrow new space. Meanwhile, the raw areas wounded by the script gradually move into the cotton, which because of its special treatment immediately staunches the bleeding and prepares the body for deeper penetration by the script. Here, when the body is rolled over again, the teeth along the edge of the harrow rip the cotton from the wounds, hurl it into the pit, and the harrow then has more work. And so it keeps writing deeper and deeper for those twelve hours. During the first six hours, the condemned man remains alive almost as before, he only suffers pain. The felt is removed after two hours, for the man has no strength left for screaming. Here, at the head end, warm rice pudding is placed in this electrically heated basin, and if he likes, the man can take whatever he manages to lap up with his tongue. No man ignores the opportunity. I know of no one, and I've had lots of experience. He doesn't lose his pleasure in eating until the sixth hour. Usually I then kneel down here and observe this phenomenon. The man seldom swallows the last morsel; he merely rolls it in his mouth and spits it out into the pit. At that point, I have to duck—otherwise it would hit me in the face. And how quiet the man becomes at the sixth hour! Even the stupidest man is now enlightened. It starts around the eyes. From there it spreads out. A look that might lure you into joining him under the harrow. Nothing else happens, the man simply begins to decipher the writing; he purses his lips as if he were listening. You've seen that it's not easy deciphering the script with your eyes; but our man deciphers it with his wounds. It's a lot of work, to be sure; it takes him six hours to complete it. But then the harrow forks up his entire body and dumps him into the pit, where he flops down on the cotton and the bloody water. Now the judicial procedure is over, and we—I and the soldier—bury him quickly."

The traveler had lowered his ear toward the officer and, with his hands in his coat pockets, was watching the machine working. The condemned man was also

watching it, but without comprehending. He was bent
forward slightly, following the reeling needles, when
the soldier, at a sign from the officer, took a knife
and slashed the back of the man's shirt and trousers
so that they dropped off. He tried to grab his falling
clothes to cover his nakedness, but the soldier lifted
him up and shook off his final rags. The officer
switched on the machine and in the sudden hush the
condemned man was laid out under the harrow. The
chains were loosened and the straps fastened in their
stead; in the first moment, it seemed almost a relief
for the condmened man. And now the harrow came
down a bit, for he was a thin man. When the needle
points touched him, a shudder ran over his skin; while
the soldier was busy strapping in his right hand, he
stretched out his left hand, not knowing where; but
it was toward where the traveler was standing. The
officer kept gazing at the traveler from the side, probing his face as if to read the effect made on him by
the execution, which he had at least outlined for him.

The wrist strap tore; the soldier must have drawn
it too tight. The officer had to step in; the soldier
showed him the torn-off scrap. The officer walked over
to him and said, facing the traveler: "The machine is
extremely intricate, something is bound to rip or break
now and then; but that shouldn't interfere with one's
overall opinion. Anyway, the strap can be replaced
immediately: I'll use a chain. Of course, it will interfere with the delicacy of the vibrations for the right
arm." And while fastening the chains, he added, "The
wherewithal for maintaining the machine is greatly
reduced now. The former commander granted me an

unlimited budget for this sole purpose. We had a depot here, where all possible spare parts were stored. I confess, I was practically a spendthrift—I mean earlier, not now, as the new commander claims—he uses anything as a pretext for battling old institutions. Now he oversees the machine budget himself, and if I order a new strap, the torn one is demanded as evidence; it takes ten days for the replacement to arrive, but it's an inferior brand and not worth much. And meanwhile, no one cares how I'm supposed to run the machine without a strap."

The traveler pondered: It's always risky interfering decisively in other people's business. He was a citizen of neither the penal colony nor the country it belonged to. If he were to condemn or even obstruct this execution, he might be told: You're a foreigner, keep quiet. He couldn't have responded to that, he could only have added that he was surprised at himself in this case, for he traveled purely with the goal of observing but in no way altering judicial methods in other countries. Of course, the situation here was highly tempting. The injustice of the procedure and the inhumanity of the execution were beyond all doubt. No one could assume any self-serving motives on the traveler's part, for the condemned man was a stranger to him, a foreigner, and no one he sympathized with. The traveler himself had letters of recommendation from high places, had been welcomed here with great cordiality, and his being invited to this execution even seemed to indicate that they were asking his opinion about this legal action. And this was all the more probable in that the commander, as the traveler had now heard loud and clear, was no supporter of this procedure and was almost hostile toward the officer.

Suddenly the traveler heard a shriek of rage from the officer. He had just shoved the felt stump into the condemned man's mouth, not without some effort, when the man, unable to fight his nausea, had shut his eyes and vomited. The officer hastily pulled him up from the stump and was about to turn the man's head toward the pit; but it was too late, the vomit was already flowing down into the machine. "It's all the commander's fault!" the officer shouted and in his daze he shook the brass rods in front. "My machine is being soiled like a stable!" With trembling hands, he showed the traveler what had happened. "Haven't I spent hours at a time trying to make the commander understand that no food should be served to the condemned man a whole day before the execution? But our new mild policy reflects a different attitude. The commander's ladies stuff the man's belly with sweets before he's taken away. All his life he's eaten nothing but stinking fish, and now he has to eat sweets! Still, it could be possible, I would not object—but why don't they get a new felt gag, which I've been requesting for the last three months? How can a man help feeling nauseated when he gets that felt into his mouth after over a hundred men have sucked and gnawed on it while dying?"

The condemned man had laid down his head and he looked peaceful; the soldier was busy cleaning the machine with the man's shirt. The officer went over to the traveler, who, with some vague foreboding, stepped back; but the officer grabbed his hand and pulled him aside. "I want to speak to you privately," he said, "may I?"

"By all means," said the traveler, listening with downcast eyes.

"At present, this procedure and this execution, which you now have a chance to admire, no longer have any open supporters in the colony. I am their sole representative and simultaneously the sole representative of the old commander's legacy. I can't even think of expanding the procedure any further—it takes all my energy just to preserve it as is. When the old commander was alive, the colony was full of his supporters; to some extent, I have the old commander's persuasiveness, but I entirely lack his power. As a result, his supporters have kept a low profile; there are lots of them left, but nobody admits it. If you go to the teahouse today—during an execution, that is—and keep your ears open, you may hear some ambiguous remarks. Those people are all supporters, but under the current commander and with his current views, they're completely useless to me. And now I ask you: Should such a life's work"— he pointed at the machine—"perish because of this commander and his women, who influence him? Should one put up with this? Even if one is only a foreigner visiting our island for a few days? But there's no time to lose, they're preparing some action against my judicial authority. Talks are already taking place at the commander's headquarters without my being allowed to attend. Even your visit today strikes me as characteristic of the entire situation; they're cowards and so they send you, a foreigner, ahead. How

different the executions used to be! The entire valley
was mobbed a whole day in advance: they all came
just to watch. Early in the morning, the commander
showed up with his ladies; fanfares awoke the entire
camp; I reported that everything was ready; the company (no high official dared to be absent) grouped
around the machine; this heap of cane chairs is a
wretched leftover from that era. The machine was
freshly polished and glistening; I used new replacement parts for almost every execution. In front of a
hundred eyes—all the spectators stood on tiptoe as
far as the hills—the commander himself placed the
condemned man under the harrow. Something that a
common soldier may do today was assigned to me,
the presiding judge, and it was an honor for me. And
now the execution began! No jarring note disturbed
the running of the machine. Some people stopped
watching altogether; they lay in the sand, closing their
eyes. Everyone knew: Justice was being done. In the
hush, all we heard was the condemned man's sighs,
muffled by the felt gag. Today the machine no longer
succeeds in wringing a louder sigh from the condemned man than the felt gag can throttle; but back
then, the writing needles emitted a mordant liquid,
which we are not allowed to use anymore. Well, and
then came the sixth hour! It was impossible to allow
everyone who requested it to watch from up close.
The commander, wise as he was, ordered that preference be given to the children. I, however, because
of my profession, was always permitted to stand close
by; I would often squat there with a small child in
each arm, right and left. How profoundly we took in

the transfigured expression from the tortured face, how intensely our cheeks basked in the glow of that justice, attained at long last and already fading! What wonderful times, my friend!"

The officer had obviously forgotten whom he was dealing with; he had thrown his arms around the traveler and placed his head on his shoulder. The traveler was deeply embarrassed; he gazed impatiently over the officer's head. The soldier had finished the cleanup work and had now poured some rice pudding from a can into the basin. No sooner did the condemned man, who seemed to have recovered completely, notice the pudding than his tongue began snapping at it. The soldier kept shoving him away, for the pudding was probably meant for some later time; but in any case, it was equally unbecoming of the soldier to reach into it with his dirty hands and eat it in front of the ravenous prisoner.

The officer quickly pulled himself together. "I didn't mean to touch you," he told the traveler. "I know it's impossible to make those times comprehensible today. Anyway, the machine is still running and it still works on its own. It works on its own even when it's alone in this valley. And ultimately, the corpse, in an incomprehensibly gentle flight, still drops into the pit even if hundreds of people no longer gather round the pit like flies, as they used to do. Back then, we had to install a sturdy railing around the pit, but it was torn down long ago."

The traveler, wanting to get his face away from the officer, glanced about aimlessly. The officer assumed he was contemplating the desolation of the valley; he therefore took hold of the traveler's hands, circled around him to meet his eyes, and asked: "Are you aware of the disgrace?"

But the traveler held his tongue. The officer left off him for a brief while; with legs apart, hands on hips, he stood silently, gazing at the ground. Then, with an encouraging smile, he said: "I was near you yesterday when the commander invited you. I heard the invitation. I know the commander. I instantly understood what he was up to. Even though he has enough power to take action against me, he doesn't dare as yet; but he does want to expose me to your judgment—that of a distinguished foreigner. He is meticulous in his calculations: this is your second day on the island, you didn't know the old commander or his ideas, you are trapped in European attitudes—perhaps you're opposed on principle to capital punishment in general and this kind of mechanical execution in particular. Furthermore, you watch the execution take place without public participation, dismally, on a somewhat defective machine. Given all these things, would it not (the commander thinks) be highly possible that you do not consider my procedure appropriate? And if you do not consider it appropriate, you will not (I am still speaking from the commander's point of view) hold back your opinion, for you must certainly rely on your tried-and-tested convictions. True, you have gotten to know and respect many peculiarities of many nations. You will therefore probably not state your wholehearted opposition to this procedure as you might in your own country. But the commander doesn't even need that: a casual, a simply careless word would be enough. It doesn't have to express your conviction so long as it merely seems to comply with his wishes. And he *will* question you very insidiously—of that I am certain. And his ladies will sit around in a circle and prick up their ears. You will say something like, 'In my country a judicial procedure is different,' or, 'In my country the defendant is interrogated before the verdict,' or, 'In my country the condemned man is informed of the verdict,' or, 'In my country there are other forms of punishment besides capital punishment,' or, 'In my country torture existed only in the Middle Ages.' Those are all remarks that are as correct as they may sound natural to you—innocent remarks that do not discredit my procedure. But how will the commander receive them? I can see him, the good commander, instantly shoving his chair aside and hurrying out to the balcony, I can see his ladies thronging after him, I can hear his voice now (the ladies call it a thunderous voice), and he says, 'A great researcher of Western Civilization, assigned to investigate judicial operations in all countries, has just said that our procedure, an old custom, is inhumane. With this verdict from such a personage, it is naturally no longer possible for me to tolerate this procedure. As of today I therefore order . . . etc.' You try to cut in: you did not say what he is proclaiming, you did not call my procedure inhumane—quite the contrary: on the basis of your deep understanding you regard it as thoroughly humane and human; you also admire this machinery—but it's too late: you don't even get out on the balcony, which is already crowded with ladies; you try to draw attention; you try to shout; but a lady's hand covers your mouth—and I and the old commander's work are doomed."

The traveler had to suppress a smile; so the task he had thought so hard was that easy. He said evasively, "You overestimate my influence. The commander has read my letter of recommendation, he knows I am no expert in judicial proceedings. Were I to express my opinion, it would be that of a private individual, no more significant than anyone else's opinion, and in any case far more insignificant than the opinion of the commander, who, as I am led to believe, has very far-reaching powers in his penal colony. Now if his opinion is as firmly set as you believe, then I fear that the end has come for this procedure with no need for my modest help."

Did the officer see the light? No, not yet. He emphatically shook his head and glanced back at the condemned man and the soldier, both of whom flinched and stopped eating the rice; then the officer walked up very close to the traveler, looked at something on his jacket instead of at his face, and said more softly than before:

"You don't know the commander, you are—please forgive the expression—somewhat innocent in regard to him and indeed all of us. Your influence, believe me, cannot be assessed high enough. Why, I was in seventh heaven when I heard that you would be attending the execution all by yourself. This order from the commander was aimed at me, but I will now turn it to my advantage. Undiverted by false insinuations and scornful looks—which could not have been avoided if a greater audience had come to the execution—you have heard my explanations, viewed the machine, and are now about to watch the execution. Your verdict must already be formed; should you feel any minor uncertainties, then the sight of the execution will eliminate them. And now let me request something of you: please help me in regard to the commander!"

The traveler did not let him continue. "How could I?" he exclaimed. "That's quite impossible. I can help you as little as I can harm you."

"You *can*," said the officer. With some dread the traveler saw the officer clenching his fists. "You *can*," the officer repeated more urgently. "I have a plan that is sure to work. You believe that your influence does not suffice. I believe that it does suffice. But even granting that you are right: is it not necessary to try anything, even something that may be insufficient, in order to preserve this procedure? So then listen to my plan. For me to carry it out, the most essential thing today is that in the colony you conceal your verdict on the procedure as much as possible. If you are not asked outright, you must say nothing at all; and your statements must be brief and vague. People should notice that it is hard for you to speak about it, that you are embittered, that, in case you should talk openly, you would absolutely swear and curse. I am not asking you to lie. Not on your life. But your answers should be brief, say: 'Yes, I watched the execution,' or 'Yes, I heard all the explanations.' Just that, nothing more. There are reasons enough—though not what the commander may think—for the embitterment that people will notice in you. Naturally he will misunderstand it altogether and construe it by his lights. That is the basis of my plan. Tomorrow, at his headquarters, the commander will preside over a major conference of all the higher administrative officials. Naturally the commander knows how to turn such a meeting into a public spectacle. A gallery was built, and it is always packed with spectators. I am forced to take part in the conferences, but I shake with disgust. Now you are bound to be invited to the session in any case; if you act in accordance with my plan, the invitation will become an urgent plea. But if for some unfathomable reason you are not invited, then you have to request an invitation; you will then receive one beyond any doubt. Thus tomorrow you will be sitting with the ladies in the commander's box. He will frequently glance up to make sure you are there. After various indifferent, ridiculous agenda items discussed purely for the audience's benefit— and mostly concerning harbor construction, always that harbor construction!—the issue of the judicial procedure will be raised. If it is not brought up by the commander, or not soon enough, then I will see to it that it is brought up. I will get to my feet and deliver my report on today's execution. Very briefly, just this report. Such a report is not usual there, but I will deliver it anyway. The commander will thank me, as always, with a friendly smile and now he cannot hold back, he will seize the favorable opportunity. 'The report,' he will speak like that more or less, 'on the execution has just been delivered. I would like to add to this report only that this execution was witnessed by the great explorer, who, as you all know, has been paying us the extraordinary honor of visiting our colony. Our meeting today has likewise been made more important by his presence. Should we not ask this great explorer what he thinks of the old, traditional mode of execution and the preliminary procedure?' Naturally there will be applause everywhere, general concurrence, I will be the loudest. The commander will bow to you and say, 'Then I shall ask you on behalf of us all.' And now you will step over to the railing. Put your hands down so they will be visible to everyone, otherwise the ladies will grab them and play with your fingers. And now you finally take the floor. I don't know how I will endure the suspense of waiting until then. You must put no restraints on your speech. Blast out the truth, lean over the railing, yell, yes indeed, yell your opinion, your unshakable opinion, at the commander. But perhaps you don't wish to, it's not in your character, people in your country may act differently in such situations. Well, that's all right too, that suffices fully, don't stand up, just say a few words, whisper them so that only the officials below you just barely catch them— that will suffice, you do not have to talk about the poor turnout for the execution, about the screaking gear, the torn strap, the repulsive felt gag—no, I will take over for you, and believe me, if my speech does not drive him from the hall, then it will force him to his knees and he will have to avow: Old commander, I bow to you. . . . That is my plan; do you want to help me carry it out? But naturally you want to— more than that, you have to."

And the officer grabbed both the traveler's arms

and peered, heavily breathing, into his face. He had shouted the last few sentences so loudly that even the soldier and the condemned man had taken notice; although they understood nothing, they stopped eating and gazed over at the traveler while chewing.

From the very outset, the traveler had no doubt about the answer he had to give; he had experienced too much in his life to waver here; he was basically honest and unafraid. Nonetheless, within sight of the soldier and the condemned man, he now hesitated for a heartbeat. Finally, however, he said as he had to: "No."

The officer blinked several times, but did not avert his eyes.

"Would you like an explanation?" asked the traveler. The officer nodded mutely. "I oppose this procedure," the traveler now said. "Even before you took me into your confidence—naturally I will never betray this confidence under any circumstances—I was already wondering if I had the right to intervene against this procedure and if my intervention could have even a tiny prospect of success. It was clear to me whom I should turn to first: the commander, of course. You made it clearer to me but without hardening my resolution—on the contrary, your sincere conviction is touching even though it cannot deter me."

The officer remained mute, turned to the machine, clutched one of the brass rods, and then, leaning back slightly, looked up at the draftsman as if checking whether everything was in order. The soldier and the condemned man seemed to have made friends with one another; the condemned man, difficult as it was because of the tight straps, made signs at the soldier; the soldier bent toward him; the condemned man whispered something, and the soldier nodded.

The traveler went after the officer, saying, "You don't yet know what I intend to do. I will give the commander my opinion of the procedure, but privately and not in a meeting. Nor will I be staying here long enough to be called in for any kind of meeting; I am sailing tomorrow morning or at least boarding ship."

It did not look as if the officer had listened. "So the procedure has not convinced you," he said to himself, smiling the way an old man smiles at a child's nonsense but hides his true thoughts behind the smile.

"Well, then it's time," he finally said, and his clear eyes, which contained some kind of challenge, some kind of appeal for cooperation, suddenly rested on the traveler.

"Time for what?" asked the traveler nervously, but received no answer.

"You are free," said the officer to the condemned man in his native language. The condemned did not believe it right off. "Well, you're free," said the officer. For the first time life actually came into the condemned man's face. Was it true? Was it merely a passing whim for the officer? Had the foreign traveler obtained clemency for him? What was it? That was what his face seemed to be asking. But not for long. Whatever it might be, he wanted, if he were allowed, to be really free and he began struggling to the extent that the harrow permitted.

"You're ripping my straps," shouted the officer. "Lie still! We're unbuckling them." And together with the soldier, to whom he signaled, he got to work. The condemned man laughed to himself wordlessly; he kept turning his face alternately left, toward the officer, and right, toward the soldier, nor did he forget the traveler.

"Pull him out," the officer ordered the soldier. Care had to be taken on account of the harrow. Because of the condemned man's impatience there were already a few small rips in his back.

But from now on the officer paid him scant heed. He walked over to the traveler, pulled out his small leather portfolio again, leafed through the papers, finally located the page he was seeking, and showed it to the traveler. "Read this," he said.

"I can't," said the traveler, "I've already told you I can't read this."

"Just take a close look at the page," said the officer, stepping nearer to the traveler in order to read with him. But when that did not help either, then, as if the page must not be touched no matter what, he raised his little finger and moved it high across the paper to make it easier for the traveler to read. The traveler also made an effort to at least accommodate the officer, but it was impossible. Now the officer began to spell out the inscription and then he read out the words. " 'Be just!'—that is what it says," he said, "now you *can* read it."

The traveler bent so close to the paper that the officer, fearing any touch, pulled it further away. The traveler said nothing now, but it was obvious that he still could not read it. " 'Be just!'—that's what it says," the officer repeated.

"Could be," said the traveler, "I believe that that is what it says."

"Fine," said the officer, at least partly satisfied, and climbed the ladder with the page. He very carefully bedded the page in the draftsman and apparently readjusted the gears entirely. It was very arduous work, some of the gears must have been very tiny; the officer had to examine the gear unit so precisely that at times his head vanished completely inside the draftsman.

The traveler uninterruptedly watched this work from below; his neck grew stiff, and his eyes smarted because the sky was streaming with sunlight. The soldier and the condemned man were occupied only with each other. The condemned man's shirt and trousers, already lying in the pit, were fished out on the point of the soldier's bayonet. The shirt was dreadfully filthy, and the condemned man washed it in the pail of water. When he then put on his shirt and trousers, both the soldier and the condemned man burst into loud guffaws because the backs of the garments were sliced in half. Perhaps the condemned man felt obliged to entertain the soldier; in his slashed clothes he turned all around in front of the soldier, who squatted on the ground, laughing and slapping his knees. Nevertheless they did restrain themselves out of deference to the gentlemen.

When the officer was eventually done up above, he smiled as he once more surveyed the whole apparatus in all its parts and shut the lid of the draftsman, which had been open until now. He climbed down, looked into the pit and then at the condemned man, who, he was pleased to note, had taken out his clothes. The officer now went over to the pail of water to wash his hands, recognized the repulsive filth too late, felt sad that he could not wash his hands, finally plunged them into the sand (this surrogate did not satisfy him, but he had to make do), then stood up, and began unbuttoning his tunic. As he did so, the two ladies' handkerchiefs tucked under his collar fell into his hands. "Here are your handkerchiefs," he said, tossing them to the condemned man. And by way of explanation he told the traveler, "Gifts from the ladies."

Despite his obvious haste in discarding his tunic and then stripping down, he handled every clothing item very lovingly; his fingers even purposely stroked the silver piping on his service coat, shaking a tassel into place. It was, however, inconsistent with this caution that as soon as he was done handling an item, he angrily flung it into the pit. The last remaining object was his short sword with its belt. He drew the sword from its sheath, smashed it, then gathered everything together—the sword fragments, the sheath, and the belt—and hurled them away so violently that they banged against each other in the pit.

Now he stood there naked. The traveler bit his lips and said nothing. He knew what was about to happen, but he had no right to hinder the officer in any way. If the judicial procedure that the officer revered was really on the verge of being eliminated—possibly because of the traveler's intervention, which he considered his duty—then the officer's action now was entirely correct; the traveler would have acted no differently in his place.

At first the soldier and the condemned man understood nothing, they were not even watching. The condemned man was delighted that he had gotten back the handkerchiefs, but he could not delight in them for long, because the soldier snatched them from him quickly and unforeseeably. Now the condemned man tried to pull them out from behind the soldier, who had stowed them in his belt, but the soldier was alert. Thus they fought half playfully. It was only when the officer was stark naked that they noticed him. The condemned man in particular seemed struck by an inkling of some great sudden change. What had happened to him before was now happening to the officer. Perhaps he would go all the way. The foreign traveler had probably given the order. So this was revenge. Without having suffered to the end he would nevertheless be avenged to the end. A broad, soundless grin now appeared on his face and did not vanish.

The officer, however, had turned to the machine. If it had been plain earlier that he quite understood the machine, it was now almost staggering to see him running it and the machine obeying him. His hand merely approached the harrow, and the harrow rose and dropped several times until it was in just the right position for receiving him; he merely touched the edge of the bed, and it already began quivering. The felt stump came toward his mouth, they saw that the officer did not really want to have it, but his qualms lasted only an instant, he promptly yielded and took it in. Everything was ready, only the straps still hung down the sides; but they were obviously unnecessary, the officer did not have to be strapped in. Now the condemned man noticed the loose straps, to his mind the execution was incomplete unless the straps were buckled in; he eagerly signaled the soldier, and they ran over to strap in the officer. The officer had already stretched out one foot to kick the crank that started the draftsman. Now he saw that the two men had come; he therefore pulled back his foot and allowed himself to be strapped in. But now his foot could not reach the crank; neither the soldier nor the condemned man would find it, and the traveler was determined not to stir. It did not matter; hardly were the straps tightened when the machine began working; the bed quivered, the needles danced on the skin, the harrow floated up and down. The traveler had been staring at it for a while when it struck him that a gear in the draftsman should have been screaking; but everything was quiet, not the slightest humming could be heard.

Because of this stillness the machine simply escaped all notice. The traveler peered over at the soldier and the condemned man. The condemned man was the livelier of the two, everything about the machine interested him: he kept bending down or stretching out, constantly pointing his forefinger to show the soldier some detail. The traveler was annoyed. He was determined to see it through, but he would not have endured the sight of them for long. "Go home," he told them. The soldier might have been willing to do so, but the condemned man regarded the order as an out-and-out punishment. Clasping his hands he begged to be left here, and when the traveler shook his head, refusing to give in, the condemned man actually knelt down. The traveler saw that orders were useless here, he decided to go across and drive the two men away. But then he heard a noise overhead, in the draftsman. He looked up. Was that cogwheel causing trouble after all? It was something else, however. Slowly the lid of the draftsman surged and then clapped wide open. The cogs of a gear surfaced and rose, soon the entire gear emerged; it was as if some tremendous force were squeezing the draftsman together, leaving no room for this gear. The gear turned all the way to the edge of the draftsman, fell down, trundled upright over a stretch of sand, and then lay flat. But now a further gear was already rising up above; it was followed by many others, large, small, and barely discernible ones. The same thing happened to all of them. Whenever the onlookers figured that the draftsman must be empty by now, a new, very large group appeared, rose, plummeted, trundled across the sand, and lay flat. During this process, the condemned man forgot all about the traveler's order, he was utterly absorbed in the gears; he kept trying to grab one, simultaneously urged the soldier to help him, but withdrew his hand in fright for another gear would promptly follow, terrifying him, at least when it began rolling.

The traveler, however, was alarmed; the machine was obviously falling to pieces; its tranquil operation was deceptive. He felt he had to look after the officer, since he could no longer take care of himself. But while the tumbling cogwheels had monopolized his attention, he had failed to observe the rest of the machine. Now, however, when, after the final gear had left the draftsman, he bent over the harrow, he

225

had a new and even harsher surprise. The harrow was not writing, it was only pricking, and the bed was not rolling the body, it was only lifting it, quivering, against the needles. The traveler wanted to do something, perhaps stop the machine: this was no torture, such as the officer was aiming for, it was full-blown murder. The traveler stretched out his hands. But the harrow with the forked-up body was already turning aside, which it normally did only in the twelfth hour. The blood flowed in a hundred streams—not mingled with water; the small water pipes had likewise failed this time. And now the very last element failed: the body did not separate from the long needles, it poured out its blood but dangled over the pit without dropping. The harrow was about to return to its old position, but as if noticing that it had not yet freed itself of its burden, it remained above the pit.

"Do something!" the traveler shouted at the soldier and the condemned man and grabbed the officer's feet himself. He wanted to push against the feet while the other two men grabbed the head at the opposite end so that the officer could be eased off the needles. But the two men could not make up their minds to come over; the prisoner even turned away. The traveler had to go over and violently shove them toward the officer's head. In so doing, he reluctantly saw the face of the corpse. It was as it had been in life; no sign of the promised redemption was perceptible; the officer had not found what all the others had found in the machine. His lips were squeezed tight, his eyes were open, with the same expression as in life, his gaze was calm and convinced, the point of the large iron spike had passed through the forehead.

When the traveler, with the soldier and the condemned man behind him, reached the first few houses in the colony, the soldier pointed to one, saying, "That's the teahouse."

On the ground floor of a house lay a deep, low, cavernous room with smoky walls and ceiling. It was open full-breadth toward the street. Even though it barely differed from the colony's other houses, which, except for the commander's palatial headquarters, were all very decrepit, the teahouse nevertheless looked like a historic relic to the traveler, and he felt the power of earlier times. He stepped closer, walked, followed by his companions, between the small, unoccupied tables on the street in front of the teahouse, and breathed in the cool, dank air coming from the interior.

"The old man is buried here," said the soldier. "The priest refused to let him lie in the cemetery. For a while they couldn't decide where to bury him. Finally they buried him here. The officer probably told you nothing about that, for naturally this is the thing he is most ashamed of. A few times he even tried to dig the old man up at night, but he was always chased away."

"Where is the grave?" asked the traveler, unable to believe the soldier. Instantly both the soldier and the condemned man ran ahead of him, stretching out their hands toward the location of the grave. They took the traveler all the way to the back wall, where patrons were seated at several tables. They were probably dockworkers, strong men with short, shiny black beards. None of them wore a jacket, their shirts were ripped, they were poor, humiliated creatures. When the traveler approached, a few stood up, hugged the wall, and gazed at him.

"He's a foreigner," the whispers circled the traveler, "he wants to look at the grave." They pushed aside one of the tables, underneath which there actually was a gravestone. It was a simple stone, low enough to be concealed under a table. It bore an inscription in very tiny letters; the traveler had to kneel down to read it. It said: "Here lies the old commander. His followers, who must remain anonymous now, have dug him this grave and set up the stone. There is a prophecy that the commander will be resurrected after a certain number of years and lead his followers from this house to reconquer the colony. Have faith and abide!"

Upon reading this and getting to his feet, the traveler saw the men standing around him, smiling, as if they had read the inscription with him, had found it ridiculous, and were asking him to concur in their opinion. The traveler pretended not to notice. He distributed a few coins among them, waited until the table had been pushed back over the grave, left the teahouse, and headed toward the harbor.

In the teahouse, the soldier and the condemned man had found acquaintances, who held them back. But they must have soon shaken them off, for the traveler was still midway down the long stairway leading to the rowboats when they came running after him. They probably wanted to force the traveler to take them along in the last moment. While the traveler was below, negotiating with a ferryman to row him to the steamer, the two men dashed down the stairs, holding their tongues, for they did not dare shout. But by the time they arrived below, the traveler was already in the rowboat, and the ferryman was already casting off. They might have jumped into the boat, but the traveler pulled up a heavy, knotted rope from the floor and threatened them with it, thereby preventing them from jumping in.

A COUNTRY DOCTOR

To My Father

THE NEW LAWYER

We have a new lawyer, Dr. Bucephalus. Little in his appearance recalls the time when he was the warhorse of Alexander of Macedonia. But anyone familiar with the circumstances will notice a thing or two. Yet recently, on the perron of the courthouse, I saw even a very simpleminded court usher, who, with the expert eye of a small-time patron at racetracks, was marveling at the lawyer as, lifting his thighs aloft, he climbed from step to step, his footfalls ringing on the marble.

In general, the bar approves of Bucephalus' admission. With astonishing insight, people tell themselves that Bucephalus, given the modern social system, is in a quandary and that in any case, he deserves a friendly reception for that reason and also for his significance in world history. Today—no one can deny it—there is no Alexander the Great. Some people do know how to murder; nor do they lack the skill of hurling a lance across a banquet table and striking a friend; and for many, Macedonia is too confining, so that they curse Philip, the father—but no one, no one can lead us to India. Even in those days, the gates of India were unattainable, yet their direction was pointed out by the tip of the royal sword. By now those gates have been carried off to some other location altogether and today they are wider and higher; no one points out their direction; many people hold swords, but only to brandish them wildly; and the gaze that tries to follow them grows confused.

So perhaps it is best to bury oneself in the law books as Bucephalus has done. Free, in quiet lamplight, far from the uproar of Alexander's battle, his flanks not squeezed by the rider's loins, he reads, turning the pages of our ancient tomes.

A COUNTRY DOCTOR

I was in a great predicament: an urgent trip lay
ahead of me; a dangerously ill patient awaited me in
a village ten leagues away; a heavy blizzard filled the
vast space between me and him; I did have a wagon,
lightweight, with large wheels, just the right kind of
wagon for our country roads. Bundled up in my fur
coat, holding my instrument bag, I stood in the courtyard, ready to travel; but the horse was lacking, the
horse. My own horse had died the previous night
because of its overexertion in this icy winter. My
housemaid was now running around the village, trying
to borrow a horse; but it was hopeless, I knew it; and
covering up with more and more snow, becoming more
and more immobile, I stood there forlorn.

My maid appeared at the gate, alone, swinging the
lantern. Naturally: who would lend someone a horse
at such a time for such a trip? I strode back across
the courtyard; I could think of no solution. Confused, tormented, I kicked the brittle door of the
pigsty, which had not been used in years. The door
opened, banging to and fro on its hinges. Warmth
and aroma emerged, as if from horses. A dim stable

lantern swayed inside on a rope. A man, cowering in the low shed, exposed his open, blue-eyed face.

"Should I harness up?" he asked, creeping out on all fours. I could think of nothing to say, so I stooped down only to see what else was in the sty. The maid stood beside me. "You never know what you've got in your own house," she said, and we both laughed.

"Hey, Brother, hey, Sister!" shouted the stableman, and two horses, mighty creatures with strong flanks, tucking their legs in close to their bodies, lowering their well-shaped heads like camels, shuffled out one behind the other solely by twisting their rumps out of the doorway, which they filled completely. But then they promptly stood upright, on high legs, with densely steaming bodies.

"Help him," I said, and the willing girl dashed over to hand the wagon harness to the stableman.

But no sooner did she reach him than he clutched her and banged his face against her. She screamed and fled back to me; the red imprint of two rows of teeth were left on the girl's cheek.

"You swine," I yelled furiously, "do you want a whipping?" But then I promptly remembered that he was a stranger, that I did not know where he came from, and that he was helping me voluntarily while everyone else had refused.

As if knowing my thoughts, he does not hold my threat against me; instead, still busy with the horses, he turns toward me only once. "Get in," he then says, and indeed: everything is ready. I have never, I note to myself, ridden with such a beautiful pair of horses, and I get in cheerfully.

"But I'm driving," I tell him, "you don't know the way."

"Certainly," he says, "I'm not going with you anyhow, I'm staying with Rosa."

"No," Rosa shouts and runs into the house with a correct foreboding of her inescapable fate. I hear the jingling chain that she draws across the door; I hear the lock snap; I also see her dashing through the hallway and the rooms, putting out all the lights to avoid being found.

"You're coming along," I tell the stableman, "or I won't go, as urgent as this trip may be. I wouldn't dream of giving you the girl as the price of this trip."

"Giddyap!" he says, clapping his hands. The wagon is yanked away, like a log in a current. I hear the door of my house bursting and splintering under the stableman's onslaught; then my eyes and ears are filled with a roar that penetrates equally to all my senses. But even that lasts only a moment, for, as if my patient's farmyard opened up right in front of my gates, I am already there. The horses stand calmly; the snow has stopped falling; moonlight all around. My patient's parents hurry out of the house, his sister behind them; they practically lift me from the wagon. I glean nothing from their confused chatter; the air in the sickroom is almost unbreathable; the neglected hearth oven is smoking. I will push open the window; but first I want to look at the patient. Gaunt, no fever, not cold, not warm, with vacant eyes, shirtless, the boy heaves himself up under the featherbed, clings to my neck, whispers into my ear, "Doctor, let me die." I peer around; no one has heard it. The parents stand mute, leaning forward, waiting for my verdict; the sister has brought a chair for my bag. I open my bag and search through my instruments. The boy keeps groping for me from the bed to remind me of his plea; I take hold of some pincers, check them in the candlelight, and put them down again. "Yes," I think blasphemously, "in such cases the gods help, sending the missing horse, adding a second one because of the urgency, bestowing the stableboy on top of everything else—"

Only now do I think of Rosa. What do I do, how can I rescue her, how can I get her out from under that stableboy, ten leagues away, uncontrollable horses in front of my wagon?—these horses, which have now somehow loosened the reins, pushed open the windows, I don't know how, from the outside; each has stuck its head through a window and, undaunted by the family's shrieks, they gape at the patient.

"I'm driving right home," I think, as if the horses were asking me to travel; but the sister believes I am dazed by the heat, and so I put up with her removing my fur coat. A glass of rum is set down for me. The old man pats me on the back—the sacrifice of his treasure justifies this familiarity. I shake my head; I feel nauseated within the narrow circle of the old man's thoughts; that is the only reason why I refuse to drink. The mother stands by the bed, luring me over; I obey and, while a horse neighs loudly toward the ceiling, I place my head on the boy's chest, and he shudders under my wet beard. It confirms what I know: the boy is healthy, his circulation a bit poor— he is saturated with coffee by the worried mother, but

healthy, and it would be best to kick him out of bed.
I am no do-gooder and so I let him lie. I am employed
by the district and perform my responsibility thoroughly, almost overdoing it. Though badly paid, I am
generous and helpful with the poor. I still have to
take care of Rosa, then the boy can have his way,
and I too will want to die. What I am doing here in
this endless winter!? My horse has died, and no one
in the village will lend me his own. I have to pull my
team from the pigsty; if they did not happen to be
horses, then I would have to ride with sows. That is
how it is. And I nod to the family. They know nothing
about it, and if they did know, they would not believe
it. Writing prescriptions is easy, but communicating
with people is hard. Well, then I am done with my
visit, once again they have summoned me for nothing,
I am used to it, with the help of my night bell the
entire district torments me; but having to give up Rosa
this time—that lovely girl, who has lived in my home
for years, barely noticed by me—this sacrifice is too
great, and I have to come up with sophistry, devise
some makeshift solution to avoid pouncing on this
family, who, after all, cannot for the life of them return
Rosa to me. But when I close my bag and signal for
my fur coat, and the family members stand together,
the father snuffling over the rum glass in his hand,
the mother probably disappointed in me (just what do
people expect anyway?), tearfully biting her lips, and
the sister flourishing a bloodstained towel, I am somehow willing to admit, if need be, that the boy may be
sick after all. I go to him, he smiles at me as if I
were bringing him the strongest soup of all—ah, now

both horses are neighing: the noise, probably ordained by a higher power, is meant to facilitate the examination. And now I find: Yes, the boy *is* ill. In his right side, near the hip, a hand-sized wound has opened up. Pink, in many nuances, dark in its depth, lighter toward the edges, soft-grained, with uneven clots of blood, and open like the surface of a mine. That much from the distance. A closer inspection reveals a complication. Who can look at that without whistling softly? Worms, equal in length and thickness to my little finger, rosy in color and also splashed with blood, caught inside the wound, with tiny white heads, with many tiny legs, wriggle up to the light. Poor boy, there is no helping you. I have located your big wound; you are being destroyed by that blossom in your side. The family is happy, they see me doing something; the sister says so to the mother, the mother to the father, the father to several guests who, balancing with outstretched arms, tiptoe in through the moonlight of the open door.

"Will you save me?" the boy whispers, sobbing, utterly blinded by the life in his wound. That is what the people are like in my area. Always demanding the impossible of a doctor. They have lost the ancient faith; the pastor sits at home, unraveling his liturgical vestments one by one. But the doctor is supposed to accomplish everything with his delicate surgical hand. Well, whatever: I did not offer myself; if you people misuse me for sacred purposes, then I will put up with that too. What more could I ask? I, an old country doctor, bereft of my housemaid! And so they come, the family and the village elders, and undress me. A school chorus with the teacher at its head stands outside the house, singing these words to an extremely simple tune:

> Strip him, then he'll heal,
> And if he doesn't heal, then kill him!
> He's only a doctor, only a doctor.

Then I am stripped bare and, my fingers in my beard, my head bowed, I calmly gaze at the people. I am quite composed and superior to them all and will remain so, even though it will not help me, for now they take me by my head and feet and carry me to the bed. They place me along the wall, on the side with the wound. Then they all leave the room; the door is closed; the singing dies out; clouds pass across the moon; the bedding lies warm around me; in the windows the horses' heads waver like shadows.

"You know," someone says into my ear, "I have very little confidence in you. Why, you were only shaken off here, you didn't come on your own two feet. Instead of helping me, you crowd my deathbed. I would love to scratch your eyes out."

"Right," I say, "it *is* shameful. But I *am* a doctor, after all. What should I do? Believe me, it is no easier for me."

"I should content myself with that excuse? Oh, I have to. I always have to content myself. I came into the world with a lovely wound; that was my only endowment."

"Young friend," I say, "your problem is that you don't have an overall grasp of things. I, who have been in all sickrooms, far and wide, say to you: Your wound is not so bad. Created at a sharp angle with two strokes of the ax. Many people offer a side and barely catch the sound of the ax in the forest, much less hear it getting closer to them."

"Is that really so or are you deceiving me in my fever?"

"It is really so—take a district physician's word of honor."

And he took it and fell silent.

But now it was time to think about saving myself. The horses were still standing faithfully in their places. Clothes, fur, and bag were quickly snatched up; I did not care to waste time dressing. If the horses raced as they had coming here, I would leap from this bed to mine, as it were. Obediently a horse backed away from the window; I tossed the bundle into the wagon; my fur coat soared too far, it clung to a hook by only one sleeve. Good enough. I swung myself on the horse. The reins loosely trailing behind, one horse barely tied to the other, the wagon bumbling behind them, the fur was the last thing in the snow.

"Giddyap!" I said, but the movement was not lively. Slowly, like old men, we moved through snowy wasteland. For a long, long time, we could hear the new but defective singing of the children:

> Cheer up, all you patients,
> The doctor has been placed in your bed!

Never will I come home at this rate; my flourishing practice is doomed; a successor robs me, but to no avail, for he cannot replace me. The disgusting stableman rages in my home; Rosa is his victim; I refuse to picture it. Naked, at the mercy of the frost in this most wretched era, with an earthly wagon, unearthly horses, I, an old man, wander about. My fur coat hangs from the back of the wagon, but I cannot reach it, and not one of my agile patients, that riffraff, will lift a finger. Deceived! Deceived! Once you have responded to the false alarm of the night bell—it can never be made good.

UP IN THE GALLERY

If some frail, consumptive equestrienne on a reeling horse in the ring, in front of a tireless audience, were uninterruptedly driven around in a circle for months on end by a ruthless, whip-cracking ringmaster, whirring on the horse, blowing kisses, swaying at the waist, and if this performance under the incessant roar of the orchestra and the ventilators were to continue into the ever-widening dreary future, accompanied by applause that kept waning and swelling up again, from hands that are actually steam hammers—then perhaps a young gallery visitor might hurry down the long stairway through all the tiers, plunge into the ring, and shout "Halt!" over the fanfares of the ever-adjusting orchestra.

But since it is not like that—since a beautiful lady, in white and red, comes soaring in through the curtains that the proud liveried footmen open before her; since the ringmaster, devotedly seeking her eyes, breathing toward her in an animal stance; since he lovingly hands her up on the dapple-gray horse as if she were his utterly beloved granddaughter taking off on a dangerous journey; since he cannot make up his mind to signal with the whip; but finally pulls himself together and cracks it smartly; runs alongside the horse, his mouth open; follows the rider's leap with sharp eyes; scarcely believes her skill; tries to warn her by shouting in English; furiously admonishes the grooms, who clutch hoops, to be very attentive; since before the great breakneck leap he raises his hands, beseeching the orchestra to hush; since he finally lifts the girl down from the trembling horse, kisses her on both cheeks, and considers no tribute from the public satisfactory enough; while she herself, supported by him, high on the tips of her toes, in a whirl of dust, her arms outspread, her head thrown back, tries to share her bliss with the entire circus—since this is so, the gallery visitor puts his face on the railing and, sinking into the concluding march as into a heavy dream, he weeps without realizing it.

AN ANCIENT MANUSCRIPT

It is as if a great deal had been neglected in the defense of our fatherland. Previously, we paid no attention and went about our work; however, the recent events have given us cause for concern.

I have a cobbler's shop on the square in front of the imperial palace. No sooner do I open up at the crack of dawn than I see that the entrances to all the streets running into the square are occupied by armed men. These are not our soldiers, however, they are obviously nomads from the north. In some manner that I cannot fathom they have penetrated all the way into the capital, even though it lies very far from the border. Well, at any rate, they are here; and there seem to be more of them every morning.

As is their nature, they camp out under the open sky, for they despise houses. They keep busy honing swords, sharpening arrows, practicing horsemanship. This peaceful square, which was always kept scrupulously clean, has been turned into an absolute stable. Sometimes we do try to run out of our shops and clear away at least the worst of the filth, but we now do so

246

less and less often, for our efforts are pointless, and besides, we also risk being trampled by the wild horses or injured by the whips.

It is impossible to speak with the nomads. They do not know our language—indeed, they barely have one of their own. They communicate with each another like jackdaws. We keep hearing those jackdaw shrieks. They neither understand, nor care about, our way of life, our institutions. Consequently, they are also impervious to any sign language. You can dislocate your jaw and wrench your hands out of your wrists, but they still have not understood you nor will they ever understand you. They often make grimaces: then the whites of their eyes twist up and foam drools from their mouths; yet they are not attempting to say anything or frighten anyone; they grimace because that is their way. Whatever they need they take. It cannot be said that they resort to violence. When they reach for something, we merely step aside and relinquish it to them.

They have also taken a good item or two from my stock. But I cannot complain when I see what is happening to, say, the butcher across the road. No sooner does he bring in his wares than everything is snatched away and devoured by the nomads. Their horses likewise eat meat; often a rider lies next to his mount, and both of them feed on the same hunk of meat, each from a different end. The butcher is fearful and does not have the nerve to halt the meat deliveries. We understand this, however, and so we all chip in to keep him going. If the nomads did not get meat, then who knows what they might think of next; indeed, who knows what they will think of even though they do get meat every day.

Recently the butcher figured he could at least spare himself the drudgery of slaughtering, and so he brought in a live ox in the morning. He must never try that again. I lay flat on the floor, way in the back of my workshop, for something like an hour, after piling all my clothes, blankets, and pillows on top of me, just so as not to hear the bellowing of the ox, which the nomads were pouncing on from all sides, ripping out chunks of its warm flesh with their teeth. The square had been silent for a long time before I ventured out again; like drinkers around a wine cask, they were sprawling wearily around the remains of the ox.

It was precisely at this point that I thought I spotted the emperor himself in a window of his palace; normally he never comes to those outer rooms; he always lives only in the innermost garden; but this time he was standing, or at least so it seemed to me, at a window, gazing with a lowered head at the tumult in front of his palace.

What will be the upshot? we all wonder. How long will we endure this burden and torment? It was the imperial palace that lured the nomads here, but it does not know how to drive them out again. The gates remain locked; the guards, who always used to march in and out ceremonially, now stay behind barred windows. The rescue of our fatherland has been entrusted to us craftsmen and shopkeepers; but we are not equal to such a task; nor have we ever boasted of being capable of it. This is certainly a misunderstanding, and it is destroying us.

BEFORE THE LAW

Before the Law stands a gatekeeper. To this gate-keeper comes a man from the countryside and requests admittance to the Law. But the gatekeeper says that he cannot admit him just now. The man reflects and then asks whether he will be able to enter later on.

"It is possible," says the gatekeeper, "but not now."

Since the gate to the Law is open as usual and the gatekeeper steps aside, the man bends over to look through the gateway, into the interior. When the gate-keeper notices this, he laughs and says, "If it entices you that strongly, then try to go on in despite my prohibition. But mind you: I am powerful. And I am only the lowest of the gatekeepers. And from hall to hall gatekeepers stand, each more powerful than the last. I myself cannot endure the sight of even the third one."

The man from the countryside did not expect such difficulties; after all, the Law, he thinks, is supposed to be always accessible to everyone. But when he now takes a closer look at the gatekeeper in his fur coat, his large pointed nose, the long, thin, black Tartar beard, he decides he would rather wait until he receives permission to enter. The gatekeeper hands him a stool and lets him sit down at the side of the door.

There he sits for days and years. He makes many attempts to be admitted and tires the gatekeeper with his requests. The gatekeeper often puts him through minor interrogations, asks him about his home town and about many other things; but these are aloof questions, such as great lords ask, and in the end he always tells him that he cannot let him in as yet. The man, who equipped himself thoroughly for his trip, uses anything, no matter how valuable, to bribe the gatekeeper. The gatekeeper accepts everything, but says, "I'm accepting it only so you won't think you've neglected anything."

During these many years the man keeps his eyes on the gatekeeper almost uninterruptedly. He forgets all about the other gatekeepers, and this first one strikes him as the only obstacle to getting into the Law. He curses his poor luck—in the first few years loudly and relentlessly, and later on, when he grows old, he merely grumbles to himself. He becomes childish, and since during his years of studying the gatekeeper he has also gotten to know the fleas in his fur collar, he also asks the fleas to help him and to change the gatekeeper's mind.

Eventually his eyesight starts dimming, and he does not know whether his surroundings are actually darkening or his eyes are merely deceiving him. However, in the darkness he does recognize a glow breaking inextinguishably from the door of the Law. Now he does not have much time left.

Before his death all his experiences of the entire

period gather in his mind as one question that he has never asked the gatekeeper. He beckons to him since he can no longer raise his rigidifying body. The gatekeeper bends way down to him, for their difference in size has changed greatly to the man's disadvantage.

"What else do you want to know?" the gatekeeper asks. "You are insatiable."

"All people strive for the Law," says the man. "How come in these many years no one but me has asked to be let in?"

The gatekeeper realizes that the man is approaching the end, and so, in order to reach his waning hearing, he yells at him:

"No one else could be let in here, for this entrance was meant for you alone. Now I'm going to go and shut it."

JACKALS AND ARABS

We were camping in the oasis. My companions were asleep. An Arab, tall and white, walked past me; he had attended to the camels and was going to the sleeping area.

I flopped backwards into the grass; I tried to sleep; I couldn't—the keening howl of a distant jackal; I sat up again. And something that had been so far away was suddenly near. A swarming of jackals all around me; eyes gleaming in matte gold and fading; lithe bodies in agile, regular motion as if under a whip.

One jackal came up from behind, squeezing under my arm and against me as if needing my warmth; then stood before me and spoke to me, almost eye to eye:

"I am the eldest jackal far and wide. I am happy to be greeting you here. I had already given up all hope, for we have been awaiting you for an eternity; my mother waited and her mother and every one of their mothers all the way back to the mother of all jackals. Believe me!"

"I'm amazed," I said, forgetting to kindle the stack of wood, which lay ready to fend off the jackals with its smoke; "I'm very amazed to hear that. I just happen to be coming from the far north and I am taking a brief trip. What can I do for you jackals?"

As if encouraged by my perhaps all-too-friendly reception, they drew in closer around me; all of them were panting and snarling.

"We know," the eldest began, "that you come from the north, that is exactly what we are setting our hopes on. The north has the intelligence that is not to be found here among the Arabs. Not a spark of intelligence can be struck from their cold haughtiness. They kill animals in order to eat them and they scorn carrion."

"Don't talk so loudly," I said, "there are Arabs sleeping nearby."

"You are truly a foreigner," said the jackal, "otherwise you'd know that never in the history of the world has any jackal feared an Arab. Fear them? We? Isn't it enough of a misfortune to be banished among such a people?"

"Could be, could be," I said, "I don't presume to have an opinion about things that are so remote from my life; it sounds like a very ancient quarrel; so it must be in the blood; and perhaps it may only end with blood."

"You are very smart," said the old jackal; and they all started panting harder, with harried lungs, even though they were standing still; a rank smell, which at times I could endure only by gritting my teeth, poured from their open maws, "you are very smart; your words are consistent with our old teachings. So we will draw their blood, and the quarrel will be ended."

"Oh!" I said more vehemently than I meant to say, "they will defend themselves; they will take their muskets and mow you down in swarms."

"You misunderstand us," he said, "in human fashion, which apparently is not lost even in the north. We—we are certainly not going to kill them. The Nile would not have enough water to cleanse us. Why, we run away at the mere sight of their living bodies, into purer air, into the desert, which is our home for that very reason."

And all the jackals around me, who had meanwhile been joined by many others from far away, lowered their heads between their front legs, polishing them with their paws; it was as if they wanted to conceal a repugnance so dreadful that I felt a strong urge to jump high and flee from their circle.

"Well, then what do you plan to do?" I asked, trying to stand up; but I couldn't; two young beasts had dug their teeth into the back of my jacket and shirt; I had to remain seated.

"They are holding your train," the old jackal earnestly explained, "it's a mark of respect."

"Make them let go!" I cried, turning to and fro between the old one and the youngsters.

"Naturally they will," said the old one, "if that is your wish. But it will take a while, for they have bitten in too deep, as is customary, and now they have to extricate their jaws very slowly. In the meantime, listen to our request."

"Your behavior has not made me very receptive," I said.

"Don't make us pay for our clumsiness," he said, relying for the first time on the keening tone of his natural voice, "we are poor animals, we have only our teeth for anything we want to do, good or bad, all we have is our teeth."

"Well, just what can I do for you?" I asked, only slightly placated.

"Sir," he cried, and all the jackals howled; it sounded very remotely like a melody; "Sir, we would like you to end the quarrel that tears the world apart. You look exactly like the person who our forebears said would do it. We must have peace from the Arabs; breathable air; our view cleansed of them all around the horizon; no shriek of lament from a sheep slaughtered by the Arab; all creatures should perish quietly; undisturbed, they should be drained by us and cleansed, purified down to the bones. We want purity, nothing but purity"—and now all of them were weeping, sobbing—"just how do you endure this world, you noble heart and sweet innards? Dirt is their white; dirt is their black; their beards are horrors; one must spit at the mere sight of their eye sockets; and when they raise an arm, hell opens up in the armpit. Therefore, oh sir, therefore, oh dear sir, with the help of your all-powerful hands, with the help of your all-powerful hands, cut their throats with these scissors!" And, obeying a jerk of his head, a jackal came over, a pair of small sewing scissors covered with old rust was dangling from his fang.

"So at last the scissors and that will be the end of it!" shouted the Arab leader of our caravan; he had stolen over to us upwind and was now cracking his gigantic whip.

The jackals all dashed away; but then they halted

at some distance, huddling together, the many animals, so close and rigid that they appeared to be packing into a tiny pen surrounded by flitting will-o'-the-wisps.

"Well, sir, now you have seen and heard this spectacle," said the Arab, laughing as merrily as his tribal restraint permitted.

"Then you know what the animals want?" I asked.

"Naturally, sir," he said, "why, it's notorious; as long as Arabs have existed, that pair of scissors has been wandering through the desert and will wander with us until the end of time. It is offered to every European for the great work; every European happens to strike them as precisely the destined man. These beasts have an absurd hope; they are fools, utter fools. That is why we love them; they are our dogs; more beautiful than your dogs. Just look, a camel died during the night, I've had it brought here."

Four porters came trudging over with the heavy carcass and dumped it in front of us. No sooner was it lying there than the jackals raised their voices. As if drawn, each one irresistibly, by ropes, they came, haltingly, their bellies brushing the ground. They had forgotten the Arabs, forgotten their hatred; they were bewitched by the all-extinguishing presence of the strongly reeking cadaver. One of them was already at its throat, and his first bite found the jugular vein. Like a small, raging pump trying both urgently and hopelessly to douse a raging fire, every muscle of his body strained and stiffened in its place. And by now, all the jackals were piled high on the corpse, performing the same work.

And now the Arab leader snapped his sharp whip crisscross over them. They raised their heads; half conscious in their euphoria; saw the Arabs standing before them; felt the whip on their muzzles; retreated in leaps and bounds, running backwards for a stretch. But the camel's blood was already lying there in pools; smoking upward; the body was shredded in several places. They couldn't resist; they were back again; the Arab leader raised his whip again; I grabbed his arm.

"You are right, sir," he said, "we will leave them to their occupation; besides, it is time we broke camp. But you *have* seen them. Wonderful animals, aren't they? And how they hate us!"

A VISIT TO THE MINE

Today the chief engineers were down in our mine. The management issued some kind of order to drive new tunnels, and so the engineers came to do the preliminary surveying. How young these men are and yet already so diverse! They have all developed freely, and their sharply defined characters are independently revealed while they are still young.

One man, black-haired, lively, has eyes that dart everywhere.

A second one, with a notebook, jots down things while walking, looks around, compares, takes notes.

A third one, his hands in his coat pockets, so that everything on him is taut, walks upright; maintains his dignity; only his constant biting of his lips reveals his impatient, irrepressible youth.

A fourth one provides the third with explanations that the latter does not ask for; shorter than he, running alongside him like a tempter, his forefinger always in the air, he seems to be delivering a litany about everything that is to be seen here.

A fifth man, perhaps the highest in rank, brooks no companion; he is now ahead, now behind; the group adjusts its pace to his; he is pale and weak; responsibility has hollowed his eyes; often, when reflecting, he presses his hand on his forehead.

The sixth and the seventh walk slightly bowed, head close to head, arm in arm, in intimate conversation; if this were not obviously our coal mine and our station in the deepest tunnel, one could mistake these bony, beardless, bulbous-nosed gentlemen for young clergymen. One of them usually laughs to himself, purring like a cat; the other, likewise with a smile, does the talking, his free hand beating out some sort of time. How certain these two gentlemen must be of their position—indeed, despite their youth, what services they must have performed for our mine if they were allowed, during such an important inspection, to occupy themselves so steadfastly, under the boss's very eyes, purely with their own concerns or with concerns not relevant to the present task. Or could it be that, for all their laughter and all their inattentiveness, they do in fact notice everything that is necessary? One may scarcely pronounce a definite verdict about such gentlemen.

On the other hand there can be no doubt that, say, the eighth man is incomparably more absorbed in the task than these two—indeed more than all the other gentlemen. He has to take hold of everything and tap it with a small hammer that he keeps taking from his pocket and returning there. Sometimes, despite his elegant clothing, he kneels in the dirt and taps the ground; then again, but only while walking, the walls or the ceiling over his head. Once he even stretched out on the ground and lay there silently. We thought

some accident had occurred, but then he sprang up,
his lithe body wincing slightly. He had once again
merely examined something. We believe we know our
mine and its rock formations, but what this engineer
keeps examining in this fashion is beyond our grasp.

A ninth man pushes a kind of baby carriage con-
taining the measuring devices. Extremely costly devices, embedded in the softest cotton. This carriage
should actually be pushed by the clerk, but it is not
entrusted to him; an engineer had to be called upon,
and he enjoys doing it, as we can see. He is probably
the youngest, perhaps he does not understand all the
apparatuses, but his gaze keeps resting on them—
which sometimes almost causes him to bump the carriage into the wall.

However, there is another engineer, who walks next
to the carriage and keeps it from bumping. He obviously understands the devices thoroughly and seems
to be their real custodian. From time to time, without
stopping the carriage, he removes a component of
some device, peers through it, unscrews or screws,
shakes and taps, holds it to his ear and listens; and
finally, while the carriage pusher usually stands still,
this engineer puts back the tiny thing, barely visible
from afar, and lovingly replaces it in the carriage. He
is a bit domineering, this engineer, but only for the
sake of the devices. Ten paces ahead of the carriage,
we are supposed to move aside at a wordless sign of
his finger, even if there is no room to move aside in.

Behind those two gentlemen walks the unoccupied
clerk. It goes without saying, given their great knowledge, that the gentlemen have long since discarded

all arrogance; the clerk, by contrast, seems to have gathered it inside himself. His one hand in back of him, the other in front, rubbing his gilded buttons or the fine cloth of his livery jacket, he often nods to the right or the left, as if we had greeted him and he were responding, or as if he assumed that we had greeted him but that he was unable to check it from his great height. Naturally we do not greet him; but at the sight of him one might almost believe that there is something tremendously distinguished about being a clerk for the mine management. Behind his back, admittedly, we laugh, but since not even a lightning bolt could induce him to turn around, he remains as something incomprehensible in our esteem.

Today there will be little more work; the interruption has been too extensive; such a visit carries off all thoughts of work. It is far too tempting to peer after the men in the darkness of the test tunnel, where they have all vanished. Besides, our shift is almost over; we will not witness the return of the gentlemen.

THE NEXT VILLAGE

My grandfather used to say: "Life is amazingly brief. Now it is so concentrated in my memory that, for example, I can hardly understand how a young man can make up his mind to ride into the next village without fearing that—aside from unfortunate accidents—even a normal, happy lifetime is far too short for such a ride."

AN IMPERIAL MESSAGE

An emperor on his deathbed, we are told, sent a message to you, the only one, the wretched subject, the insignificant shadow who had fled from the imperial sun to the most distant distance—you of all people. He ordered the messenger to kneel at his bedside and he whispered the message into his ear; it was so important to him that he had the messenger whisper it back to him. By nodding his head, he confirmed the correctness of the words. And before the entire throng attending his death—all hindering walls are torn down and the grandees of the empire stand in a ring on the wide- and high-swinging staircase—in front of all these men he dispatched the messenger. The messenger instantly set out; a strong, a tireless man. Stretching out now one, now the other arm, he forces his way through the crowd; if he meets with resistance, he points to his chest, to the symbol of the sun. He advances easily like no one else. But the crowd is so large; their dwellings are numberless. If he could reach an open field, how lightly he would fly, and soon, no doubt, you would hear the splendid banging of his fists on your door. But instead, what useless efforts he makes; he is still pushing his way through the rooms of the innermost palace. He will never make it; and if he succeeded, nothing would be gained: he would have to fight his way down the staircases; and if he succeeded, nothing would be gained: he would have to stride across the courtyards; and after the courtyards the second enclosing palace; and again staircases and courtyards; and again a palace; and so on for thousands of years. And if he finally plunges through the outermost gate—but it can never, never happen—the entire imperial capital, the center of the world, still lies before him, piled high with its sediment. No one gets through here, and certainly not with a dead man's message. But you sit at your window and dream up the message when the evening comes.

THE ANXIETY OF THE HEAD
OF FAMILY

Some say the word "Odradek" is of Slavic origin, on which basis they try to prove its development. Then again, others believe it stems from German and is only influenced by Slavic. Now the uncertainty of both interpretations justifies our conclusion that neither is correct, particularly since neither helps us to find a meaning for the word.

Naturally no one would get involved in such studies if there were no such thing as a creature named Odradek. At first glance it looks like a flat, stellar spool for thread, and indeed it seems to be covered with thread. However, these can only be odds and ends, old torn threads of the most disparate sorts and colors, knotted together, but also ensnarled. Yet it is not just a spool: a small oblong stick emerges from the middle of the star, and another small stick is joined to the first one at a right angle. With the help of this second stick on one side and a point of the star on the other side, the whole thing can stand erect as if on two legs.

One is tempted to believe that this structure used to have some practical form and is merely broken now. But this does not seem to be the case: at least no sign of this can be found. Nowhere can we see hints or breaks that would indicate anything of the sort; the whole thing seems senseless, yet complete in its fashion. No further details, incidentally, can be pinpointed since Odradek is extraordinarily agile and eludes capture.

He lingers by turns in the attic, the staircase, the corridors, the vestibule. Sometimes he remains unseen for months on end; so he must have moved to other houses; but then he inevitably returns to our house. Sometimes when you step through the door and he happens to be leaning on the staircase banister down below, you feel like speaking to him. Naturally you ask him no difficult questions, you simply treat him—his very tininess inveigles you into doing so—like a child.

"What's your name?" you ask him.

"Odradek," he says.

"And where do you live?"

"No permanent residence," he says, laughing. But it is the sort of laughter that can only be produced without lungs. It sounds fairly like the rustling of fallen leaves. This usually ends the conversation. Incidentally, not even these answers can always be elicited: often he remains dumb for a long time, like the wood he seems to be.

Futilely I wonder what will happen to him. Can he die? Everything that dies has had some kind of goal, some kind of activity, and they have worn it down; but this is not true of Odradek. Might he then someday roll down the stairs, dragging his threads, at the very feet of my children and children's children? He clearly harms no one; but the idea that he might survive me is almost painful.

ELEVEN SONS

I have eleven sons.

The first is very unattractive in his appearance, but earnest and smart; nevertheless, while I love him as I do all my children, I do not think very highly of him. His mind strikes me as too simple. He looks neither right nor left nor into the distance; he keeps running around or rather spinning in his small circle of ideas.

The second is handsome, slender, well-built; it is a delight seeing him in an on-guard fencing position. He too is smart, but also sophisticated; he has been around, and that is why even the nature of our homeland seems to speak more familiarly with him than with the stay-at-homes. Yet this advantage is certainly not only and not even essentially due to his travels; it is part of the child's inimitable character, which, for example, is acknowledged by everyone who wants to imitate his wildly controlled dives, his multiple somersaults into water. The imitator's courage and desire last up to the end of the diving board; but once there, instead of diving, he abruptly sits down and lifts his arms apologetically. Yet despite all that (I

should really be blissful about such a child), my relationship to him is not unmarred. His left eye is a bit
smaller than his right and it winks a lot—only a minor
blemish, granted, which makes his face look even
more audacious than it might otherwise, and, given his
reclusive, unapproachable nature, no one will notice,
much less condemn this smaller, winking eye. I, the
father, do so. Naturally what hurts me is not this
physical blemish so much as a minor irregularity in
his psyche, something that somehow fits that defect,
a kind of poison wandering through his blood, a kind
of inability to round off his full potential, which is
visible to me alone. Then again, that is precisely what
makes him my own true son, for this defect of his is
also the defect of our entire family and merely blatant
in this son.

The third son is likewise handsome, but not in a
way that appeals to me. It is the singer's beauty: the
curving lips, the dreamy eyes, the head that requires
a drapery behind it in order to be effective, the
boundlessly bulging chest, the readily startled and
far-too-readily sinking hands, the legs that move del-
icately because they cannot carry much. And moreover: his voice does not have a full, round tone; it
deceives you for an instant; makes the connoisseur
prick up his ears; but then its breath promptly fails.
Nevertheless even though everything generally entices me to show off this son, I much prefer keeping
him hidden. He himself is unobtrusive about it—
not because he knows his faults, but out of innocence. He also feels alien in our time: as if belonging
to my family, but also to another family, one lost to

him forever, he is often sullen, and nothing can cheer him up.

My fourth son may be the easiest of all to get along with. A true child of his time, he is understood by everyone, he stands on the ground that is common to all men, and everyone feels like nodding at him. Perhaps it is because of this universal acknowledgment that there is something easy about his character, something free about his movements, something light-hearted about his judgments. One would like to keep quoting some of his statements—only some, of course, for on the whole he suffers from all too much glibness. He is like a man who soars off admirably, slices the air like a swallow, but then hopelessly ends up in the bleak dust, a nothing. Such thoughts envenom the very sight of my child.

The fifth son is dear and good; he promised much less than he has kept; used to be so insignificant that one felt downright alone in his presence; but he did manage to gain some prestige after all. If asked how this came about, I could scarcely reply. Perhaps innocence most easily passes through the raging of the elements in this world, and he *is* innocent. Perhaps all too innocent. Friendly to everyone. Perhaps all too friendly. I confess: I feel queasy when someone praises him to me. After all, one makes praising too easy on oneself if one praises an obviously praiseworthy person like my son.

My sixth son appears, at first glance anyway, to be the most pensive of all. A moper and yet a chatterbox. That is why it is not easy to get at him. If he faces defeat, he lapses into invincible melancholy; if he gets the upper hand, he maintains it by chattering. Yet I will not deny that he has a certain self-oblivious passion; in broad daylight he often struggles through thoughts as if in a dream. Without being ill—in fact, he enjoys very good health—he sometimes staggers, especially at twilight, but needs no help, never falls. Perhaps this phenomenon is to be blamed on his physical development, he is much too tall for his age. This makes him unattractive overall, despite remarkably attractive details—for example, his hands and feet. Incidentally his forehead is also unattractive: both its skin and its bone formation are somehow stunted in their development.

The seventh son belongs to me perhaps more than all the others do. The world does not appreciate him; it does not understand his special brand of humor. I do not overestimate him; I know that he is trivial enough; if the world had no other defect than its failure to appreciate him, it would still be flawless. But within my family I would not care to do without this son. He brings disquiet as well as respect for tradition, and he fuses both, at least to my mind, into an unassailable whole. However, he himself knows least of all what to do with this whole; he will not get the wheel of the future to start rolling. But this aptitude of his is so encouraging, so hopeful; I wish that he had children and that they in turn had children. Unfortunately my wish does not appear to be coming true. In a self-complaisance that I neither understand nor desire, but that contrasts marvelously with the verdict of the people around him, he wanders about alone, has no interest in girls, yet will never lose his good mood.

My eighth son is my problem child, and I really know of no reason for this. He looks at me strangely, and yet I feel a fatherly closeness to him. Time has made up for a lot; but I sometimes used to shudder at the mere thought of him. He goes his own way; has broken all ties to me; and with his hard skull, his small athletic body (only his legs were quite weak for a boy, but this may have righted itself by now), he will manage to succeed in whatever he likes. I often felt like calling him back, asking him how he was, why he was cutting himself off from his father, and what he was basically after; but now he has gone this far, and so much time has already passed—let him stay as he is. I hear that he is my only son to wear a full beard; naturally it is not attractive on such a short man.

My ninth son is very elegant and has that melting gaze meant for women. So melting that he can occasionally seduce even me, though I know that all it takes is a wet sponge to wipe away this unearthly glamour. But the odd thing about this boy is that he has no intention of seducing; he would be satisfied to spend his entire life on a couch and waste his gaze on the ceiling or far more preferably let it remain under his eyelids. If he is in this favorite position of his, then he likes to talk, and does so rather well; he is terse and vivid; but only within narrow limits; if he goes beyond them, which is unavoidable because of their narrowness, his talk becomes quite empty. One would motion him to stop if one had any hope that his sleep-filled gaze would notice the gesture.

My tenth son is said to have an insincere character.

I do not wish to deny this defect entirely, to confirm
it entirely. But it is certain that whoever sees him
approaching with a solemnity far exceeding his age,
in an always buttoned frock coat, in an old but pains-
takingly brushed black hat, with his immobile face,
his somewhat jutting chin, his lids arching heavily
over the eyes, the two fingers sometimes raised to the
mouth—whoever sees him like that thinks: This man
is an absolute hypocrite. But you should just hear
him speak! Sensibly; thoughtfully; laconically; par-
rying questions with wicked liveliness; in amazing,
self-evident, and cheerful harmony with the universe—a harmony that necessarily stiffens the neck
and lifts the head. Many people who consider themselves very intelligent and who, for this reason—
they thought—were repelled by his looks have been
strongly attracted by his words. Then again there are
people who are indifferent to his looks, but who find
his words hypocritical. I, as his father, do not wish
to decide, but I must admit that the latter critics
should in any case be taken more seriously than the
former.

My eleventh son is delicate, probably the weakest
of my sons; but deceptive in his weakness: you see,
at times he can be strong and resolute; but even then
he has an underlying weakness. Yet it is no shameful
weakness, but something that seems like a weakness
only on this our earthly ground. Is not a readiness to
fly a weakness, since it is a wavering and fluttering
and unsteadiness? My son displays something along
those lines. Naturally a father is not delighted by
such characteristics; after all, they obviously tend to

destroy the family. Sometimes my son looks at me as if to say, "I will take you along, Father." At that point I think, "You would be the last person I would trust." And his eyes seem to answer: "Well, then at least let me be the last."

Those are my eleven sons.

A FRATRICIDE

It has been proved that the murder took place in the following way:

Schmar, the murderer, stationed himself toward nine P.M., in the moonlit night, at the corner where Wese, the victim, had to turn from the street where his office was into the street he lived on.

Cold night air sending shudders through everyone. But Schmar was wearing only a blue suit; furthermore, his jacket was unbuttoned. He felt no cold; besides, he was constantly moving. He kept a tight grip on his murder weapon, half bayonet, half kitchen knife, fully exposed. He peered at the knife against the moonlight; the blade flashed; not enough for Schmar; he banged it against the pavement bricks, striking sparks; regretted it perhaps; and to fix the damage, he drew the blade over the soles of his boots like a violin bow while, standing on one leg and leaning over, he also listened to the grinding of the knife on his boots, though alert to any sound from the fateful side street.

Why was all this tolerated by Pallas, a private citizen, who was nearby, watching everything from his window on the second landing? Try and fathom human nature! With his collar turned up, his dressing gown belted around his wide waist, he peered down, shaking his head.

And five houses further on, catercorner from his house, Mrs. Wese, her fox fur over her nightgown, was peering out for her husband, who was taking an unusually long time today.

At last the bell on the door of Wese's office rings, too loudly for a bell on a door, across the city, up to the sky, and that is where Wese, the diligent night worker, still invisible in this street, heralded only by the bell signal, emerges from the house; instantly the pavement counts his quiet steps.

Pallas leans out far; he must not miss anything. Mrs. Wese, reassured by the bell, shuts the clattering window. But Schmar kneels down; since he has nothing else exposed, he presses only his face and hands against the stones; where any other person freezes, Schmar burns.

Wese halts precisely at the borderline separating the two streets, he only props himself on his cane into the next street. A whim. The nocturnal sky has enticed him, the dark blue and the gold. Unknowing, he glances at it, unknowing, he runs his hand through his hair beneath the raised hat; in the sky nothing forms a pattern as an omen of his imminent future; everything remains in its absurd, unfathomable place. It is actually quite sensible of Wese to keep walking, but he walks into Schmar's knife.

"Wese!" shouts Schmar, standing on tiptoe, his arm outstretched, the knife sharply lowered. "Wese! Julia is waiting in vain!" And Schmar stabs to the right into the throat and to the left into the throat and the third thrust deep into the belly. Water rats, slit open, emit a sound similar to Wese's.

"Done," says Schmar and hurls the knife, the superfluous bloodstained ballast, against the nearest house front. "Bliss of murder! Relief, ecstasy at the flowing of another man's blood! Wese, old nightshade, friend, beerhouse crony, oozing out into the dark ground of the street. Why aren't you simply a bladder filled with blood so I could sit on you and you would vanish altogether? Not everything comes true; not every dream that blossoms bears fruit; your heavy remains lie here, already impervious to any kick. What's the point of the tacit question you are thereby asking?"

Pallas, chaotically choking down the poison in his body, stands in his two-winged front door which flies open. "Schmar! Schmar! Everything's been noticed, nothing's been overlooked." Pallas and Schmar peruse one another. Pallas is satisfied, Schmar reaches no conclusion.

Mrs. Wese, flanked by a crowd, dashes over with a face thoroughly aged by terror. The fur coat opens; she collapses upon Wese; her nightgowned body belongs to him; the fur, closing over the couple like the lawn over a grave, belongs to the crowd.

Schmar, barely stifling the last of his nausea, pressing his mouth into the shoulder of the policeman, who, stepping lightly, takes him away.

A DREAM

Josef K. was dreaming:

It was a beautiful day and K. wanted to go on a walk. But no sooner had he taken a few steps than he was already at the graveyard. Its paths were highly artificial, impractical in their windings, yet he glided along such a path as if hovering unshakably over raging water. From far away, he spotted a freshly dug burial mound at which he wanted to halt. This burial mound exerted an almost enticing effect on him, and he felt he could not get there fast enough. At times, however, he could barely glimpse the mound, it was covered with flags that twisted and flapped powerfully against one another; the flag bearers could not be seen, but there appeared to be great rejoicing.

While his eyes were still riveted in the distance, he abruptly saw the burial mound next to the path—indeed almost behind him by now. He hastily leaped into the grass. Since the path continued rushing along beneath his feet as he leaped off, he staggered and fell to his knees right in front of the mound. Two men were standing behind the grave, holding a headstone between them in the air; the moment K. showed up,

278

they thrust the stone into the earth, and it stood there as if cemented to the ground. Instantly, a third man emerged from the bushes, and K. promptly identified him as an artist. He was wearing only trousers and a misbuttoned shirt; a velvet cap was on his head; in his hand, he clutched an ordinary pencil, drawing figures in the air even as he approached.

He now applied this pencil to the top end of the stone; the stone was very high, he did not even have to lean down, but he did have to bend forward, since he did not wish to step on the burial mound, which separated him from the stone. So he stood on tiptoe, steadying himself by propping his left hand against the surface of the stone. Through some extremely skillful manipulation, he succeeded in producing gold letters with that ordinary pencil; he wrote: "HERE LIES—" Each letter came out clean and beautiful, deeply incised and in purest gold. After writing those two words, he looked back at K.; K., who was very eager to see what would come next in the inscription, gazed at the stone, paying little heed to the man. And in fact, the man was about to continue writing, but he could not, something was hindering him, he lowered the pencil and turned to K. again. This time, K. looked back at the artist, who, he noticed, was very embarrassed but unable to indicate the reason for his embarrassment. All his earlier liveliness had vanished. As a result, K. likewise felt embarrassed; they exchanged helpless glances; there was some kind of awful misunderstanding between them, which neither of them could clear up. To make matters worse, a small chime began tinkling inopportunely from the tomb chapel, but the artist waved his raised hand wildly, and the chime stopped. After a brief pause, it started in again; this time very softly and then promptly breaking off with no special admonition from him; it was as if it merely wanted to test its own sound. K. was inconsolable about the artist's dilemma, he began to cry, sobbing into his cupped hands for a long time. The artist waited for K. to calm down, and then, finding no other solution, he decided to keep writing all the same. His first small stroke was a deliverance for K., but the artist obviously managed to execute it only with utmost reluctance; moreover, the penmanship was not as lovely—above all, it seemed to lack gold, the stroke moved along pale and unsteady, only the letter became very large. It was a *J*, it was almost completed; but now the artist furiously stamped one foot into the burial mound, making the dark soil fly up all around. At last, K. understood him; there was no time left to apologize; with all his fingers he dug into the earth, which offered scant resistance; everything seemed prepared; a thin crust of earth had been set up purely for show; right beneath it a huge hole with sheer sides gaped open, and K., flipped over on his back by a gentle current, sank into the hole. But while, with his head still erect on his neck, he was welcomed down below by the impenetrable depth, his name, with tremendous embellishments, rushed across the stone up above.

Enraptured by this sight, he woke up.

A REPORT FOR AN ACADEMY

Honored Gentlemen of the Academy:

You have accorded me the honor of asking me to submit to the Academy a report on my previous apish life.

Unfortunately, I am unable to comply with the terms of your request. Almost five years separate me from my apehood—a period that is perhaps short if measured on the calendar, but infinitely long when one gallops through it, as I have done, accompanied for stretches by excellent people, advice, applause, and orchestral music, yet basically alone, for in order to remain in the picture, anyone accompanying me kept far away from the barrier. My achievement would have been impossible had I wished to cling obstinately to my origin, to the memories of my youth. Indeed, renouncing all obstinacy was the supreme commandment that I imposed on myself; I, a free ape, knuckled under to this yoke. As a result, however, my memories were closed off more and more. While initially I had the choice, should people have wanted it, of returning freely through the full gateway that the sky forms over the earth, that selfsame gateway, as my development

281

was whipped forward, simultaneously became ever lower and narrower: I felt more comfortable and more thoroughly included in the human world; the storm that blew after me from my past calmed down; today it is merely a draft that cools my heels; and the distant aperture through which it passes and through which I once passed has grown so small that even if I had sufficient strength and desire to run back that far, I would have to flay the very hide from my body to squeeze through. Frankly, much as I like to use images for these things, your apehood, gentlemen, insofar as you have anything of that nature behind you, cannot be more remote from you than mine from me. Yet anyone who walks here on earth feels a tickling in his heel: from the small chimpanzee to the great Achilles.

In its most restricted sense, however, I may be able to reply to your inquiry after all, and I even do so with great delight.

The first thing I learned was: how to shake hands; a handshake attests to frankness; although now that I am at the peak of my career, that first handshake may have been joined by frank speech. It will probably contribute nothing essential for the Academy and fall far short of that which has been asked of me and which I cannot convey, try as I might—but still and all: it ought to show what guidelines a former ape has observed when penetrating the human world and establishing himself here. Yet I could not articulate even the following insignificant information if I were not utterly sure of myself and if my position were not consolidated and unshakable on all the major vaudeville stages of the civilized world:

I come from the Gold Coast. In regard to how I was captured, I must rely on reports by others. One evening, a safari of the Hagenbeck Zoo Company (incidentally, I have since drained many a good bottle of red wine with the leader) was lurking in the underbrush along a watering hole when I ran over to its bank in the midst of a herd of apes. They fired; I was the only one hit; I got two wounds.

One in the cheek; it was light, but left a large, red, naked scar, which has earned me the repulsive, thoroughly inappropriate name—which only an ape could have come up with—of Red Peter, as if the red spot on my cheek were all that distinguished me from that locally popular trained ape-animal Peter, who recently died. (I mention all that merely in passing.)

The second bullet lodged below my hip. The wound was severe; it still causes me to limp slightly today. In a recent essay by one of the ten thousand newshounds that carry on about me in newspapers, I read that my ape nature is not yet fully suppressed; the proof being that whenever I have company, I always take down my trousers to show the entry point of the bullet. That scoundrel should have every finger of his writing hand blasted off one by one! I—I have the right to take down my trousers in front of anyone I care to; people will find nothing there but a well-groomed fur and the scar left—to avoid any misunderstanding, let us choose a specific word for a specific purpose—the scar left by a *heinous* shot. Everything is open and straightforward, we have nothing to hide; when it comes to plain truth, great minds will shed the very finest of manners. If, on the other hand, that pen pusher were to take down his trousers for visitors, he would be cutting a very different figure, and I am willing to view it as a sign of his good sense that he refrains from doing so. But by the same token—let him stay out of my hair with his delicacy of feeling!

After those shots, I awoke—and this is where my own recollection gradually begins—inside a cage in the steerage of the Hagenbeck steamer. The cage did not have four sides; it consisted of only three sides and was attached to a crate, which formed the fourth wall. The structure was too low to stand up in and too narrow to sit down in. I therefore had to crouch with bent knees that constantly trembled, and since at first I probably wanted to see no one and remain in the dark, I kept facing the crate while behind me the bars sliced into my flesh. People see an advantage in keeping wild beasts like that during their early confinement, and today, after my own experience, I cannot deny that this is truly the case from a human point of view.

But back then it never crossed my mind. For the first time in my life, I had no way out; at least I could not move forward; right in front of me was the crate, board joined solidly to board. Between the boards, of course, there was a continuous gap, which, upon first discovering it, I hailed with the blissful howling of ignorance; however, this gap was not wide enough for me to slip even my tail through it, nor was I able to widen it with all my apish strength.

Supposedly, as I was later told, I made unusually little noise, which led them to conclude that I would either die soon or, if I managed to survive the initial critical period, become highly trainable. I did survive that period. Dull sobbing, painful flea-picking, tired licking of a coconut, banging my skull against the crate wall, sticking my tongue out at whoever approached—those were my first activities in my new life. But in all those things, all I felt was: no way out. Today, naturally, I can use only human words to depict my then apelike feelings and therefore I merely distort them; but while I may be unable to capture the old ape truth, then it at least lies in the direction I have indicated—of that there can be no doubt.

Previously, I had had so many ways out, and now I had none. I was stuck. My freedom of movement would not have been further reduced even had I been nailed to the spot. Why? You can scratch the flesh raw between the toes on your feet, but you will not find the reason. You can squeeze your back against the bar until it almost slits you in half, but you will not find the reason. I had no way out, but I had to find one, for I could not live without it. Always up against that crate wall—I would have unquestionably died. However, for the Hagenbeck Zoo Company, apes belong up against the crate wall—well, so I had to stop being an ape. A fine, lucid train of thought, which I must have somehow concocted with my belly, for apes think with their bellies.

I fear that people may not understand exactly what I mean by "a way out." I am using the term in its fullest and most widespread sense. I am deliberately avoiding the word "freedom": I do not mean that grand sense of freedom on all sides. As an ape, I may have been familiar with it, and I have met human beings who yearn for it. But for my part, I did not want freedom then nor do I want it now. Incidentally: human beings all too often deceive themselves about freedom. And just as freedom is considered one of the most sublime feelings, the corresponding disillusion is likewise one of the most sublime. Often, while waiting to go on for a vaudeville performance, I have watched some pair of acrobats fiddling about on trapezes under the ceiling. They swung, they rocked, they leaped, they floated into each other's arms, one carried the other by clenching his hair in his teeth. "This too is human freedom," I thought to myself, "high-handed motion!" You mockery of Holy Nature! No theater could hold out against the laughter of apery at this sight.

No, it was not freedom I wanted. Just a way out; right, left, wherever—that was all I demanded. Let the way out be a mere delusion—my demand was small, the delusion would be no greater. Keep going, keep going! Just don't stand still with raised arms, squeezed against a crate wall!

Today I can see clearly: without utmost inner calm I could never have escaped. And indeed I may perhaps owe everything I have become to the calm that took hold of me after my first few days in the ship. And that calm I owed in turn to the crew of the ship.

They were good people, despite everything. Even today I fondly recall the sound of their heavy steps, which echoed in my drowsing. Those men were in the habit of tackling everything very slowly. If one of them wanted to rub his eyes, he would lift his hand like a suspended weight. Their jokes were coarse but hearty. Their laughter always had a bark to it, which sounded dangerous, but was of no significance. Their mouths always had something to spit out, and it made no difference to them where they spit. They always griped that my fleas jumped over to them, yet they were never seriously angry at me for that; they simply knew that fleas thrived in my fur and that fleas are jumpers; they accepted it. If they were off duty, a few of them would sometimes gather around me in a half circle, barely speaking, just grunting at one another; stretching out on crates and smoking their pipes; slapping their knees if I so much as stirred; and every so often, one of them would take a stick and tickle me in a pleasant place. Were I to be invited to sail on that ship today, I would certainly decline the invitation, but it is equally certain that not all the memories haunting me in steerage would be ugly.

More than anything else, it was the calm I acquired among those men that kept me from attempting any escape. In retrospect, it strikes me that I must have had at least an inkling that I ought to find a way out if I wanted to live, but that this way out could not be found by escaping. I no longer know whether escape was possible, though I believe it was; for an ape, escape should always be possible; the way my teeth are today, I have to be careful even when doing something as ordinary as cracking nuts; but back then, I would no doubt have eventually succeeded in chewing through the lock on the door. I did not do so. And what would have been gained by it anyhow? No sooner would I have poked my head out than I would have been recaptured and locked up in an even more awful cage; or else, unnoticed, I could have fled to other animals, perhaps the giant pythons across the hold, to perish in their embraces; or I might even have managed to steal all the way up to the deck and leap overboard, then I would have bobbed up and down in the ocean for a while and finally drowned. Desperate acts. I did not reckon in such human terms, but under the influence of my milieu I behaved as if I *were* reckoning.

I did not reckon, but I did observe at leisure. I watched those men going back and forth; always the same faces; the same movements; it often looked to me as if there were only one man. And this man or these men were going about unhampered. A lofty goal beckoned. No one promised me that if I were to become like them the cage door would be pulled up. Such promises in return for seemingly impossible achievements are not given. But if one succeeds in doing the impossible, then the promises belatedly appear in the very place where one sought them earlier to no avail. Now there was nothing particularly enticing about those men. Were I an adherent of the above-mentioned idea of freedom, I would certainly have preferred the ocean to the way out that emerged in the dismal gazes of these human beings. But in any event, I had been observing them for a long time before I ever thought of such things—in fact, it was my accumulated observations that first pushed me in this specific direction.

It was so easy imitating these people. I already knew how to spit on the very first day. We would then spit into one another's faces; the only difference was that I would lick my face clean afterwards, and they would not. I soon smoked a pipe like an old-timer; and when I then actually pressed my thumb into the bowl of the pipe, the whole crew shouted with glee; the only thing I was in the dark about for a long time was the difference between an empty and a stuffed pipe.

My worst trouble was with the liquor bottle. The smell was agonizing; I forced myself with all my strength; but weeks went by before I overcame it. Strangely enough, the crew took my inner struggles more seriously than anything else about me. I cannot tell the men apart in my memories, but there was one who kept coming back; alone or with friends; by day, by night; at any hour; he would station himself in front of me with the bottle and give me lessons. He did not understand me, he wanted to solve the enigma of my being. He would slowly uncork the bottle and then peer at me as if checking whether I had understood; I confess that I always watched him with wild, with rash vigilance; no human teacher would find such a human student anywhere on earth. After uncorking the bottle, he would lift it toward his mouth; I peering all the way into his throat; he would nod, satisfied with me, and put the bottle to his lips; I, entranced with my gradually dawning knowledge, would squeal and scratch the length and breadth of my body, wherever; he rejoiced, put the bottle to his lips, and took a swallow; I, desperately impatient to emulate him, soiled myself in my cage, which in turn gave him great satisfaction; and now, holding the bottle far away and then swinging it to his mouth while leaning backwards, the more vividly to instruct me, he would drain it at one swig. I, worn out with overpowering desire, could no longer follow him and I hung limply on the bars while he ended the theoretical instruction by grinning and rubbing his belly.

And now the practical training began. Was I not already utterly exhausted by theory? No doubt, utterly exhausted. That was part of my fate. Nevertheless I reached for the proffered bottle as well as I could, trembling as I uncorked it; with each success new energy gradually developed; barely differing from the original model by now, I lifted the bottle, put it to my lips and—and hurled it away in disgust, in disgust, even though it was empty and filled only with the smell, hurled it to the floor with disgust. To my teacher's sorrow, to my own greater sorrow—nor did I placate him or myself by remembering, after hurling the bottle away, to rub my belly superbly and grin while doing so.

All too many lessons unfolded like that. But to my teacher's credit: he was never angry at me; granted, he sometimes put the burning pipe to my fur until some area that I could barely reach began to smolder; but then he would put it out himself with his own kind, gigantic hand; he was never angry at me; he realized that the two of us were on the same side, fighting against my apish nature, and that mine was the harder task.

And then what a victory it was both for him and for me when one evening in front of a large group of spectators (they may have been having a party, a gramophone was playing, an officer was sauntering among the men)—when that evening, in an unobserved moment, I grabbed a liquor bottle left inadvertently near my cage, uncorked it, as I had been taught, amid the growing attention of the company, put it to my mouth, and now, not hesitating, not twisting my lips, an expert drinker, with roundly rolling eyes, a sloshing throat, I really and truly drained it, tossed it away no longer as a desperate creature but as an artist, I did forget to rub my belly, but instead, because I had no choice, because it got the better of me, because my senses were reeling, I curtly exclaimed, "Hey!" breaking out in human sounds, plunging into human society with that cry, and feeling its echo, "Listen, he's talking!" like a kiss over my entire sweat-soaked body.

I repeat: it did not entice me to imitate human beings; I imitated because I was seeking a way out, and for no other reason. Besides, little was accomplished with that victory. My voice instantly failed; it took months for it to come back; my repugnance toward the liquor bottle grew even more intense. My direction, though, was established once and for all.

When I was handed over to my first trainer in Hamburg, I soon recognized the two possibilities that were open to me: zoological garden or vaudeville. I did not waffle. I told myself: Do anything you can to get into vaudeville; that is the way out; the zoological garden is merely another barred cage; once you're in it, you're doomed.

And I learned, gentlemen! Ah, one learns if one must; one learns if one wants a way out; one learns relentlessly. One supervises oneself with the whip; one mangles oneself at the least resistance. My ape nature, rolling head over heels, rushed out of me and away, so that my first tutor almost turned apish himself in the process, soon gave up teaching, and had to be carted off to a mental hospital. Luckily, he was soon released.

But I went through many tutors—indeed, even several at once. As I grew more confident of my abilities, with the public following my progress, and my future beginning to look bright, I engaged tutors myself, had them sit in five successive rooms, and learned simultaneously from all of them by leaping incessantly from room to room.

That progress! That penetration of my awakening brain by rays of knowledge from all sides! I do not deny it made me happy. But I also admit that I did not overrate it, certainly not back then, and how much less today. By dint of a strenuous effort, which has never been repeated on this earth, I have achieved the average education of a European. This may be nothing in itself, but it is something inasmuch as it helped me out of the cage, opening up this special way out, this human way out. There is a marvelous German idiom: "to slink off into the bushes"—meaning "to see something through"—and that was what I did: I slunk off into the bushes. There was no other way, so long as I could not choose freedom.

In surveying my development and what I have achieved so far, I neither complain nor am satisfied. With my hands in my trouser pockets, my bottle of wine on the table, I half lie, half sit in the rocking chair and gaze out the window. If a visitor comes, I receive him as is proper. My personal manager sits in the vestibule; if I ring, he comes and listens to what I have to say. I perform almost every evening, and my triumphs could hardly be greater. When I come home late at night from banquets, from scientific societies, from social get-togethers, a small, half-trained female chimpanzee is waiting for me, and I have a good time with her in apish fashion. By day, I do not want to see her; for she has the madness of the confused trained beast in her eyes; I alone recognize it and I cannot endure it.

In any case, I have, all in all, attained what I set out to attain. Let no one say it was not worth the bother. Besides, I am not intent on any human verdict; I only want to spread knowledge; I only report; for you too, honored gentlemen of the Academy, I have only reported.

TRANSLATOR'S NOTE: The selection of stories in this collection has been dictated by copyright constraints on the original German material. The contents follow the chronological order of Kafka's publications and their integral structures. Thus, in *Contemplation*, the stories appear in the same sequence as in the original German edition.

ABOUT THE TRANSLATOR

Joachim Neugroschel, who has won three
PEN translation prizes as well as the translation prize of the French-American Foun-
dation, has translated more than 140 books,
including works by Paul Celan and Georges
Bataille plus Nobel laureates Elias Canetti
and Albert Schweitzer.